HOME TO KENTUCKY

THE MCCOYS:
BEFORE THE FEUD
BOOK 2

THOMAS A. MCCOY

ISBN 978-1-7325140-7-2 (paperback)

FOREWORD

At the sounds of the shots behind and above him, Ben saw a silhouette shadow emerging above the dull yellow straw grass. The contrast of dark and light was so distinct, he could clearly see a man getting on one knee and bringing a pistol up to aim at him. Quickly, Ben brought the end of his pistol's barrel to the center of the shadow and pulled the trigger. The man slumped forward, pulling the trigger on his pistol and sending out a wild shot and making dirt fly as he fell into the grass, face first.

Seeing him drop and then lay still, Ben came out of the rocks and started toward him to make sure he was not going to be trying to get off another shot. At that moment, the thief who had gone below and around the side of the hill where Ben had been positioned came up to the crest and stood at the top of it, taking aim at Ben. The sergeant, the leader of the outlaws, was at the wagons and couldn't see James anymore, who was heading toward Lawrence. Not having another target, the sergeant took aim at Ben. The two thieves had Ben in their sights, and he had no idea he was about to get drilled from two different directions.

PROLOGUE

It had been more than six weeks since the McCoys' last raid on the North's stockpiles of Southern valuables. The general's attempt to find the raiders had not been fruitful, and his investigation had all but died out. It had been weeks since anyone had come to the ranch asking questions.

It was finally time for the band of raiders to break apart; if anyone wanted to leave, they could do so without too much suspicion falling back on them. And four of them did: Benjamin McCoy from the 10th Regiment (Diamonds) Kentucky Cavalry, Wiley McCoy from the Second Battalion Kentucky Mounted Rifles, and Lawrence and James McCoy from the Hunters Indiana Volunteers, the Southern military's name for the First Regiment Chickasaw Infantry.

It had been decided that the paintings, silver serving sets, and the other trinkets of the rich they had stolen from storage sites would just draw suspicion, so they had taken all of it to the pastor in Harrisonville shortly after the bounty from the last raid was delivered to the church, where it would be split among the townspeople.

The remaining bounty had been divided evenly between all of the McCoys, and the four who were heading home to Kentucky had their share to take with them. Except for the large tent Wiley was carrying, the contents of each man's wagon were identical. The wagons were light weight; similar to a buckboard wagon with the sides made taller and a board across the back. They still didn't know how they were going to be able to spend the gold coins without getting caught. They would have to use some of it for traveling expenses, which meant they would be leaving a trail of money for someone to follow. But it was a long trip from Lawrence, Kansas to eastern Kentucky, and the men knew that anything could happen along the way.

CHAPTER 1

A GOOD GROUP OF MEN

It was a journey that would take them all the way from the Kansas City, Kansas region, across the length of Missouri and Kentucky, passing through Daniel Boone's territory and the Cumberland Mountains. Lawrence and James would be the first to see their families, as their homes were closest, near where the Tennessee and Virginia borders grazed Kentucky. Lawrence was going to the Pine Mountains, and James was going to Wallins Creek, near the middle fork of the Kentucky River, just a short distance away.

Ben and Wiley were both headed to Pike County, about eighty-five miles farther east; Wiley was going to Belcher, and Ben to Beaver Bottom, which was only five miles distant.

They were all accustomed to being in the saddle for long stretches of time. None of them, however, were used to riding on the seat of a wagon for more than a few hours, the sitting cushions they were bringing would become a necessity before long. It was going to be a lengthy haul, and a dangerous one. Many of the soldiers who found they had nowhere to go after the war had turned into highwaymen, forming small groups of robbers who preyed on those who traveled the main roads that cut across the states and territories.

Benjamin, or Ben as everyone was now calling him, was tall like the others—at least six feet. He had rugged features and a pointy chin, with sky blue eyes and dark brown hair above it. He was not stocky—more like lanky and lean—but much stronger than he appeared to be.

His specialty was horses, taking care of them, breaking them to a saddle, and training them to do things on his signal, like stopping hard, backing up, coming to him, or taking off on the run in the case of danger or attack.

He'd taught his own horse, the one he'd picked from those at the ranch, all of this, plus to kneel and drop to his belly on the ground and keep very quiet, skills mainly used when he was hunting. He still sorely missed his horse from back home, Midnight, a beautiful black Morgan. He had brought the horse with him to the war, but the gelding had been stolen by the Yanks during a surprise attack.

Wiley was the tallest and biggest of the travelers. At six-foot-six, thick-chested and broad-shouldered with no fat on his frame, he was by far the most handsome of their group. He had hazel eyes, a square jaw and chin, light brown hair, and a warm disposition. When he was feeling good, a friendly smile that went from ear to ear, showing all of his teeth. He was one of the few McCoys over thirty-five who still had a full set.

People said he was strong as an ox but mean as a bear when riled. He was particularly good with a rifle. Using the new Spencer carbine, he could shoot a pheasant out of the air one hundred fifty yards away, and he could hit a quail sitting on the ground at two fifty.

He had brought with him the .50 caliber buffalo gun he'd used in the war as a sniper, and he could hit his target at over five hundred yards up or downhill, and on a flat plane at almost six hundred. Growing up poor had trained him to shoot well. Bullets were hard to come by; each shot had to be well-placed, so he wouldn't waste a shell or ruin a lot of the meat. In the war, he'd had to be even more careful, because if he missed, he was likely to get killed.

Lawrence was a bit taller than Ben. He was broad-shouldered, with a thick chest and long arms and legs, and weighed over two hundred pounds. He had eyes so dark, sometimes they seemed almost black, especially when he was angry. Lawrence had a flame of vengeance burning inside him for the way his life had been turned upside down because of the war and how he had been mistreated by neighbors and kinfolk before going off to fight. They'd looked down on him for not taking advantage of his knack for book learning. Because he was smart as a whip, people used to say he was wasting his gift of intelligence, but he just didn't want to go to school or live in the city. He only wanted to be in the mountains and prosper from what nature would provide.

Before the war, he and his cousin James used to hunt well enough to supply food for several families. They had become known as the best trackers and hunters in the county. Some joked that they were so good, they could track birds five minutes after they had flown away. Of course, that was impossible, but the two excelled at finding and following a trail. They could track across rock, find and follow a several-day-old trail through forest and streams, thick woods or prairie, and catch any animals they wanted to find. They were even able to tell pretty accurately how long ago the tracks had been put there, just by looking at the signs. In the war, their tracking skills had come in handy. They'd tracked many of the Indian scouts of the Northern army and took them out.

James was only six feet tall, but that was still tall for most people. He had green eyes, brown hair, a beard and mustache, and was solidly built—a good-looking young man, and also very strong. Lean and light, he could run like a deer. Like Lawrence, he was an excellent shot and was also adept at making traps for animals using only materials he found in the woods. His income before the war mainly came from setting trap lines for furs.

When it came to ambushes or snares, he could set traps where they wouldn't be found until it was too late, and whatever he was after found themselves already caught in it. He loved to sneak up on a rising trout, toss a grasshopper in front of it, and yank the fish out of the water before it knew it was hooked. He also enjoyed sneaking up on animals, just to see how close he could get without them knowing he was there. It was said that one time he snuck up on a bear and slapped it before he shot it. During the war, he figured catching the Indian scouts of the Northern army was the same as trying to trap an animal, only bigger.

The planned route home would cut straight across the bottom portion of Kentucky via the main road coming out of Independence that headed southeast toward the corner of the state where Tennessee, Kentucky, Missouri, and Arkansas pretty much came together. This road was one of the easiest to travel, as it passed through the lower elevation mountains. The four men would end up traveling through much mountainous territory on their journey back home. They knew there were going to be many obstacles on their way and wanted the least of them be the topography.

CHAPTER 2

DAMSELS IN DISTRESS

The McCoys had each gotten an equal portion of the bounty from the raids. This share amounted to one wagon, three horses, two saddles, and three strongboxes full of gold coins. Also included were five new seven-shot Spencer carbine rifles, four six-shot Colt pistols with eight extra, quick-exchange bullet cylinders; several hundred rounds for each weapon, and a two-man tent.

The only individual items in their possession were the camping necessities given by the other McCoys to help make their journey as comfortable as possible. This consisted of a single large tent, a couple of pots and frying pans, flint bars, sulfur matches, and campfire spits for roasting game they would shoot on the way. They were also given food in the form of a hind quarter of smoked beef, some dried venison, bacon, fatback, lard, salt pork, and a couple of sacks each of flour, cornmeal, salt, sugar, potatoes, carrots, and onions. Additionally, they had a water barrel, two buckets, two canteens, some blankets, a couple of sleeping cots, some ropes, a tarp, some saddle blankets, extra tack and harnesses for their horses, and a sack of oats and grain to feed to the horses on their way.

Finishing out the load were various tools they might need to build new houses. Outfitted to the gills, wagons fully loaded and covered with tarps, the group of four started out on their long journey.

They had been traveling for about a week when Lawrence noticed off in the distance two people walking along the road.

What in the heck are two people doing out here walking in the middle of nowhere? he thought.

As the wagons got closer, the pair ran off and hid in the tree line. The group stopped the wagons, and Lawrence and James jumped out and started following their trail. It didn't take long for Lawrence to catch a glimpse of one of them hiding behind a fallen tree. He looked over at James, signaled where they were, and James started working his way around behind the hidden figures.

"You there, in the woods, come on out!" Lawrence hollered. "We ain't going to hurt you! Iffen y'all need some help, we'll be glad to see what we can do." He got no answer, so he said, "I see you'ns trying to hide over there. Y'all ain't got nothin' to fear from us, so come on out." Still no answer. By now, James had worked his way up behind them; he could see them about twenty yards off, crouched low.

It was then that James got close enough to see the people they were approaching weren't men. "Ladies," he said, "don't be afraid. We aren't here to take advantage of you. We'd just like to help you out if we can, iffen you want us to." Startled at the voice coming from behind them, the women turned and saw James standing out in the open as Lawrence began walking toward them from the other direction. Realizing they were stuck in the middle, they decided there was no sense in staying crouched down.

As they stood up, the men halted and took the measure of the two hapless travelers. One looked about mid-thirties and had dishwater-blonde hair and a full, mature figure; she was really quite pretty, if one looked under all the dirt she had on her.

The other one looked like she was probably her daughter, between fifteen and eighteen. She had a fine figure, just starting to blossom, and a very pretty, innocent face. But both faces were wearing an expression of terror. It was clear that they were wondering what was going to happen to them now.

"We didn't mean to scare you," James said, "and we don't mean you any harm, but what in tarnation are you two women doing out here by yourselves?"

"We were attacked by a gang of highwaymen," the older woman replied. "We were on our way to Kansas with my husband and son. We had stopped for just a moment, so we could go in the woods and relieve ourselves." She paused. James could see she was trembling.

"While we were in the woods doing our personal business, we heard horses approach, and voices," she continued. "There were eight to ten riders. Fortunately, we were hidden when the men came up on our wagons."

Both James and Lawrence had the same thought. This story wasn't going to end well.

"My husband and son didn't tell them where we were. I heard my husband say it was just the two of them headed to Kansas to his sister's place. The men asked my husband what they had in the wagons, and he told them it was just our household goods, only what they were taking with them to their new home.

"Then the men pulled pistols out and said, 'Let's have a look.' One of them told my husband and son to put their hands up and get off the wagons. There were so many men, it would have been useless for him to try and go for his guns."

James nodded. That was the absolute truth.

"They pulled back the tarps we had covering the wagons and seemed to like what they saw under them. They took some rope and tied my husband's and son's hands behind their backs and made them get in the wagon bed. Then they drove off with our wagons, and that was the last I saw of my husband and son."

The girl next to the woman put her hands on her mouth. She was trying to stifle sobs.

"We don't know what happened to them; all we know is they went east. We stayed hidden for about thirty minutes, and then started following the road west, hoping we could find some help. That was a day and a half ago."

James looked at Lawrence, who shrugged his shoulders. "Let's go back out to the road where we have our wagons," James said. "We'll get you something to eat and drink, and we'll talk this over with our kin."

They walked out to the wagons, and Lawrence pulled Ben and Wiley aside and quietly told them what the lady had disclosed. After which, he turned to the woman and said, "I'm sorry, ma'am, I didn't ask you your name. I can't very well introduce you to my kinfolk if I don't know it."

"My name is Clarissa," the lady said, "and my

daughter is Cassandra, but we go by Claire and Cassie."

"Thank you, ma'am," Lawrence said, introducing himself and the rest of the men. When he was finished he said, "Lemme get y'all some water and something to eat."

Lawrence filled mugs from the canteens they carried and sliced them off some pieces of their smoked venison; they had a few biscuits left from the morning and he gave those to them too. He left them to eat and walked over to the other men.

"Well, boys, ya want to try to help them or just drop them at the nearest town?" he said.

"I don't know," Ben said. "We shouldn't be taking any extra risks with what we've got in our wagons and all."

Wiley was shaking his head. "Yeah, but if that was someone you knew," he said, "wouldn't you do what you could to get their family back together? Nobody knows what we got, and as long as we keep it covered and don't talk about it to anyone, no one will know. I say we go to where that gang took their wagons and see if we can't find their trail. If we can find something to follow, we can go in easy and take a look from a distance and see if we might be able to do anything to save their menfolk and their belongings. If we decide we can't help them, we go to the nearest town and drop them with the sheriff."

The others nodded in agreement. "Yeah, okay," Ben said. "We'll go to the spot and see what we find."

Wiley nodded. "If there's a trail we can follow, Lawrence and James, you can track it since you're better trackers," he said. "We'll make a camp somewhere close by and wait for you to come tell us if you found anything."

James and Lawrence exchanged a glance. Tracking was a lot more exciting than the ranch work they'd been doing for the last few months.

"If you haven't found anything within, let's say, a day or two at most," Wiley said, "then come back, and we'll take these ladies to the nearest town. Is that okay with the rest of you?" They were all in agreement.

Lawrence walked back to the wagon and said, "Miss Claire, me and the fellows would like to see if we can help y'all out. If you don't mind, we'll take ya to where they took yer wagons and see if we can find a trail."

Claire dropped her eyes. Her hands were twisting a fold of her skirt.

"Me and James are pretty good trackers," Lawrence continued, trying to put her at ease. "If there's a trail to be found, we'll find it. If we find one, you'll have to stay with the wagons. Ben and Wiley will watch out fer ya till we get back from trailing that gang. Hopefully, they'll have a hideout somewhere nearby, cuz I can't see them taking your wagons, without having a place to hide them fairly close by. Gangs don't usually travel any distances with wagons. We'll trail them for a couple days if we have to, but if they haven't stopped somewhere by then, I don't know what we'll be able to do. But we're willing to give it a try, if you'd like us to."

She lifted her head, looked him in the eyes, and with tears in her own, replied, "We would be very grateful if you would try and see what you can find. I feel so hopeless and helpless right now, but if there's anything I want, it's to do everything I can to get my husband and boy back. I'll gladly show you the place where they took our wagons. I just hope there's still some kind of a trail to follow."

Her face was quickly tear-streaked, and his heart went out to her. "Then I guess you better climb up on the seat of one of these wagons., and we'll get on our way," Lawrence said. She quickly climbed up in the seat of the closest wagon. Cassie started to follow her, and Lawrence took her hand to help her climb.

As soon as the rest of the men heard her say she would like them to help her find her family, they climbed aboard their own wagons and delivered a clicking sound to their wagon horses. On command, the horses headed down the road the women had been walking on for a day and a half.

They figured they may have covered thirty miles, but it couldn't be much more than that. Since it was only a couple of hours before midday, they figured they might make it to the place before nightfall. They were traveling at a good pace but tried to talk to the women, asking them about their homes, what the war had done to them, and what they were hoping to do with the rest of their lives. Lawrence was only about six or seven years older than Cassie, and the pair kept sneaking curious glances at one another whenever the opportunity presented itself.

Lawrence thought she was quite pretty and looked as if she was starting to generously fill out in a womanly way. Claire noticed their glances but being a wise woman, she pretended she didn't. They had to move along quite quickly in order to keep up with the lead wagons. Bouncing in the seat so much meant they couldn't talk a lot.

The men in the lead were setting a fast pace because they knew the longer it took them, the less their chances were of finding a trail. At about dusk, the lead wagons slowed and stopped. Lawrence asked the women if it would be all right if they made camp there, because they didn't want them to miss any sign of where the abduction occurred, and it was getting dark.

"That's not problem for us," Claire said, "and it's probably the best, all things considered."

The men started setting up the camp and gathering wood for their fire. They put two cots and blankets in one of their two-man tents, which they hoped would make the women more comfortable than sleeping out in the open like they usually did.

When that was done, Wiley and Ben went about unhitching the horses and untying the ones that had been traveling behind the wagons. They had stopped in this area because they saw an area where a stream would be running between some trees.

Leading the horses through a thicket of small trees, they came to an opening with nice grass for the animals to eat. They hobbled the horses there, checked out the stream, then came back and took the horses two at a time for a drink. A row of tall oak trees extended the whole visible length of the creek, giving them shelter and protection.

When all of the horses had been watered, they left them hobbled in the clearing to eat all they wanted and headed back to the campsite. On the way, they decided they had to post a guard. They figured they had gotten close to where the gang had taken the wagons and didn't know whether they had been spotted from a distance, or were being watched even then.

Coming into the campsite, they saw that Lawrence and James had cut some of the beef and were frying it in a skillet, and the ladies were making biscuits and slicing potatoes and onions.

Wiley turned to James and Lawrence. "Why don't you give us your canteens, and we'll go fill them down at the creek," he said.

Handing them the canteens, Lawrence said, "Don't be long. Vittles will be ready in about fifteen minutes."

"That should be just about time enough," Ben answered. The beef was done, and the potatoes were almost finished when the ladies pulled the biscuits away from the fire.

They sat down as the women served up the food and passed them each a full plate, then served up their own. "I'm so hungry, I could eat three plates!" Claire said. "It's been almost two and half days since we've had a decent meal."

Cassie was busy filling her mouth with food. Finally, she paused long enough to say, "You men sure did come well equipped. You could probably feed ten people for a month with what's in that wagon."

Lawrence smiled "We all have the same thing in our wagons," he said. "It was our payment for working on a ranch for the last couple of months, and believe me, we did a lot of work."

When they finished eating, there wasn't a single bite of anything left. The women offered to take the plates and pans down to the creek to wash them. While they were gone, the men started discussing what they were going to do for the night. "I think it's best if we make a half circle around our campfire and the ladies' tent with the wagons," Wiley said. "We should post a guard by the wagons and one up higher on the hillside, just before the crest of it. There're some boulders about two thirds of the way up. They can offer some cover. From there, we'll be able to see the campsite and out around us a good distance."

The others nodded in agreement.

"We should take four-hour shifts," Wiley continued. "Then we'll split the last four hours, with the last shift standing guard while we prepare breakfast and get things ready to move out, just in case someone decides to try to jump us at daybreak as we're getting ready to leave." They all agreed that sounded good, so he asked, "Who wants first watch?

"Not me," Ben said. "I think it would be better if Wiley and me took second watch, so that we can have Wiley up by those rocks with his buffalo gun and one of the carbine rifles at first light, watching over us while we get ready to go."

"Yeah," James said. "That way he can knock off one or two of them before they get anywhere close to within range of any regular rifles. By then, the rest of us should be ready for them."

Wiley agreed, and they started to push the wagons into a semi-circle. When they were done, everyone got their bedrolls out and laid them by the wheels of the wagons, so they had some cover but were still close to the fire. The women came back into the camp and put the pots, pans, and plates on the end of one of the wagons, ready for the morning.

Wiley told Claire she should try to get a good night's sleep and not to worry. "We're posting two guards throughout the night to keep watch," he said.

She felt grateful they were thinking about protection. It was then she realized she was staring at him and thinking about what a big handsome man he was. She looked away quickly, scolding herself for thinking that way.

"It's been a while since we've been able to get a full night's sleep," she said. "We want to thank you boys for helping us, and for all your hospitality."

Lawrence piped up, "Don't you worry about anything. We'll have you awake just after first light, so we can make a fine breakfast and get things ready to roll. You just make yourself as comfortable as you can with what we have, and we'll take care of the rest."

Claire and Cassie both smiled. "Well then, good night y'all," they said in unison and went to their tent. Wiley and Ben went to their bedrolls and wrapped up, trying to get to sleep as soon as they could. Lawrence and James decided that Lawrence would go up on the rocks, and James would stay down at the campsite. Lawrence grabbed his blanket and one of his carbine rifles and went toward the rocks.

James started looking around for more wood to use during the night. He found a fallen tree not far from the campsite and started breaking off as many branches as he could carry; he made several trips to the fallen tree and stopped when he had a very large pile of wood.

It turned out to be plenty enough to last the night. The shift changes went smoothly, and not a soul tried to sneak up on the campsite.

• • •

At first light, Wiley thought he saw something way up on the hill, more than a quarter mile away—but wasn't sure what it was. When he came down from his post to have breakfast with the rest of the group, he told them about it.

Wiley thought about it and had more to add. "When we move out, keep your eyes peeled for anything moving along the sides of us or anything way out to the front," he said. "The last wagon needs to keep checking behind us every so often, just to make sure nothing comes up from behind without us knowing."

The women made ham steaks and bacon and biscuits and gravy, with plenty of hot coffee, for their breakfast. Once again, the women went to the river to wash the plates and pans, and the men got the horses and prepared everything to leave. When the women came back, they packed away the cooking things in the back of Lawrence's wagon and climbed on it for the trip. As they started out, Wiley asked the ladies to keep their eyes sharp for the place they had last seen their wagons. They moved at a slower pace than they'd taken the day before. They didn't want to seem like they were a hurry if someone was watching, and they didn't want the women to miss the place the gang had come up on them.

By the time the women started saying they thought they recognized the area, they had been traveling for a couple of hours. Claire said she remembered where they went off into the trees to do their personal business, because there was a large, towering oak about ten yards inside the tree line. She said there'd also been three clusters of trees on the other side of the road about a hundred yards away. With these landmarks to look for, they thought it shouldn't be very hard to find the right spot. Ben, being up front in the first wagon, was the first to see the towering oak. He slowed his horse and turned in his seat. "Is that the one?" he said to Claire. "That big oak tree over yonder?"

Claire stood up to get a better look. "I think so," she hollered. "I can't be sure from here, but I tied a piece of the lining of my dress to a branch of a small tree close by it. We need to get there to make sure."

When they'd gotten as close as they could to the tree, Claire climbed down from the wagon before Lawrence could get down and get over to that side to help her out, but he was in time to hand Cassie down from the wagon. As her feet touched the ground, she ran to catch up with her mother. Together, they walked toward the trees; her mother knew exactly where the cloth would be, if this was the right place.

It only took a couple of minutes before they were coming back out of the trees. Claire had the strip of her dress in her hand. The men had gathered between the second and third wagon and were standing there, waiting. As Claire approached them, she was looking out past the wagons, remembering the last image she had of her husband and son as they'd been dragged off by the gang.

"This is it!" she exclaimed. She showed the men the piece of dress material she'd pulled from the tree. Then pointing down the road, she said, "They took the wagons the way we're headed. That was the last I saw of them," and she started to cry.

Wiley, being the one standing next to her, reached out to put his arm around her, drawing her to his shoulder to comfort her. "Try not to cry," he said. "We'll do our best to find your husband and son. Hopefully we're not too late, and they'll still be alive."

At the thought of that, she abruptly stopped crying. "Oh, God, yes. We must hurry!" she said.

"We can't be in too much of a hurry," Wiley replied. "We don't want to miss where they left the road."

Wiley asked the two women if they could handle driving a wagon at a slow pace. "Because from here forward, me and Ben will keep an eye out all around us," he said. "I'll be in the first wagon, and Ben will be in the last, but Lawrence and James need to be freed up to look for tracks or a trail where they left the road. That means they need to walk, so they won't miss anything."

Both women affirmed that they could handle a horse and wagon.

"We've had to do it quite often," Claire said, "whenever the men would go hunting to look for something to eat. They always stayed within sight, but sometimes they'd get a couple hundred yards or more off the road. We stayed on the wagons, moving them slowly forward, keeping up with them."

James and Lawrence went to their wagons and got one of their carbine rifles. They started out walking down the road in front of the wagons. Wiley helped Claire get up on the second wagon, and Ben helped Cassie get on the third. Then Ben went to the last wagon and Wiley to the first, and they started moving down the road slowly, staying behind Lawrence and James.

Ben and Wiley kept their eyes scanning the countryside to the sides, with Wiley in front, looking out as far as he could, to see if they saw anyone watching or coming up on them. Ben monitored the road behind them.

After about an hour, Lawrence stopped and studied

the ground off to the left. James came to his side to see what he was looking at. They walked off the road for about twenty yards and conferred for a minute, and then turned around and headed back to the wagons.

"There's a trail here," James said. "You can't see any horse tracks or wagon tracks, but you can see where they used some brush to wipe them out. If it's not the gang we're after, it's awful strange. Most people won't try to hide their trail. If we follow it a ways, we should be able to see the trail of the wagons or where the grass was broken and hasn't come back up."

Lawrence shifted his carbine from hand to hand, suddenly restless. "Me and James are going to take a couple horses, ride back in there a little ways, and see if we can find anything." They saddled the horses that had been trailing their wagons.

Wiley looked around and saw where the road went down and out of sight into what they knew back home as a "holler." That was a place that was too big to be called a ravine but too small to be called a valley. Someone might holler from one hillside to the other and be heard, hence the name.

Wiley said, loud enough for everyone to hear, "I'm going up ahead to take a look at where the road dips out of sight. It that might be a good place for us to wait till Lawrence and James get back. We may have to wait a day or two. Hopefully not, but we might as well be prepared." He took his wagon to the rise to have a look.

When he got to the top of the rise, he saw a large clearing down around the tree line that ran through the bottom of the holler. It looked like a fair place to make a camp, and there were a couple of good places for a guard to be up high to view the whole clearing. He could see the road coming from both directions and the area where it dipped down. He turned the wagon around and went back to the group.

By then, Lawrence and James had prepared their horses and some food and water to take with them. "We'll be waiting for you just below that rise in the road," Wiley told them. "There's a nice sized clearing off to the right, down by the tree line that runs through the bottom. You boys be careful and try not to be seen; if we're going to have any chance of saving those two, we can't let them know someone's tracking them."

Lawrence gave him a look as if he was telling them something they already knew very well. "We'll do our best to keep a good look out up ahead of us while we're following their trail," he said. "If we do catch up with them, or if they have a hideout somewhere, there's going to be a lookout. I just hope we see him before he sees us!"

Lawrence had to add his own warning to Wiley. "You need to be careful here too. You know they're watching this road, so they can rob people. You should be okay down between those hills. Just try not to make too much smoke with your fire, or better yet, wait till dark before you make one. Make sure your lookout post is up high enough, so you can see anyone coming down the road from either direction and along the edges of that holler."

"Yes, sir," Wiley responded. "Ya think maybe that's why I like that place to make camp?"

"Sorry," Lawrence replied, a little embarrassed. "I forgot that's why you were the platoon sergeant, but I think maybe you forgot me an' James have been tracking and taking out more than a few Injun scouts. We'll get back as soon as we find something, or if we think they just kept on going."

Lawrence and James left, following the trail, and the others took the wagons down over the rise into the holler. When they got to the clearing near the bottom of the hill, they climbed down from the wagons.

"Hold up a minute before you start unloading anything," Wiley told them. "I want to take a look around and see if this really is the best place for us to camp." He walked through the trees at the far side of the clearing and went out of sight. A few minutes later, he came back, saying he'd found a better place.

"We'll have to clear a path for the wagons to get through," Wiley said. "Ben, grab your ax, and I'll grab mine."

He looked at Claire and said, "You two stay here with the wagons and keep an eye out. Come and get us if you see anyone coming."

The women looked at each other, and a shudder of fear went through them as they remembered what had happened before. Their determination to be strong and do whatever they had to do to find their menfolk won over. Claire nodded at Wiley. "Okay," she said. "We'll stay alert for anything and let you know."

It took a little more than an hour to clear a path wide enough to get the wagons through. When the men came back through the trees, the women let out a sigh of relief.

"Through those trees," Wiley said, pointing into the thicket, "about thirty yards, there is an even bigger clearing where we can fit everything and be out of sight from anyone traveling on the road."

The men hadn't cleared all the low branches from the

path, and the horses ducked their heads as they walked the wagons through. The men could have ridden on the wagons but would have had to lay on the bench seats in order not to be hit by branches. Once through the pathway, the ladies saw a large grassy clearing and heard water moving off to the side, where there was a fast-flowing creek splashing over rocks in the stream bed.

They looked at each other and smiled. "This is a real pretty place," Cassie said. "I like it here."

Ben added, "Yeah, seems we lucked out for now." He turned to Wiley and said, "Let's go take some of those small trees we cut and put them across the front of the path, so it looks like there is no path in here."

Wiley turned to Claire. "You two can have a look around. Just don't go too far. We'll be back shortly." He went with Ben to cover the opening.

While they were gathering the small trees they'd cut to get inside the clearing, Ben turned to Wiley and said, "Looks like you have taken a liking to Claire. She's a pretty one, but don't forget she has a husband." He avoided his eyes.

"A man can't help but notice a pretty woman," Wiley said. "And don't you worry. I know my manners."

When they thought they had enough trees across the opening, Wiley went out toward the road to see if someone could tell they had covered an entrance from out there. From that perspective, he decided that unless someone got up close and was really trying to see an opening, it wasn't noticeable. They went back through the trees to the wagons.

The women were just coming back from the stream when Ben and Wiley came into the clearing by the wagons. "We found a nice little pool downstream a little ways," Claire said, "and thought we might go take a bath. The water's pretty cold, but at this point, I'd take a bath in ice to get all this dirt off me and wash my clothes."

Wiley nodded. "If that's what you want to do, go right ahead," he said. "I have some soap you can use. Just be careful and keep an eye out in case someone comes down from the hillsides trying to get to the stream. If you want, I'll come down with you and stand guard. I'll keep my back turned, but you'll have to watch out on the other side of you."

She smiled at him and said, "I think it'd be better if we just went alone."

"Suit yourself," he replied. "Just yell real loud if you run into any trouble."

He got the soap and gave them a couple of blankets to wrap up in while their clothes dried, and off they went to take their bath. He turned to Ben. "We better get to setting up this campsite, so we don't go down and spy on those girls," he said. "Even though I'd like to take a peek, it wouldn't be gentlemanly. I wouldn't want them thinking anything about us other than that we are gentlemen, so let's just get things ready to have us a nice lunch." Ben grinned.

They went about gathering stones for a fire pit, clearing the spot for it and setting up a roasting spit, which would also hold a pot. They cut some wood for their fire, then remembered what Lawrence had said about not making the fire until dark, so smoke wouldn't give them away.

Wiley admired their work. "Looks like the campsite's ready," he said, "and seeing it's an hour or so before noon, we're going to have to have a cold lunch. We can make a fire for dinner after dark. One of us ought to get up on that hillside among those rocks and start keepin' an eye out. I'll go first, and let's break it up into two-hour shifts till after supper. Then we can take four-hour shifts and split the last one before daylight."

Ben agreed. "Sounds okay to me," he said. "I think I'll take me a nap."

About an hour and a half later, the women came back to camp. Claire decided to make a fire and started looking around for the matches. Wiley had seen the women making their way back upstream toward the camp from up above them on the hill. He walked down into camp, figuring they would want to dry their clothes. By the time he got there, Claire had found the matches. "What do you think you're doing?" he said to her.

She looked at him dumbfounded, thinking it was quite obvious. "I was just going to light a fire, so we can dry our clothes; they didn't dry very well during the time we laid them out in the sun."

He smiled, "Yeah, I was going to light a fire earlier and make us a nice lunch, then I remembered, we don't need any campfire smoke to be spotted by anyone."

She looked at him with embarrassment for having forgotten. "Oh shoot, we'll have to stay in these blankets till after dark. That's going to be a little tricky trying to keep ourselves covered."

With an interesting grin, Wiley said, "Yeah, it just might be. I'll set up your tent for you and you can just go inside and have a nap till it gets dark." He woke up Ben, and told him it was his turn to take the lookout duty. Then he went over to the wagon where they had put the tent from the night before and pulled it out. He set it up with one flank to the fire pit. Claire and Cassie had draped their clothes over the side of one of the wagons and were standing around, waiting for him to finish.

They followed him over to the tent when he carried over the cots. They waited to go inside till after he finished setting them up. When he came back out, Claire looked at him with a big smile and curtsied. "Thank you, kind sir. Your graciousness is greatly appreciated," she said, and moved past him into the tent. Cassie followed behind.

He laughed as he watched them. "You're quite welcome, my lady. I always come to the rescue of a damsel in distress."

As Ben was about to go up to the lookout point, Wiley told him he was going to try his luck fishing; Ben wished he'd thought of that instead of napping.

"Some fresh fish would be good tonight," he said. "I hope you catch enough for all of us," He left the campsite, carrying a rifle and his canteen.

Wiley found the fishing line and hooks he had brought for just this kind of occasion and headed down to the stream to look for a likely spot for some fish. He walked a little way downstream and found the pool where the women had bathed. There was a rim of soap residue they'd left along the shoreline.

He continued downstream, looking for any pools that might hold fish. After about fifty yards he came across a nice one, probably thirty yards long and maybe half as wide, and decided he'd try fishing in the shadows from the far bank. He cut across upstream of the pool and started hunting on the hillside for grasshoppers to use as bait.

He caught three or four of them, put the grasshoppers in his shirt pocket, then pulled some grass and put it on top of them to hold them in there. He went back to the pool and stealthily snuck up to the bank, where the shadows were extending out into the water. He tied his line to the end of the branch he'd cut to make his fishing pole, put his hook on the line, and a grasshopper on the hook. He tossed it out into the shadows, staying well back from the edge of the pool. His first two tries didn't have any results, so he moved down another fifteen feet and cast out again. Almost immediately, the grasshopper on the end of his line was swallowed by a large fish. Fortunately, the fish swam upstream. He followed it past where he had been fishing, to a spot where the bank was not as steep as where he had first hooked it, so he could drag it up on shore without breaking the branch he had chosen for his pole.

It was a trout of about two and half pounds.

He took it back to the steep banked area of the pool where he was fishing when he hooked it and laid it up on the hillside. He tried again in the same place and caught another one, not quite as large. He tried again with no results and moved down the pool another fifteen feet. He caught two more, about a pound a half each, from that same pool. He worked his way downstream and fished in two other ponds. He ended up with ten nice fish, but he had traveled about a quarter of a mile downstream to catch them.

As he broke a branch to put through their gills so that he could carry them back, he realized he'd been fishing for a good while and that it must be close to his time to be the lookout again. It took him a while to get back to the campsite. When he got there, Claire told him Ben had been there and asked for him, because it was his turn on watch.

He showed them the fish, and asked if they knew how to clean them, saying that he couldn't because he was late for his turn on watch. Cassie said she did. She just needed a knife. He got one from his wagon and gave it to her, grabbed his rifle, and canteen, and went out to where Ben was.

Cassie checked her clothes to see if they were dry. Since they were just damp mostly, she dressed and went down to the stream to clean the fish. Claire told her to be careful and to stay within shouting distance.

Ben came into the campsite a few minutes later, saying, "It's almost dusk. I think we can go ahead and start a fire," so they did.

Claire took her clothes and tried to put them by the fire without getting them dirty.

Ben saw what she was doing and said, "Hold on there, I'll make you a rack you can put them on; that way they won't be on the ground. They might end up smelling like wood smoke if the wind changes, but at least they'll get completely dry."

He had finished making the rack from tree branches, and Claire was laying out her clothes, trying desperately to keep herself covered with the blanket, when Cassie came into camp with the cleaned fish. She saw the rack and said, "Oh, good. I was starting to get cold in these damp clothes of mine." She set the fish down on the back of the wagon and went to the tent. She came out of the tent wrapped in her blanket and walked over to the rack and laid her clothes on it.

As the two women stood by the fire getting their blankets nice and warm, Claire noticed Ben was looking at them. She said, "I guess we're warmed up enough for now. Let's get into the tent and stop bothering this man. I can see he's not very comfortable with the two of us standing here with just a blanket around us."

"No, you're not bothering me," Ben said quickly, "and I didn't mean to be staring at you, if I was."

Claire smiled. "It's okay," she said. "You can let us know when our clothes are dry."

"Okay. In the meantime, I'll get started on making dinner for all of us." And he started assembling the makings of their meal.

He checked the clothes before he started putting the pans on the fire; they were dry, and so that they wouldn't smell like fish or fried potatoes, he took them to the tent and gave them to Claire.

While the fish were cooking, Lawrence and James came into camp with Wiley. They said they had found the trail and followed it until it started getting dark. Afraid they might lose it if the gang changed directions, they got their bearings and decided to come back and spend the night in camp. The pair decided that they would head out in the morning, prepared to stay overnight, if necessary.

They ate all of the fish, potatoes, and biscuits; the men had two big fish each, and the women had only one, but said they were completely full. As everyone sat around the fire, Lawrence said, "It looked like there were eight single horses and two wagons that had made the trail we were following. They'd quit brushing out the trail after about a couple hundred yards from the road and left an easy one to follow after that. Let's all try and get a good night's sleep. Tomorrow, we'll be able to ride fast to the place we turned around at and pick it up again easily." He was hoping to comfort the women with his words.

Wiley said, "Sounds good to me. I'm tired; I didn't take a nap like Ben here. I went and caught our dinner."

Ben had to add, "I'm not much of a fisherman, anyway. With all of us here, we can take three-hour shifts on lookout and all be able to get plenty of sleep. I'll take first watch." He grabbed his rifle and canteen and started up to the lookout point. The women went to wash the pans and plates in the stream. By the time they came back, all three of the men were already in their bedrolls, and two were snoring. The women put the stuff in the wagon and went into their tent for the night.

CHAPTER 3

FINDING THE HIDEOUT

The night went smoothly until about three in the morning, when Lawrence was on guard. He heard horses on the road so he laid down on the rocks and put his rifle against his side, so the moon wouldn't reflect off of it. He saw six riders go past him, heading east. *This must be the gang. Who else would be riding out here at this time a night?* he thought. None of the riders even looked in his direction; it seemed they had no worries about anyone looking for them.

By the end of his watch, nothing else had happened. He had seen a few deer, but nothing else. He went to wake James for his turn and told him about the riders and to be sure to stay low and not silhouette himself because they may be coming back.

At first light, James went back to camp. Everyone was awake and doing things to either prepare breakfast or prepare the horses and gear for the day's tracking.

"No one's come back down the road so far," he told them. "If it was them, they're still out, and we need to be careful of them coming up from behind us while we're following the trail. Whoever's going to be on watch here needs to get to a place they can be well hidden from the road. Those rocks are too open. It's a good spot for a night watch, but not for the daytime."

Wiley said, "There's a clump of trees that has some brush around them on the other hillside that we can stay hidden in. We'll still be able to see the camp and in both directions on the road."

James replied, "Yeah, I saw what I think you're talking about on my way back down here, and it looked like a pretty good place. Not much cover from bullets, but good to hide in."

They had their breakfast and coffee, put out their fire as the sun was coming up, and the women went to wash the dishes. Lawrence and James mounted up and went off at a fast trot to get to where they had left the trail the day before. Wiley went up to the clump of trees on the other hillside.

When they reached the place where they had turned around the day before, they reigned the horses. Lawrence said, "I'll take the high ground. I can keep watch behind us for the riders coming back. You make sure we're on the right trail."

"All right," James replied, "but make sure you give me enough time to get out of sight from anyone coming up behind us."

Lawrence turned his horse in a tight circle. "I'll give my best whistle, and you'll know to hightail it to the closest place you can hide," he said.

They had been tracking for a couple hours when James heard a loud whistle from above. He quickly looked around him for somewhere to hide and spotted a small ravine off to his right. He couldn't tell how far down it went, but it was the only place he would have a chance to reach that might hide him and his horse, as trees were pretty sparse in the area they were in. He made his horse take off on the run and started down the hillside into the ravine, not stopping until the edge of it was well over his head. He stopped his horse beneath an outcropping, where a tree was clinging to the edge of the embankment. After a few minutes, he heard a wagon rumbling fast across the hard ground he had been tracking on, followed by the sound of running horses, so he stayed as still as possible and hoped his horse wouldn't make any noise. After a few minutes, he heard a whistle and went back up the ravine the way he came.

When James got to the trail, Lawrence was there. "That has to be the gang," he told him. "They were going pretty fast down this trail, and it looked like they had rustled another wagon from somebody. There were five men on horses and one in the wagon, pulling another horse. They probably stranded whoever's wagon it was, or they killed them and dumped them somewhere on the way."

James started his horse down the trail. "Let's get a move on and see if we can follow them to their hideout. Keep an eye out for their lookout, and let's move."

They were following the trail for about a mile when Lawrence saw something reflecting the sunlight far up ahead. He told James, "Hold up. We need to see what that is, up there on the hill."

They stopped and found a good place to hide their horses, where they wouldn't be seen from the trail or from up above. Once the horses were settled, they grabbed their rifles and started out on foot. As soon as there was enough cover to get over to the back side of the hill where Lawrence saw the reflection, they went across the trail and started climbing the hill.

Staying low, they approached the top of the hill. Just slightly below the crest, they found a place to sit behind some brush that offered a wide view of the area below. Lawrence saw the reflection again, took a guess about how far away it was, and noted there was a lone tree about ten yards from the rocks where he had seen the reflection. James looked out toward the opposite hillside and saw down around the base of it was a large cluster of oak trees. There were some horses tied underneath them.

They decided to go back over the hill and try to come back up to the top a good distance beyond where Lawrence had seen the sun reflecting off whatever it had been. They moved quietly along the far side of the hill to a point a hundred yards or more beyond the reflection, then crawled up over the hill's crest.

They crept to a vantage point where they could get a good look at the cluster of oak trees below and above the rocks close to where they had seen the glimmer. Both thought it would be an ideal place for the gang's lookout, and their intuition had been right. A man was sitting behind the rocks with his rifle leaning up against the hillside, sunlight sparkling brilliantly off its barrel. Looking downward through the trees, they could see there was a cabin below. A wagon rolled out from under the tree cover and started heading farther into the little box canyon that the hillsides formed.

They watched as it traveled about a quarter mile and turned off down into a gully. A few minutes later, a rider came back on the horse that had been pulling the wagon and quickly vanished into the woods by the cabin. They figured he had hidden the wagon back beyond the cabin, so that if anyone came around snooping, they wouldn't see anything suspicious. They could see that if someone did go back that way to snoop around, the outlaws could ambush them on their way back. Because of the steep hillsides, there appeared to be only one way in and out on horseback.

They decided to circle around below the crest of the hills to get to the other side of the box canyon. They crawled back over the hilltop till they could stand and not be seen from the other side, then started hiking at a fast pace. It was imperative to get a look at the place where the wagon had been left, along with a view of the land and cabin area from that side.

When they thought they had gone far enough, they slowly approached the crest of the far hill, then went down on their bellies again and crawled to the top. Looking down, they saw a deer trail that would take them into the trees at the end of the ravine. The woods obscured the view down there, which meant they would have to go there to see.

They looked around carefully to make sure there wasn't a guard. And once again, they crawled until they were well hidden by the trees, then started to walk, crouched low, down the deer trail toward the bottom of the ravine.

A little more than halfway down, the terrain flattened out, creating a plateau large enough for the road, the area of the cabin, and the cluster of trees that hid it all. Along the edge of the plateau, the terrain dropped off even farther into a deeper ravine. There was a trail there that seemed to have been made by a lot by wagons. It ended in a sheer cliff that looked like it had been formed by water runoff forceful enough to have washed away the end of the plateau. When they finally made it to where they could see the bottom of this deeper ravine, the men were both astounded by what they saw.

Underneath the cliff's hundred foot drop-off was a splintered mountain of wood. It looked like ten or more wagons had been rolled off the cliff and broken apart upon hitting the bottom. Underneath it all lay what looked like three human bodies. James and Lawrence turned to face each other. "This doesn't look good for Claire and Cassie's kinfolk," Lawrence said.

James shook his head. "We need to get down there," he said, "and see if there's not something we can take back that might identify who those men are."

The pair stayed low as they followed the deer trail toward the carnage. When they got to the wagons, they had to put bandannas over their faces. The smell of decomposing bodies was gut-wrenching. They decided to take the boots from the bodies and a piece of their shirts. It was no use trying to imagine what the faces were like while they were alive because of decomposition and what the birds and animals had done to them. After getting the boots and the pieces of the shirts, they hurried back out the ravine and up over the hillside.

They made their way, crawling, toward the crest of the area where they had first sneaked past the guard. Coming up to it, they realized they had actually gone a little farther than they'd needed to, but upon seeing there was still plenty of cover to hide them, they decided it was actually a safer way for them to come down to get to their horses.

They made it to them as the sun was starting to go down. It would soon be below the hills. They stuffed the shirt pieces deep into their saddlebags and ran some leather straps they were carrying through the boot strappings and around their saddle horns several times so they wouldn't lose them. Then they walked the horses down the ravine a good distance before coming back up onto the trail they used to come in on where they finally mounted up and took off running, hoping to get back to the campsite before it was completely dark. They slowed to a trot eventually, realizing that they didn't need to push the horses so hard. Delivering the news more quickly was not going to change anything.

It took a couple of hours to get back to their campsite. Darkness had been blanketing the terrain and sky for a good while.

Chapter 4

Delivering the News

Ben was on watch and heard their horses before he saw them. When he realized the riders were Lawrence and James, he came down from the rocks to meet them at the entrance to the campsite to see what they had learned.

When Lawrence and James got to the edge of the trees, they dismounted. As Ben drew close enough to see their faces, their expressions told him the outcome wasn't good. "We found the gang's hideout," James said, "and we think we found Claire's husband and son, along with some other unfortunate soul."

Lawrence shook his head. "I really hope we didn't find them, but I think we did," he said.

They moved the branches covering the entrance to their hideout and then unstrapped the boots from the saddle horns and pulled the pieces of shirts from the saddlebags. Ben took the horses to where the other horses were and hobbled them while James and Lawrence stacked the branches back across the front of the entrance. They felt terrible carrying the items they knew were sure to break the ladies' hearts. They walked slowly toward the camp fire.

The items were an emotionally weighty load. They'd potentially mean that life and family as Claire and Cassie had known it had been destroyed.

Wiley saw them coming and started toward Lawrence, motioning for him to wait where he was. When he reached them, he asked what they had found.

Lawrence held out the boots and shirt scraps. In a low voice, he said, "I hope this is not theirs, but I fear the worst."

Wiley examined the items. The scent of death still clung to them.

"How should we go about showing them what we found?" Lawrence said.

"There is not really any easy way we can do it except just to tell them," Wiley said. "You found what we think is the hideout and want to know if they recognize what you brought back."

As Lawrence looked at him, he felt a pain in his heart. The women would be devastated. "I think I'll let you do that," he said and handed Wiley the pieces of the shirts and the boots. Ben had finished caring for the horses and joined the men.

Claire and Cassie were standing near the campfire. Their expressions were a mixture of eagerness and fear.

As the men all reached the fire pit, Claire was able to get a clear look at the cloth scraps and boots Wiley was carrying. Tears welled in her eyes as she reached out and took them from Wiley. As she brought them close to her bosom, the dam inside her burst, and she started sobbing uncontrollably. She dropped the cloth and boots and ran to the tent, crying her heart out.

Cassie looked at the men in bewilderment, not

wanting to believe her worst fears were being turned into reality. "Can I see them?" she said. Ben picked up the boots and handed them to her, and Wiley handed her the pieces of the shirts. Cassie stared at the shirt scraps and ran to the tent with them, bursting into tears on the way.

The men stood silently for a minute. It was clear from their reaction they had found who they were looking for. They walked away from the tent, so they wouldn't be heard, and Lawrence asked, "Well, what are we going to do about this?"

Wiley responded, "What should we do? You know darn well this needs to be turned over to the sheriff."

Ben shook his head. "There is no sheriff for thirty-five miles, and those boys just killed someone else for their wagon. If we wait to go get a sheriff and get him back here, who knows how many more they will kill. Heck they may even find our campsite!"

Wiley's face became serious. "There's at least eight murderers holed up back there from what Claire said. What else can we do?"

"We should just go in there and give them what they deserve," James said. His voice was cold and angry.

Lawrence held up his hands. "Let's see what the women want us to do."

They walked back to the fire pit and waited until the crying and sobbing slowed down a bit before having the courage to interrupt their pain. Wiley went over to the tent, Lawrence following close behind. He called Claire's name and asked if he could come inside, then entered without waiting for them to respond.

He sat down next to her on the cot, pulled her close, and held her while she cried. Lawrence went in the tent and did the same for Cassie, holding her tight as she sobbed.

After a few moments, Claire wiped her face. "Did you take them off our men, or did you just find them somewhere?" she said.

Wiley responded, his voice very soft, "I'm sorry, but they were taken off of them."

She started crying very hard again, with gut-wrenching sobs between gasps for air. She'd gotten final confirmation that she had lost her husband and son.

The men stayed with the two women for quite a while, trying to comfort them in their loss. Eventually, Claire asked if she could be alone with Cassie, and of course they complied with her wishes. As they got up to leave, they picked up the boots and one of the pieces of the shirts to remove the visual reminder of their loss. The other piece was gipped in Claire's fist, and she wasn't letting it go.

Wiley and Lawrence went out of the tent and over to the other men.

"I think we should try to make some supper for us," Wiley said. "Maybe they'll want to eat something in a little while." They went about getting the food ready and started cooking.

When supper was ready, Wiley went to the women's tent with two plates of food. "You ladies need to eat something," he said. "It might help you feel a little better if you have something in your stomachs." He left the plates on the ends of the cots and then went back to the men and said, "I think we'll have to wait until tomorrow morning to find out what they want us to do about this. For now, let's eat our supper and try to get some sleep.

I'll take first watch up on the hill."

The night was a quiet one, and when his watch was over, Wiley went to the tent and looked in. The plates were empty, and both women were sleeping. They looked like they'd cried themselves to sleep. As he picked up the plates, Claire woke up. "Thank you for everything," she said. "This just hurts so much."

He looked at her puffy, tear-streaked face, and struggled for a way to help her feel better. "I know how it feels when you lose someone you love," he finally said. "I lost my wife to consumption before I joined the war. It's terrible when something like this happens and there's nothing you can do can change it. You can't believe it's happened, and you can't do anything about it. You ask yourself what your life is now worth. You have an emptiness inside that you can't seem to fill, and you believe that nothing ever will close that hole in your heart. I really felt like my life was not worth even living without her. That's why I joined in the fight between the North and the South; I just didn't care if I got killed or not."

Wiley sighed. The memory was still so painful. "In the end," he said, "I realized that God was not through with me yet, otherwise I would have died in a battle somewhere. There must be some other purpose for me here on this earth." His words were louder now, more forceful. "Maybe that's why you were not taken when they were—there's another purpose for you. You just don't know what it is yet, like me. We can only hope that someday we find out what that purpose is."

He shook his head, as if to clear his sad thoughts. It was time to get her mind on something else. "The men and I were wondering if you want us to go get a sheriff and bring him back here," he said. "Although, I don't know how far ahead the next town is, I do know the one behind us is about thirty or so miles back. It would probably take two or three days before I could get back here with a posse."

She looked back at him through red eyes. "I don't know. What do you think we should do?"

"Well," he answered, "we can't very well just go in there and string them up ourselves. That would just make us vigilantes and killers just like them, without giving them a fair trial."

She looked in his eyes, desperation showing heavily on her face. "What are we going to do?" she said. "We have no home or family left or any place to go. Would you go get the sheriff?"

Wiley nodded. "Sure, if that's what you'd like us to do. But who knows what that gang will do during the time it takes to go get him."

She brought her hands up and smoothed her hair as if trying to regain her composure, "I'm not a murderer," she said, "and I don't want you boys to turn into murderers, even though I'd like to go shoot them myself."

He saw the hatred in her eyes and felt the desire for revenge in her words.

"Let me talk to the boys and see what they think would be best."

When he'd rejoined the rest of the men, Wiley told them that what she'd asked. They looked at each other and agreed that that would be the best, so they wouldn't be getting themselves into any trouble that they might not be able to handle.

"I'll go back to the last town we passed," Wiley said, "and see if I can get the sheriff to get a posse together. I might as well start out now, as I'm rested and it's a clear night. I should be able to cover twenty miles before daylight."

He asked Ben if he would saddle up a fresh horse for him and asked Lawrence to put some food together. Then he asked James to fill his canteens while he went and talked to Claire. The men moved quickly to do what he'd asked.

This time, when he asked if he could come inside the tent, he waited before stepping in.

As he sat down on a cot and looked at Claire, tears welled up in his eyes; he felt like he was reliving the pain he'd felt when he'd lost his wife.

"I'm going to ride back to the last town we passed and tell the sheriff what we know," he told her. "I'm going to leave in a few minutes; you should be safe here with the other three to protect you. Try and get some sleep. I'll be back as soon as I can."

Then he gave her a hug and turned to leave. "Please be careful," she said, her voice trembling with anguish that she couldn't hold back. As he came out of the tent, Ben was bringing his horse over by the wagons, where his food and canteens were waiting. He put the food in a saddlebag and looped the strap of the canteen over the saddle horn. Then he grabbed the reins of his horse, and before walking through the opening in the trees. "You boys be real careful and take care of those women till I get back. I'll be back as fast as I can."

After Wiley had left, the others put back the branches to cover the opening. They went to the campfire and sat around talking about how to go about taking down that gang. Lawrence offered the idea of just blowing up the cabin while they were sleeping. Ben asked, "How do you plan to do that?"

He smiled. "I just happen to have brought a few of those cannon charges with me," he said. Ben and James turned to each other with surprise, and they started to laugh.

Lawrence looked at them, confused. "What's so funny?"

Still laughing, James said, "Well, we just happen to have some too."

And with that, they were all laughing.

After the mirthful moment had passed, Lawrence said, "We should go up there and watch the place while Wiley's gone, so we can kind of know the routine they have for the lookout and what they do around there." His tone was once again, very serious. "It takes about three hours of an easy ride to get to where we could keep a watch on them," he continued. "Since we've been there, me and James could take shifts. I can go a few hours before sunup, and he can come relieve me just before sundown. We can run those kinds of shifts, spying on them till Wiley gets back. We'll split the lookout duty here, so that whoever has to go out to spy on them can get some sleep before he has to go back. What do ya think?"

Ben and James agreed that it sounded like the best way for them to do something useful while they were waiting for Wiley to return.

"I'm going to turn in," Lawrence said. "You two split up the lookout watch and wake me a few hours before sunup."

The lookout shifts went without incident. As requested, a few hours before sunup, they woke Lawrence. He grabbed some food and his canteens and headed out to find a good spot to keep an eye on the gang's hideout. Before he left he turned to James. "I'll leave my horse on the far side of the hill from where their lookout was," he told him. "It will be well hidden. I'll try to find a place up above and beyond the lookout, where I can see the whole layout of the place and stay hidden, just to give you an idea where I'm going to be positioned."

Lawrence headed to the area close to where they had gone behind the hill the last time. He made it before sunup and walked his horse along the bottom of the hill till he came to a good-sized cluster of trees to hide in before hobbling him. Then he started making his way up the hill beyond the lookout, hoping he would still be able to see the cabin once he got to the top.

The sun was just starting to come over the horizon as he was crawling. He crested the hill, heading to a spot where he was well hidden but could still see the things he wanted to keep an eye on. As daylight came over the hill, he found the lookout's position again and saw the man seemed to be asleep, his hat pulled down over his eyes. He looked down around the tree area and the cabin; there was no movement at all. He managed to find a place he could lie down and look out underneath the brush. He made sure to keep his rifle underneath him, so he wouldn't give away his position like their lookout had.

It was hard to stay there like that, but he knew that's what he had to do. It was just like before when they had watched the Northern army's storage sites. The man on watch had woken up when the sun's rays reached him. About an hour after sunup, a relief lookout came up to him. A relief lookout was sent about every four hours to change with the man on watch.

There wasn't much activity around the cabin. Once in a while a man came outside to go off in the trees to relieve himself or take a look at the horses. Not long after the third lookout change, a couple of men came outside and started playing horseshoes in front of the cabin. Other than that, there was no other activity. As the sun was going down, he heard something making noise in the brush above him and saw James crawling around through the brush. He threw a pebble at him to get him to look his direction. When the pebble hit him, he looked in the direction it came from and saw Lawrence lying underneath the brush and crawled over to him. Lawrence told him what he had seen during the day and whispered, "Keep a good estimate on the time intervals when they change the lookout during the night. You should be able to hear them, as they talk loud when they change guards, even if you can't see them."

James let him know he'd left his horse in the same place as his. As he was leaving, Lawrence said he'd be back before sunup and crawled his way back up, over and down the other side of the hill till he was able to stand and be out of sight. He walked his horse out along the bottom of the hill until he felt he was far enough away he could ride so no one would hear the horse's hooves. Riding back to the campsite, he kept a wary eye on the trail ahead.

As he walked his horse through the opening in the trees, he saw Ben coming down the hill to meet him. He caught up with him as he reached the wagons. "Well, how did it go? What did you see?" Ben said.

"They're a bunch of lazy no-accounts," Lawrence said, and even he could hear the bitterness in his voice. "But it's been only one day, so I can't say for sure. I did see a way we can sneak in at night behind the cabin. They don't have a guard back that way or anywhere close to it."

Then he added with less acrimony, "I think if we took out the lookout, we can sneak close enough to put some charges at the front door and on the corners and behind the cabin. We can then get behind the bigger trees and be plenty close enough to hit the charges easily and blow the place to smithereens."

"Good," Ben said. "That's just what they deserve. I know I'd sure like to do that right now, but we need to wait and see what the sheriff thinks."

The next day went pretty much the same without any deviations from the routine they had seen. On the third morning, Lawrence and James watched six riders leave the cabin just after sunup. James waited an extra hour before leaving the observation post to head back to the campsite in case someone turned around and came back to the cabin. He didn't want to be seen on the trail into the place. Wiley hadn't returned by just before sundown when James left the campsite to relieve Lawrence.

When Lawrence made it back to the campsite, Wiley was there with the sheriff and a paltry four men that had come as his posse. He told them about the six riders leaving and not having come back yet.

The sheriff said, "I want to wait a little while and see if those riders come back with a wagon or something. I want to have them all together at the hideout, if we can. I'll post one of my men up on the hillside here by the campsite to watch the road tonight, and I want to put one of my men up at the place where you've been watching the hideout from." Lawrence said he would take the man there whenever the sheriff wanted him to.

The sheriff looked around at his men and nodded. "If you will take my man up there in the morning when you would normally change the lookout, that'll be fine," he replied.

The women prepared dinner for everyone that had showed up after James had left, Ben and James had already eaten. Lawrence got his plate, and Claire gave him dinner. When he was finished, he turned to the sheriff and said, "Will you wake me up a few hours before sunup? If we leave three hours before sunup, we should get there just before first light."

"I want to go along and take a look at the layout of the place before we go in there to arrest them," the sheriff replied. I'll go along and will watch for a little while, then me, you, and your man that's up there will come back here and go over a plan to get those boys. For now, my men will take three-hour shifts on the lookout above the campsite; that way they can try to get some rest so we'll all be fresh for tomorrow."

It was almost three in the morning when the sheriff woke Lawrence and told him it was time; Lawrence ready to go in less than ten minutes. The sheriff had coffee ready, so he drank a couple of quick cups before they left. Then the three men walked their horses through the opening, mounted up, and rode in the direction where James was. Two others who woke as they were getting ready to leave replaced the cut trees across the opening when the men and horses had passed through.

It took them only two and a half hours. Lawrence knew the way well and could go at a quick pace.

He led them to the place where they would leave the horses. He told them to watch their steps and to be quiet, and that he would motion to them when they needed to get down and crawl the rest of the way. Daylight was breaking through the darkness as they topped the hill.

James heard more than just one person coming up on him. *Oh crap! Somebody must have seen me.* He crawled farther under the bushes, but then he saw Lawrence, so he crawled back out. He saw the sheriff's star and that another man was with them. "We're going to leave the sheriff's man here," Lawrence told him. "He'll watch the place till we get back." They each crawled to a position where they would be hidden, but still had a good view, and waited. James told them that the riders hadn't come back yet.

The sheriff looked at the place and all of the surrounding area, and said, "Okay, I think I've seen enough. Let's get back to the campsite and talk about how I think we should do this."

They made it back to the campsite well before midday. When the man on watch came down the hill to see the sheriff, the sheriff told him, "You need to go back up and hold tight because the gang hasn't come back to the cabin yet. And make sure you stay out of sight of the road but can still watch it."

They led their horses through the opening and put back the cut trees that hid it. James took the horses over to the other horses and watered and hobbled them.

When he got back to the wagons, the sheriff had told all the men to come around and listen to what he had to say.

"I think we should wait and see if the other riders come back today," he said, "and if they do, we'll go in there tonight after dark and try to surround them. Some of us will go the long way around the far side of the hills to get into position to come in from behind the cabin, and some of us will sneak up from the front after we take out their lookout."

Lawrence cleared his throat. "I have some cannon charges that I kept from the war," he said. "I was going to use them on a mining claim I have back home, but maybe we can set them up against the walls and the front of the cabin. They'll explode if we shoot them, and they pack a wallop. One of them can probably take out a whole wall of that place."

The sheriff thought this was a good idea. "They probably aren't going to come out peacefully," he said, "and I personally don't like the idea of having a shootout with a bunch of killers. I mean, I can shoot pretty fair, but it'd be easier if we could take out more than one of them at a time with one shot at each of the charges—but only if we have to, of course."

And so, the sheriff agreed they should take the charges and see if they could get them in place without the thieves knowing. The first task was to see if the riders would come back sometime before nightfall. They each took two-hour shifts at the lookout point for the road. A little after midday, there was the sound of horses, and a couple wagons came moving pretty fast out on the road. After they went by, the man on lookout came down to the campsite and said, "It looked like they hadn't noticed anything and weren't worried about being followed. They turned off the road and headed toward their hideout. There were six men—four on horseback, and one man driving each wagon with a horse in tow behind."

The sheriff's response was a quick one, "Let's give them a couple of hours as a head start, so they'll feel comfortable that they got away with whatever they've done. We'll head in there this afternoon, so we can get a look at where we need to go and how to get there before sundown. We'll wait for the men that have to go around the hillside to get into position. They'll be coming down the hill behind the cabin. Hopefully, we'll be able to take out their lookout without him getting off a warning."

James nodded. "I can take out their lookout," he said with some pride in his voice. "I like sneaking up on critters and poking them before I shoot them, and I'm good at it. I used to sneak up on the Indian scouts of the North's army and take them out without a sound. I'm pretty sure I can get the lookout before he can give anyone a warning."

Lawrence was also eager to help. "I'll go around the backside of the hills with the other men, because I've been there before and can show them the best way," he said.

Ben then added, "I'll be the one that sets the charges around the building, so the rest of us can shoot them easily, if need be."

Wiley offered to help set the charges also. The sheriff was glad they took it upon themselves to do the most critical parts of his plan. He wasn't sure why, but he felt certain they were much more experienced in those tactics than his posse.

They waited close to two frustratingly anxious hours to leave the camp. When they got to the group of trees where the sheriff's man had left his horse, they all dismounted and headed up the hill to take a look at where they needed to go. At the crest, they started crawling till they reached the place where the sheriff's deputy was hiding. After about ten minutes, the sheriff motioned for everyone to pull back.

The sheriff assigned three of his men to go with Lawrence, and the last one to come with him, Wiley, and Ben. They estimated it would take the men an hour or more to go around the backside of the hills and get into position.

"Once you get to the top of the hillside behind the cabin, we need to wait till the moon is up high enough to give us some seeing distance," the sheriff said. When you're ready to start down the hillside behind the cabin, one of you strike a match, wave it, and blow it out quick, so we'll know you're ready to go down the hillside. Then we'll take out the lookout. When that's done, we'll strike a match, wave it and blow it out quick, and you can start down the hill. When you get to the bottom, spread out so you can cover the sides as well as the back. Get as close as you can to the cabin but stay behind trees big enough to give you cover from bullets."

The sheriff paused and squinted toward the cabin. It was still and quiet down below. "Once you're in position," he continued, "we should be in position in the front of the cabin. You'll wait until you hear me tell the men inside to come out and surrender before we do anything. Wiley and Ben will have put the charges in place and gotten back to some cover before I say anything." The sheriff pulled his hat off his head, smacked some dust from the brim, and set it back on. "Don't expect them to surrender," he said. "I expect as soon as I say I'm the sheriff they'll start shooting. If that happens, any of you that can see a clear shot at a charge, shoot it. After that happens, we'll try and shoot anyone shooting at us."

The men nodded in agreement, and the sheriff asked if anyone had questions as to what they were to do. When no one responded, he said, "Okay, you fellows going around the back way better get a move on." The four men mounted up and Lawrence led the way. James moved down the hillside, trying to get as close as he could to their lookout. They had to wait until the moon was high and they were able to see as well as they could with what light it was going to offer. Though only a half-moon, it was fortunately nice and bright, and there were no clouds in the sky.

The man the sheriff had left to watch the place told him that six men had come back with two wagons, stopped at the cabin, unloaded the wagons, then took them farther up the ravine. Soon after, the drivers of the two wagons came back without the wagons, on the horses that had pulled them.

"They probably just dumped them where they had dumped the others," the sheriff replied.

The moon was now up high enough to send light down into the area around the hideout. It had been quite a while since the men had gone around the backside of the hills, and everyone on the front side was getting anxious waiting for the others. Finally, Ben spotted the match signal and signaled the sheriff. The sheriff signaled

James to go take out their lookout, so he started making his way over to the spot where the lookout was hiding.

It took him a few minutes because he had to be really quiet. When he got close enough that he could see the man, the man was lying back against a rock and had pulled his hat down over his eyes. Ben didn't know if he was asleep yet, but he was surely trying to go to sleep. Ben got up right next to him and lifted up his pistol, butt forward. Then quickly, he took off the man's hat and walloped him on the head, knocking him out.

After tying the man's hands and feet and gagging him with a bandanna, he went back over to where the rest of the men were. When he reached the sheriff, he told him what he'd done. The sheriff lit a match, waved it back and forth, and blew it out. The men started down the hillsides, trying to be as quiet as possible while getting into position.

The men crept up about twenty yards away from the cabin, spreading out behind the thicker trees. Light from an oil lamp was showing behind the curtains inside. Wiley took two charges, and Ben took three, and they snuck up to the cabin. They placed one at each of the back corners toward Lawrence and his men, and then one at each front corner. As Wiley went back to the sheriff, Ben tiptoed over to the front door and placed one right in front of it.

As he was sneaking away, he heard a voice from inside the cabin. "Hey," a man said, "I just saw a shadow go across in front of the window." Ben hustled off to the side of the cabin and back to the front, where the others were in position. Just as he got behind a tree, he heard the front door creak open. Ben heard the sheriff's voice.

"This is the sheriff. I want everyone in the house to come out with your hands up. I need to talk to you about some missing wagons."

As soon as he said this, the front door closed quickly. "It's the sheriff," said a voice from inside the cabin, "and he's out front." Someone came to the window and pulled the curtain back trying to see out in the darkness. When the sheriff saw the curtain move, he said in a loud voice, "You better come out with your hands up. I have the place surrounded. You're not going to get away, so just come on out."

At that point, the man took his pistol and busted out a window pane. He shot toward the sheriff's voice, hitting the tree he was hiding behind.

"Shoot them charges first," the sheriff told his men, "then fire away."

Wiley aimed at the charge by the door. A split second later, his charge went off, blowing apart a big section of the front of the building. The other two on the front corners went off, blowing away the whole front and part of the sides of the building. A second later came another two explosions from the charges placed at the back end of the cabin. When the smoke cleared, he could see the rest of the cabin had fallen in on itself and on top of the men inside.

They waited a little while to see if anyone was still in good enough shape to start shooting at them. When nothing happened, the sheriff carefully approached what remained of the building. He heard a couple of groans underneath the piles of debris, and he saw several men on the ground, in unnatural positions looking very dead. He told his men to come in and keep their eyes peeled for anyone trying to get to a gun and take a shot at them. They started pulling the wood away and uncovering the groaning men. They made sure there were no guns within their reach.

In the end, the luckiest one was the lookout. That is, if you'd call him lucky, because he was still going to be hanged with the rest of them. The others were going to go through a lot of pain healing from their injuries before they had to walk up the gallows, but all would still swing at the end of a rope.

Once all the men were tied and the dead ones pulled out in front of the cabin, they waited for sunup, so they could take a look in the ravine where the wagons had been dumped. They found two other bodies there besides those of Claire's husband and son. They hauled them out of the ravine and wrapped them in blankets, trying to keep them together as they were pretty well decomposed, and tied them to the outlaws' horses. A couple of horses had to carry two bodies. There were eight outlaws in total; four were dead, three others were incapacitated because of their wounds, and their lookout had a bump on his head but was otherwise unscathed.

When they got back to the road, the sheriff thanked Ben, Wiley, Lawrence, and James individually for their help, and shook their hands. He told them if they ever needed his help again, to just ask and he'd be glad to oblige. James showed the sheriff which two of the four bodies were Claire's family by the shirts they had on.

"I'll take the woman's husband and son into town and give them a proper burial in our cemetery," the sheriff said. "I'm not going to take them back to your camp and let those women see their men in this condition. If they want to come into town and see where they're buried, give me a couple of days to get them planted, then bring them in, and I'll show them where they're buried."

Wiley nodded. "I'll do that, Sheriff," he said, "but I'll suggest that they'll be better off just knowing that they got a proper burial and shouldn't go through the heartache again, seeing the gravesite. If they still want to, we'll come to town and pay you a visit."

The sheriff rubbed his ear. "I hope they don't," he said. "Either way, you boys be careful on your journey to Kentucky. A lot of soldiers don't have anywhere to go, and it seems some of them have started down the wrong road, robbing people trying to move somewhere and start a new life." With that, they said goodbye. At the main road the sheriff and all of the others headed west back to their town, and the McCoys headed back to their campsite. The sun was beginning to shine brightly above the horizon, and the women were anxiously waiting, hoping that none of them had been hurt trying to avenge their loss. As Ben and James hobbled the horses while Wiley and Lawrence approached the women. They stood in front of the women silently for a moment.

• • •

Claire and Cassie were wide-eyed and a bundle of nerves. "Well, what happened?" they exclaimed in bleating voices.

The men looked at each other. Lawrence's intuition told him that he should let Wiley explain.

Wiley felt good inside about what they had done, but he didn't want to smile because he knew the women still were feeling a lot of pain.

He turned to Claire, trying to look serious and comforting as well. "None of us got hurt," he said, "and we captured all eight of the gang. We had to kill four of them, but the others are going back to town with the sheriff and his posse to go on trial for the murders of your husband and son and two others we found where they had dumped the wagons."

A look of relief came over the women's faces. "The sheriff asked that you give him a couple of days to give them a proper burial," Wiley continued, "and if you still feel you need to go to the grave site, he'll show you where they are."

Claire's eyes were shiny with tears, "I really would like to go and pay my respects to my husband and son, so I know where their last resting place is," she said in a quiet voice. He could see that Claire knew she was going to hurt again, maybe even more when she saw the graves, but it was something she had to do.

CHAPTER 5

SAYING GOODBYE,
A RAY OF HOPE

Wiley wished Claire could accept things as they were and not go to where they were buried. It would just give them more heart ache, but he knew in his heart that she had to see them for herself, for the love she had for them. He had been in her situation and had lived that feeling when he lost his wife to consumption. He'd had to place her in the ground, telling her and himself that he had tried all he could to save her, and that she would always be in his heart. It had given him some closure seeing her grave, after having watched her die from a sickness he had been unable to stop. He knew it would help them be able to move on in their lives to at least be able to say goodbye to their graves.

"We'll stay here for a couple of days. Then we can go into town so you can go to the grave site," he told her. "For now, I think we should just try to be thankful for the fact you're still alive, knowing at least those that hurt you have been caught and are going to pay for it. Why don't we try to enjoy this beautiful spot, just relaxing and doing whatever you feel like doing for a little while?"

As Claire looked in his eyes, she could see that he knew how she felt. She was relieved that it was over—that they had caught the men—but yet, she and her daughter had been left with nothing and had nowhere to go. Her heart was hurting, her body was drained, and with the reality of their situation hitting home, she couldn't stop her emotions from taking over. She started crying and ran to their tent. Cassie followed after her, bursting into tears herself.

The women cried themselves into a state of exhaustion and fell asleep holding each other. A couple of hours later, they came out of the tent and walked down to the stream to wash their tear-streaked faces, trying to regain some composure. When they walked back into the campsite, they smelled and heard the sizzle of beefsteak in a frying pan. The men had done their best to make a large meal, so Claire and Cassie could eat and sleep well, knowing they probably had no energy or desire to do any cooking.

They were pleasantly surprised at the blueberry biscuits; someone had painstakingly picked and cleaned blueberries they'd found somewhere. It was a comforting gesture that made them both smile.

After their meal, Claire turned to each of the men in turn, looking them in the eye. "We can't thank you enough for all you've done for us," she said. "We can at least wash the dishes." Cassie followed her to the stream.

When they had brought back the clean dishes and put them in the wagon, Claire asked Wiley if he would take them to town, so they could pay their last respects.

He could feel the pain from her loss when he looked

at her. "Sure, I will," he said. "I think we should wait, like the sheriff said, but I'll be glad to take you in a couple of days."

At his words, she started to turn away as tears welled in her eyes again. "I think I just want to lie down and try to come back to reality," she said. Cassie had already gone to their tent, and she went to join her.

Once inside the tent, they couldn't help but hold each other and cry again. The men could hear, although it wasn't very loud this time, their heart-wrenching sobbing. It made them all feel sad inside and remember when they had lost someone dear to them, as all of them had at one time or another.

The next day, after breakfast, Cassie asked Wiley if he would take a walk with her, as she wanted to discuss something she had talked about with her mother. They walked across the stream and up over a low hill, to where the terrain opened into a flat, grassy area with no trees. There were some wildflowers growing, and Cassie reached to pick some; as she started to talk, she plucked the petals one by one.

"My mother and I don't have any idea what we can do or how we're going to live," she said. "I was hoping…since you seem to have been through something like this… haven't you? Or am I just imagining you've felt how we feel?"

He looked into her sad eyes and said, "You're right, I've been there. I lost my wife, and I felt just as helpless as you do, only in another way. I felt like I didn't have any more purpose in life. I really didn't want to go on without her." He turned his eyes to the dirt.

"We didn't have any children, but luckily, I did have

some kinfolk who supported me through that time. They kept telling me that she would have wanted me to build the dream we'd had together. They encouraged me to try and realize that even though she was gone, she would've wanted me to make a good life.

He took a step away from her. He still didn't meet her eyes.

"For a long time, I just went through the motions of living, only doing what had to be done to survive, and nothing more. One day, it just hit me that she wouldn't have wanted me to keep grieving about her not being there anymore. I started to look around our little place and saw how it was falling apart. I decided to put it back together for her, in her memory.

"I had planned to raise some cattle for beef. But the war broke out, and I went to join the army, thinking, why not? It didn't really matter to me or anyone else if I got killed. Besides, I had done what I had promised my wife by fixing up the ranch, and my heart wasn't really in trying to do more to it.

He gave a deep sigh and turned to her.

"That's where I'm headed now; I want to go see if there's anything left. My kinfolk said they would try and keep an eye on the place till I got back. I haven't heard a word from them in three years. But I need to go back to where I felt good about my life, at least go back to the home where I feel I belonged once."

She saw in his eyes that he was speaking from his heart. She knew that before her stood a man who was good, inside and out. "At least you had somewhere to be when you went through that loss," she said, "but we have lost everything, including our family. We have no idea what to do or where to go. We can't just show up at my father's sister's doorstep and add more burden to their already burdened life. She and her husband have only been in Kansas six months, but they told us if we came out there that our two families could prosper if we worked together. If we show up now, without anything, we would just make their life even harder."

She took a deep breath before she spoke again. "Seeing that you won't have any womenfolk around your place when you get there, do you think we could come along with you? I'm sure there'd be a lot of things that we could do to help out. We are both hard workers." He didn't respond, so she kept going. "A man needs a woman's touch in his house and in his life, not that I'm saying my mother wants another man right now, but I think we could help your life a little and give ourselves some purpose with pride."

He stepped back onto the path and started to walk slowly. She followed him.

"Of course, if you want to go back and live by yourself, that's surely your right to do so. Maybe we can just come with you and stay a little while, till we find somewhere we can start over ourselves. If you wouldn't mind?"

He stopped at an outcropping of rocks and sat down, looking out to the horizon. She sat down next to him and tried to see what he was looking at.

But what he was looking at was in his mind. He was trying to see into his future. He did feel something for these two women, he just didn't know what it was exactly. Was it pity because of how they had been doing what was right and had their dreams snatched away from them so brutally? Or because Claire had stirred something in his heart?

He pondered for a moment what his wife would have wanted him to do.

He didn't know if he would ever be able to love someone else. But he realized his wife would have taken them in and helped them find a new life. She would have done it out of the goodness of her heart and the compassion she held for all people, especially those less fortunate. He decided he would ask Claire what she thought about them coming along to his place.

Cassie sat in nervous silence, waiting for his response. When he finally turned to face her, he felt a warm feeling come over him. He just knew it came from his wife. "I'd be proud to help you try to find a new life," he said. "I know my wife would've done the same."

He didn't wait for her response.

"Besides, I can definitely use a hand. I'm sure there's going to be a lot of things that need done, and some that would be done much better with a woman's input. I'm not saying I want to be a family, but we can be friends and help ourselves try and move forward in this hard world, and I'm sure we can make life easier for all of us together."

His voice and eyes told Cassie she and her mother would be safe with him. "I can't thank you enough for what you've done already," she said to Wiley, "or for what you're offering us. I can only tell you we won't make you regret it." She stood up to give him a hug and show him how greatly she appreciated the fact that he cared for their well-being.

She pulled away from him. "My mother doesn't know

I just talked to you about this," she said, "so I don't know if she even will agree to going along with you. But I think she knows as well as I do that we can trust you. She would've never even considered being so forthright as I've been, but I think she'll be glad to know that we can stay with you for a while and see what life has in store for us."

Tears were coming down her face. "I'm going back to talk to her," she said. "I'm sure she'll want to talk to you herself after I tell her."

Her tears came from a mingling of joy, emotional trauma, and the ray of hope that had just beamed down on her. She left him at the rock and ran back to the tent.

Her mother, seeing the tears streaming down her daughter's cheeks, pulled her into a loving embrace. As she held her close, hoping to comfort her from the sorrow she thought the girl was feeling again, she thought to herself, *What more can happen?*

For a moment, Cassie was too out of out of breath to speak. Finally, she was able to say "I have some great news! Wiley said we can come with him to his place until we figure out what we want to do. We won't need to be a burden to anyone, especially Pa's sister, and we won't just get dropped off in the nearest town and have to try to live off some strange people's charity!"

Claire stepped away from her. "What have you done?" she said. "Gone and begged for help from Wiley?"

"No, Mother. It wasn't like that at all," Claire said quickly. "We just went for a walk, and I started talking about our predicament and asked what his plans were for the future. He told me how he had lost his wife, and then he just offered."

Her mother blinked and took a step back.

"He's such a good man, inside and out, Mother," Cassie said. "I told him we didn't want to take any more advantage of his hospitality and offered our help to him on his journey and to help him fix his homestead back up. I told him also that we could continue going on to Pa's sister's place and be useful there, but that I really didn't want to. He asked me how we planned to get her place. I just said we'd find a way, probably catch a ride in some wagons going that direction."

Then she added some imagination to her memory of the conversation.

"He looked at me and shook his head. He said, 'Putting yourself in the hands of strangers is risky business, and most women traveling with their families wouldn't want two pretty women to join their group.'" This was true, for the most part, whether he said it or not.

"Then he offered. If we wanted to, we could go with him," Cassie said. "Besides, he thought we were doing our fair share of the chores now, without even being asked. He said he liked the idea of having a couple of women traveling with them, that it kind of kept them more civilized, which a man out in the wilderness tended to forget about sometimes."

Her mother folded her arms. Her eyes gave no sign of a decision, so Cassie kept pleading her case.

"He said he wasn't going to obligate us to anything and when we get to his destination. It's up to us to decide if we want to stay and work together, to build some kind of a life. He said he lived near the borders of Virginia and Kentucky, and there are several towns close by, and Tennessee has a big city within a day or two's ride. If we ever decided we wanted a different life, there would be plenty of possibilities to go and see what we could find."

Of course, much of this was more invented conversation, but Cassie knew in her heart it was what Wiley would've said had he found the words.

But none of it seemed to be swaying her mother.

"Oh, Mama," Cassie said, "I really would like to go with them. Can we, Ma? Please? I just feel inside that it's the right thing for us to do. We'll be okay."

Her voice was downright pleading.

But all Claire said was, "Let me go talk to Wiley and see what I think about it."

She left the tent and glanced around the campsite. She didn't see Wiley, so she went back inside and asked Cassie where they had talked. Finding out, she set out for the hill.

On the other side of the hill, she saw Wiley sitting on the stone outcropping that Cassie had mentioned. He was still looking out across the landscape, apparently deep in thought.

When she got to within about ten yards, he turned to look at her.

"I think I need to talk to you," she said as she sat down beside him. "You know I loved my husband and thought I would spend the rest of my days with him. It seems as though the good Lord has other plans. Right now, I'm hoping he's guiding me as to what I should do. I can only think that the Lord put you in our path for a reason; maybe because you could help us get my husband back or maybe because he already knew he was gone, but either way, he put you in our life."

Wiley nodded and looked down at his boots.

"You're a handsome man," she said, "strong and able to take care of yourself. You don't need a ready-made family."

Quickly he raised his eyes to hers. "Now hold on there," he said. "I'm not asking for a ready-made family. I just said you two are good company and don't have to be told what needs to be done. You pitch in and help where you see you can, and I like that."

And he pulled off his hat and held it with both hands.

"I think you would be a welcome addition to our group," he continued, "and seeing as my group is all family, I'm sure there won't be any trouble with you women being so pretty like there might be if we were just a bunch of men riding together."

His fingers curled tightly around the hat, and he paused, as if gathering his thoughts. When he spoke again, his words came out with force.

"I know how it feels to lose someone you love," he said. "But I don't want you to think I'm falling in love with you, because I don't know if I even can love someone again. When I lost my wife, I didn't know if I wanted to continue in the home we'd made, or if I needed to leave everything behind and make a new start. And though I've been away from the place for a while now, she has never really left my mind or my heart. I've sort of realized that she would've wanted me to continue on with the dream we had shared. That doesn't mean with a woman, it just means to fulfill our dream at the home we created."

He was twisting the hat hard now, bending the brim like he was trying to make a bowler out of it. "I don't think she would've wanted it to be an empty house," he said. "So, if you'd like to, we can go there and see what's left. I don't even know if there's anything still standing. I just know I have to go back."

Claire nodded. It was clear that this had not been an easy decision for him to make.

"I'm sure my wife would have appreciated a woman's touch on her home," Wiley said. "What I'm trying to say is, it's not out of pity or sympathy for your situation that I said you could come with me. It's out of seeing that we would both benefit if you did."

Claire sat still a moment, letting all he had said sink in. While thinking about this, she turned and looked out over the horizon like he had been doing. As she gazed out over the view, she realized something was making this happen, something far wiser and knowing than she could ever be. She turned back to face him. "So we'll be more like partners, right? You'll take care of the things a man is supposed to take care of, and we'll take care of the things a woman needs to take care of, is that it?"

He shifted on the rock. "Well sort of," he said. "I think we can work together on a lot of things and that will just make it easier for all of us to live."

"I think that sounds like a good thing," she said slowly. "We'll complement each other's lives, while each of us finds out what we really need inside to be content. We should be able to figure that out as time goes on without having to jump into a permanent situation neither of us are really sure we want. If that's the way it can be, then I'm all for it. I'd be proud to travel with you and help you out at your homestead."

He couldn't have been more pleased at the way she put his own thoughts into words. He felt immensely relieved that he wasn't going to have to dig himself in so deeply that he wouldn't be able to find an honorable way out.

"Well then, partner," he said, releasing the hat brim and clapping the hat onto his head, "let's go see what we can do back at the campsite."

He stood up, smiling, and held out his hand to help her up, and they walked back to camp.

At the camp, Claire went to the tent to tell her daughter what she had decided. Cassie was seated on one of the cots, her hands clasped above her knees; she seemed to have been praying. As her mother entered, she looked up at her with hope and anticipation.

"Well, Cassie," Claire said. "We are now partners in a traveling adventure and a homestead rebuilding with an open-ended agreement as to how things will play out. Is that okay with you?"

Cassie jumped up from the cot. "Yes! Yes! Oh yes!" she exclaimed. "It's exactly what I want. Thank you, Mother, thank you," she said as she gave her mother a grand hug and kissed her cheek.

She left the tent and ran toward the outcropping where she had talked to Wiley. Along the way, she grabbed handfuls of wildflowers and tossed them in the air, saying to herself, "This is great. This is going to be so great. I can't wait to see Kentucky and our new homestead." She was happier than she'd been since before they'd left their home.

Wiley was by the wagons and saw Cassie come out of the tent and start running up the hillside. When Claire came out, he smiled at her and said, "Looks like someone's really happy."

She gave him a sheepish smile. "I haven't seen her so

happy in months," she said.

"It makes me feel good after we've had so much heartache. Speaking of heartache, when can we go into town, so I can pay my last respects to my husband and son?"

Wiley's face was suddenly serious. "Is tomorrow good enough?" he said. "I think the sheriff will have had enough time to do what he needs to do. We can go after breakfast; it's only about thirty miles. We can be there late afternoon, if we leave early."

She gave him a weak smile. "I guess tomorrow's the day," she said.

She turned toward the hillside. "I'll wait a while to tell Cassie that we're going to see her father and brother for the last time tomorrow morning; no need to ruin her spirits just now."

• • •

It was a solemn ride into town the next day. When they reached the sheriff's office, Wiley told them to stay on their horses, and he would find out where they needed to go. He dismounted and went into the sheriff's office.

"The cemetery is about a half a mile outside of town," the sheriff told him. "It's up on a hill that overlooks the town. There's a sign pointing down a two-track trail with the word "Cemetery" on it. There's an arrow indicating the direction. You can't miss them; they are the two fresh graves, and each has a cross at the head of it. One says son, and the other says father. I didn't know their names, so that's what I used. The criminals were buried a few hundred yards out behind this here sheriff's office, because they got no right to be buried with decent folks.

The others are awaitin' trial."

At the cemetery, Wiley said, "I'll hold the horses while you go to the grave sites." He pointed to the two fresh mounds of dirt. "That must be them," he said. He took off his hat and held it in front of him as he watched the two women walk toward the graves.

As they took in the freshly mounded dirt, and the crosses with only the word father on one and son on the other, tears started streaming down their faces as the pain broke inside their hearts once again. They cried there together for probably twenty minutes.

Finally, each of them blew a kiss toward the graves. When they came back to the horses, neither looked up at Wiley; they just took the reins of their horses and climbed on. It was a very sad and silent ride back to town.

Upon reaching the sheriff's office, Claire said she wanted to go in and thank him for taking care of the burial.

As she came in the door, the sheriff rose from behind his desk and asked, "Did you find the place?"

"Yes," she replied, "and I want to thank you for the markers you put. I wish I had something better, but I don't; those murderers stole everything we had."

The sheriff fished in his pockets for a clean handkerchief to give her but found nothing. Feeling her sorrow, he said, "It's not much consolation, but I have some money here for you from the governor's office."

She looked dumbfounded. "What are you talking about?" she said.

"Two men in that gang had a thousand-dollar price on their heads," he replied, "and it should be yours since you showed us where they went." He turned to the safe he had behind his desk, opened it, and took out a wad of money. He set it on the desk and said, "I'll just need you to sign this receipt, and you can have it."

She looked at him in disbelief. "Oh my God, really?" she said. "Lord knows we have nothing left. I guess he's trying to provide us with something to help us go on living. Thank you very much, Sheriff. It's a lousy trade-off, but we sure need it."

She tucked the money inside her corset, signed the receipt, and shook the sheriff's hand, saying thank you once again. She didn't say anything about the money when she came out of the office. She just climbed on her horse and forced her courage to come out. "Let's go. We've got a new life waitin' on us, so we might as well get to findin' it."

They stayed the night just off the road and slept late, exhausted from all the emotions. Despite the late start in the morning, they made it back to the campsite around five o'clock in the evening, just in time for supper. The trio ate dinner in silence, and when they were finished, Wiley offered to do the dishes and took their plates. The women went inside the tent, talked for a couple of minutes quietly, and then Claire stuck her head out of the tent and told the men goodnight. As an afterthought, she said, "If you're ready to get back on the road home, we'll be ready in the morning, whenever you want to leave."

Chapter 6

Good Soldiers Turned Highwaymen

The McCoys sat around the campfire for a while. Much of their discussion was about how they were going to have to be careful on the road because of what the sheriff had said about so many soldiers turning into highwaymen.

Wiley went to his wagon and got out a rough map. He sat down by the light of the campfire to show the other men the route he thought would be best and easiest to take across Missouri to Kentucky. Using his finger to follow the route, he said, "We need to get over to Charleston. From there, we're low enough on the Mississippi River. If we cut straight across into Kentucky, we will only have to cross the Mississippi, and not the Ohio River too. I think crossing one river is plenty, if we can pull it off." The others nodded in agreement.

"Once we cross, if we stay heading northeast, we'll be able to pass above the Twin Lakes area," he said. "Those are some big, wide lakes; we'll have to cross both of them or go over a hundred and twenty miles to get around them, plus cross two extra rivers."

"That's a lot of water," Ben said. "I'm not terribly fond of getting wet."

"By heading northeast after we've crossed the Mississippi," Wiley continued, "we'll have to cross the Cumberland River, but from there, we can head southeast to Franklin past the Twin Lakes, then due east into Daniel Boone's territory.

"We'll need to stay on the north side of the Cumberland Mountains. Following them northeast will take us to Wallins Creek, which is where James is from. Then it's only another ten miles to the Pine Mountains and Lawrence's home.

After that, we just continue northeast to Pike County and Fishtrap Lake for Ben and me. It's going to be a long, hard trip, but I think if we go the way I said, it will be easiest for us and the wagons."

Lawrence nodded. "Once we get past Log Mountain, it's only about six or seven miles to Wallins Creek," he said. "Me an' James have been up there, and we just might know a shortcut to our homes. It's been a long time, so we might not remember the countryside, but then again, we might."

Ben couldn't help but say, "That's great, Lawrence, after three hundred miles of traveling, you'll know a shortcut to get home. But only when you're within six or seven miles of your house. Heck, my dog could get home from ten miles away. Some pioneer you are." They all chuckled. Even Lawrence had to laugh.

"I don't know much about any of this land on the north side of the Cumberland Mountains," Ben said. "I do know a little of Virginia and Tennessee because we lived real close to those territories. When we went hunting or trapping, it was a lot easier to stay on the south side of those treacherous mountains. I'm willing to follow any road that seems easy for these wagons. I know eventually we'll get home."

James nodded. "That's what I think too," he said. "Whatever is easiest for the wagons. I plan on living a long time, and we'll get there sooner or later. Hopefully before winter."

With the men in agreement on the route, they decided they would have a nice breakfast in the morning and set out for Charleston, Missouri.

They slept without posting a guard. In the morning, they all woke up just after sunup, anxious to get back on their way. After they'd had a big breakfast of ham steaks, potatoes, biscuits with ham gravy, and a couple of cups of coffee each, they got everything loaded up on the wagons and tied the extra horses to the backs of each wagon.

They cleared the opening and walked each wagon back through toward the road. The women had decided Claire would ride with Wiley and Cassie would ride with Lawrence. They climbed aboard and started toward Charleston. They traveled for two days, passing only a couple of travelers heading for supplies into the town where the sheriff had buried Claire's family.

On the evening of the third day, they reached a crossroad. A sign at the crossing indicated that it was twelve miles north to Charleston and fifteen miles east to the Mississippi River.

Claire asked Wiley if they could go into Charleston to buy some clothes and take a hot bath.

"That's fine with me," he responded. "Let me go ask the others if they want to come along." When he told the rest what Claire wanted, Cassie exclaimed that she was quite in favor of her mother's idea. Ben and James, however, could feel themselves getting close to Kentucky and didn't want to travel twenty four extra miles just for a hot bath. Besides, they were fine bathing in the streams and knew the Mississippi River had plenty of places to take a bath. But Lawrence said he wouldn't mind going to town.

Ben and James said they would go as far as the Mississippi River and wait for them on the Missouri side of the river. When they came back from the town, they would all cross together. As Lawrence and Wiley turned their wagons toward Charleston, Wiley told them, "We'll see you there tomorrow around noon to cross over to Kentucky."

"Okay, we'll see you then," Ben replied, and they headed toward the Mississippi River.

The sun was starting to go down when the two wagons started down the main street of Charleston. It was a good-sized town—large enough to have a post office, a bank, and two hotels that offered hot baths, with restaurants on the ground floor. There was a sheriff's office, a telegraph office, and two saloons, along with a couple of mercantile stores and three general stores.

It was a peaceful-looking town. They passed a big church on the edge of town and pulled up in front of what they thought was the nicest hotel. Wiley went inside and asked if they could get some rooms, hot baths, and how late they served dinner. "We serve till nine o'clock at night," the desk clerk replied, "but if nobody's here, we close early."

"Is there a livery where I can take our wagons and horses?" Wiley asked.

"There's one out behind the hotel about fifty yards to the back," the clerk told him.

Wiley nodded and turned to leave, but then he came back. "Is there anywhere I can buy some women's clothing?" he said.

The clerk thought a moment. "If you hurry, you can reach the mercantile, three doors down on the right. Mr. Campbell runs it, and his wife brings in all kinds of things women ask for, but I think they close at six thirty. How many rooms do you want?"

They hadn't discussed sleeping arrangements, so Wiley thought he'd be safe and get a room for each of them. "We'll take four, if you have them, and all of us want a nice hot bath."

When Wiley came outside he told the others, "We need to hurry down the street to catch the store before it closes." He climbed up on the wagon and headed down to Campbell's Mercantile, Lawrence following. Wiley stopped in front of the store, jumped down, and hurried inside. Claire wondered what he needed that was so urgent it couldn't wait till morning.

As he came through the door, Mr. Campbell looked up from the counter and said, "Well, mister, you just made it. I was about to close up."

Wiley smiled. "I have two women outside," he said, "and they need to buy themselves some new clothes. Do you have some women's clothing and maybe a dress or two?"

"Let me call my wife," the owner said. "She's in the back. She can help you better with that than I can."

As Mr. Campbell fetched his wife, Wiley went outside and told the women he thought they should come in. Wiley hurried back inside, met Mr. Campbell's wife, and handed her a fifty-dollar gold piece. "Let them get anything they want," he said. "If it costs more than this, I'll pay you when I get back from the livery; we're going to be staying in the hotel just down the street for tonight."

Mrs. Campbell smiled. "I wish my husband would do something like this for me," she said. "Fifty dollars to spend how I want! I'd be so happy, I wouldn't know where to start, like a kid in a candy store, probably."

Wiley laughed. "Just tell them to get anything and everything they want, or think they might need, and that it's already taken care of," he said.

Curiosity had gotten the best of the woman, and as they came through the door, Wiley introduced them. "They're all yours, Mrs. Campbell," he said. "Take good care of them, and I'll be back shortly."

Cassie and Claire looked at Wiley, confused. Wiley tipped his hat as he left them and went back to where Lawrence was waiting.

At the livery, the stable owner approached Wiley. "You want me to take care of your horses?" he said. "Some oats and water for them and keep an eye on your wagons? It's going to cost you six dollars a night."

"Hmm," Wiley said. "I thought the highway men were out on the road. I didn't realize they had livery stables too!"

The stable owner smiled. "Aw, I was just testing the water," he said. "I can always drop my price, but it's darned hard to raise it once I've said it. What do you think is fair?"

"I was thinking more like two dollars," said Wiley.

The owner took off his hat and scratched his head. "Okay, it's a deal," he said. "Two and a half a day."

Wiley climbed down from the wagon and turned to the owner. "You guarantee no one will touch our wagons or horses?" he said.

"You bet," he replied. "This is the best place in town. Are you staying at the hotel in front?"

"Yeah," Wiley said. "We'll be there just for tonight. We're passing through on our way to Kentucky." He reached in his pocket and pulled out three one-dollar silver pieces. "This ought to cover some oats in the morning for the horses too!" he said, handing the man the coins.

The owner smiled as he took them. "Yeah, that'll cover it. By the way, my name's Sam. Yours?"

"I'm Wiley, and this is my cousin Lawrence. Pleased to meet you!" They shook hands, and the man started untying the horses from the backs of the wagons while Lawrence and Wiley headed back to the mercantile.

As it turned out, Mrs. Campbell had found some undergarments, and a petticoat for each of them. She even found two dresses each that fit fairly well.

They also picked out soaps and combs, a couple of soft-bristled bath brushes, and some socks, along with a new pair of boots each. Then they went by the perfume case and each selected a small bottle of a perfume. Wiley and Lawrence came through the door as Mrs. Campbell was totaling up their order.

Wiley looked at the goods spread out on the counter. When his eyes met theirs, he smiled and said, "Are you going to buy out the whole store?"

Claire gave them a serious look. "Well, we don't have anything, so we need a lot of things," she said. "And besides, I'm paying for this."

He looked at her, and then at Mrs. Campbell.

"You don't have to pay for it," Mrs. Campbell said. "He took care of it."

Claire looked astounded. "No," she said, shaking her head. "We won't take any charity. We can pay for this."

Wiley cleared his throat. "This is not charity," he said. "It's just a gift from me."

As she looked at him, her ruffled feathers calmed back down. "Thank you for the offer," she said, "but we really can pay for this."

But he wasn't about to give in. "When a gentleman offers a gift to a lady," he said, "it's normally respectable and polite, if the gift is respectable, that the lady accepts his hospitality and generosity."

She had calmed enough to be able to see that if she insisted, she would hurt his ego. "Well, I suppose if you put it that way, we wouldn't want to offend the gentleman by not accepting his gift," she said. "So okay, if you really want to pay for everything, we'll let you. Thank you."

Mrs. Campbell bagged the goods and clothing and told Wiley that he still had change coming. "No, hold on to it," he said. "We'll be by tomorrow to pick up some coffee and other things we need in the morning."

When they got outside, everyone had their arms full of bags and shoe boxes.

"I thought they took everything from you?" Wiley said to Claire once they were out of range of Mrs. Campbell's ears.

"They did," she replied. "It just so happens that when I went into the sheriff's office to thank him, he said that two of them had a price on their head. He had me sign a receipt and gave me the money. So now at least were not completely broke and helpless; still a little helpless maybe, but not broke anymore."

She even laughed a little at what she'd said.

It was the first laugh Wiley had heard since he'd met her, and it made him feel good inside too. Cassie let out a little giggle, and the men laughed along with them.

They went into the hotel to the front desk, where the clerk was there waiting with their keys. "We've already started filling the tubs with hot water, and they're just about ready," he said. "If you would like to order something to eat, we could have it brought to the rooms."

The group exchanged glances. They were all thinking the same thing: that it would be fantastic to have a hot bath and a hot meal at the same time. Wiley turned back to the clerk. "Bring us up your house specialties when you get a chance. Thank you again for your hospitality."

The women had rooms on one side of the hallway, and the men's were directly across from theirs. Lawrence took the one straight across from Cassie, and Wiley the one across from Claire. The men opened the ladies' doors for them and carried in their bags, setting them down on the bed. Going back into the hallway, Wiley said, "We'll leave you to your privacy and get over to our rooms. We want to get in that hot bath that's waiting."

Cassie and Claire flopped down on their beds and reveled in the softness and comfort of real bedding and mattresses. It had been so long since they had slept in a bed. In a few minutes, there was a knock on Claire's door, and two women came in with buckets of hot water, while the desk clerk waited outside with their trays of food. The women poured one bucket in the tub, bringing the level up to near capacity and set the other one beside it, and then put the tray of food on a table. Continuing down the hall, they went to Cassie's room and repeated the whole thing.

Soon, all four travelers were luxuriating in their bounty of comforts. They all devoured the wonderful meal the hotel had prepared and climbed into their baths.

The women used the scented soaps they had bought from the mercantile; the men just used the hotel soap. When the men finished with their baths, they realized they didn't have any clean clothes.

Wiley pulled his dirty clothes on and went over to Lawrence's room and knocked. "Give me your clothes," he said when he answered the door. "I'll have the hotel wash them."

He went downstairs and found the clerk. "Do you have someone who can wash our clothes?" he asked.

The clerk said, "Sure, but you have to take them off first."

Wiley laughed. "Would you send someone up to my room to get mine? I'd appreciate it. I'll leave them outside the door."

"Sure thing," the clerk replied. "Tell anyone else to do the same if they want their clothes washed. They'll be ready in the morning. We'll put them outside your door."

Back upstairs, he knocked on the ladies' doors and told them what the clerk said about getting their clothes washed, then he went back to his room and lay out on the bed. He hadn't slept in a bed for a while. In a minute, he was deeply asleep.

The next morning, all the clothes were freshly washed and smelling good, waiting outside the doors. Downstairs, Wiley paid the bill, including breakfast for them all. While waiting, the two men sat at a table in the restaurant by a window overlooking the street.

The ladies came down, each wearing one of their new dresses and their new boots. As they came down the stairs, Lawrence and Wiley looked at each other and grinned. They were looking at two of the prettiest women they had ever seen.

With the road dirt washed off and nice new clothes, there was an absolute glow to the ladies' faces. They were hardly recognizable as the scraggly travelers they'd found by the side of the road.

The men stood as the women approached the table and pulled out a chair for them to sit on. They couldn't help staring at them, even though they saw they were making the women blush.

"Sorry, if we're staring," Wiley finally said, "but you really are a couple of very handsome women."

Not to be outdone, Lawrence added, "Yes, you are two very beautiful ladies. You'll have to excuse our gawking. Us mountain people usually only get to see pretty animals or sunsets, rarely something that can actually talk back to us." They all laughed.

They stuffed themselves on scrambled eggs, fried potatoes, steak, and bread, fresh out of the oven. When they had finished a couple of cups of coffee after eating, they were ready to get back on the road.

As they walked out the door, each lady took the arm

of the man beside her, and they walked toward the livery.

When they got there, Lawrence checked over the wagons, making sure nothing had been tampered with. Wiley found the owner in his office building and told him they were ready to leave. "I'll have my helper bring out the wagons," the owner said, "I'll have them right here in a jiffy."

"Hitch up whichever horse you want to pull and tie the other two," Wiley said.

"Let's go over to the mercantile," Wiley said to Lawrence and the two women, "and buy what we think we can use so they'll have it ready by the time the wagons are."

As they started walking toward the store, Claire commented on what a beautiful day it was, and how she felt really good for a change.

"Yeah," Lawrence said, "it was nice to have a good dinner and breakfast, clean clothes after a hot bath, and a real bed. Ben and James sure missed out."

When they got to the mercantile, they saw that the Campbells had set a couple of tables and chairs in the walkway for customers to use while their orders were being prepared. The men held the chairs for the ladies; once they were seated, they went inside the store. They ordered extra coffee, more flour, and a couple of blankets each, along with a rack for their fire pit so they could put frying pans on it, instead of just setting them on the coals. They also bought a couple of bags of oats for their animals. With that, they used up every bit of the fifty dollars.

Wiley told the ladies to wait at the front of the store and they'd be back with the wagons in a couple of minutes. When they returned, Wiley shook hands with the owner, telling him thanks for everything and to tell his wife many thanks for the help she had given to the women.

By nine, they were headed out of town. They got to the main road at about midday and headed east toward the Mississippi River.

CHAPTER 7

GETTING ROBBED

After about an hour on the road, they saw two men walking up ahead. As they got closer, they realized it was Ben and James. When they reached them, Wiley stopped his wagon. "What the heck has happened now?"

Ben looked up at him. It took a few seconds to find words. "I can't believe it. I don't know what to say. We were sitting at our campsite on the side of the river, and ten soldiers came up on horseback. We had gotten some stuff out of one of the wagons, and the tarp was still partially off, and they could see a barrel of flour that we had used to make biscuits. When they asked us where we were coming from, we told them Ohio. We told him we came down this way, so we wouldn't have to cross both the rivers, the Mississippi and the Missouri." He stopped to wipe his face with his shirtsleeve.

"The sergeant, apparently the leader of the platoon," he continued, "went over and looked in the wagon and said, 'Well, this here barrel of flour says Lawrence Mercantile on it. How is it you're coming from Ohio and this came from Lawrence?' It seemed like he was trying to tell us why he was justified in doing what they were doing. 'Me and my platoon have been out on patrol looking for some men that raided storages the Union Army had in several places along the Missouri border, one in particular over by Lawrence. The general over there sent us out on patrol to see if we could find any trail of those who did it.'

"That sergeant was a tough bird. 'It seems to me you boys are lying,' he said. 'I don't know about what or why just yet, but I think these goods are stolen, along with those horses.' Then he pulled the tarps off and found our guns and said, 'These are Union weapons. Where did you get them?'

"We told them we had worked on a ranch in Ohio and this is what we had as pay for three months work. Since we had enough to make the trip home, we were headed home to Kentucky.

"The sergeant thought about it for a minute, then said, 'You boys don't look like you could've pulled off a raid by yourselves, but I do know some of this stuff is stolen from the Union Army, and I'm going to confiscate all of it. You should count yourselves lucky that I'm not going to haul you in with it.' He grinned at us and said, 'Count your blessings that we don't string you up right here. I'm only letting you go because I can't prove you did it, but I'm taking this stuff, because I know it belonged to one of those storage areas.'"

Ben shook his head. "Then he made us take off our guns and throw them in the wagon too. The sergeant left us each a canteen and a knife and said, 'You should be able to make it back to Charleston in a couple days.'"

"They took the wagons, horses, and everything else and went off down the road toward the crossroad where we left you. We started walking, trying to track them. We saw a place where it looked like they had turned off the road and went into a valley. They had tried to wipe away their tracks where they headed off the main road, but they didn't do a very good job. We decided just to keep following the road, hoping we'd run into you. They left the road probably about seven miles back, toward the river. We don't know how far they went back into that valley, or if they just kept on going."

Wiley climbed down from his wagon, put his arm around Ben's shoulder, turned him away from the wagons and started walking down the road. He asked him in a low voice, so no one else could hear, "Did they find the gold in the wagons?"

"No," Ben said. "They didn't really go through the wagons there in front of us, but I'm sure they will. They probably got about three hours' head start from the turnoff they took."

Wiley sighed. "Climb up on the wagons. We'll go back there and see what we can do about getting our stuff back," he said.

They made it to the turnoff in about an hour. There was a tree-lined ravine where they found a place they could hide the wagons and horses from the road. The turnoff was actually a two-track trail that the soldiers had taken.

"Let's make a campsite here and go on horseback," Wiley said. "I want to follow the soldiers and see where they went."

As they were getting the horses ready, Ben whispered to Wiley, "It's a good thing we wrapped those strongboxes in blankets and put them at the bottom of those crates of blankets and tents, or they would've seen it right away. I just hope we can catch up with them before they've gone through the wagons."

Wiley buckled the throatlatch on a bridle and nodded. "Maybe they haven't gone too far and stopped to make camp. If we're lucky, they picked a place we can get close to, without them knowing we're coming."

The four of them mounted their horses and rode out to find the soldiers. They had ridden about an hour when Lawrence spotted some smoke in the air, but it was a good distance away. It was coming out of a thicket of trees against the hillside, down in a ravine.

They hobbled the horses behind some trees and started moving on foot toward the smoke, staying inside the tree line at the base of the hill.

When they got within about a hundred yards of it, Wiley gestured to the hill opposite from them. "I'll go up that hillside and get to where I can see as much as I can of their camp," he said quietly. "James, you to sneak along the bottom of this ravine and try to get a look at how they're set up. Lawrence and Ben, you get as close as you can from here to block their way out if they try to come out this way." The McCoys had each taken carbine rifles and two of the new six-shot Colt pistols with extra cylinders from Wiley's and Lawrence's wagons, with pockets full of extra bullets for each weapon.

Wiley ran as fast as he could across the open area to the other hillside, hustled up to the top, and headed in the direction of the campsite from the far side of the hill. James started up the ravine, and the other two started making their way closer. Ben and Lawrence got as close as they thought would be safe, still giving themselves a good shooting area to pick off any riders that might try coming out. James, moving as silent as a cat, crept up through the ravine. As he got closer, he could hear the sounds of talking, but couldn't quite make out what was being said. He needed to get closer, and he managed to crawl within twenty yards of the campsite.

It was a calm, sunny afternoon with no wind, so he was able to hear their voices clearly.

"Boy, Sarge," one man said, "you sure sounded convincing, telling them boys we were on patrol for the general." The man laughed as he thought of the scene.

"How you came up with that story so fast was just dandy."

"Well, hell, I did go on a patrol for the general looking for that stuff," the sergeant replied. "We never did find any clues. Who knows, maybe them guns did come from one of those storages. All I know is, I seen all that food they had, and I wanted it. I'm sure the rest of you are as hungry as I am. Speaking of, we've been sitting here almost an hour, and my stomach's talk'n up a storm. How's them vittles coming along?"

A voice from over by the campfire told him it was almost ready.

Upon hearing this, James slunk out into the ravine and made his way back toward the others. When he got to Lawrence, he waved for Ben to come over, then told the two what he heard.

"So far, they haven't gone through the wagons," he said. "We need to tell Wiley!"

"We surely do," Lawrence said. "I'll go up over the hill and get him."

At the top of the hill, he headed in the direction that

Wiley would've taken and kept his eyes peeled. He finally found him laid out behind a fallen log in a group of trees. When he got close, he gave a low whistle.

When he told him what James had said, Wiley thought for a minute, looked back over at the campsite and then at the surrounding area. Coming up with an idea, he said, "Come on, let's go to the others, and I'll tell you what I think we can do."

They made it back to Ben and James quickly. "If James can get back to where he was when he heard them talking," Wiley said, "I can sneak down the front of the hillside and get to within thirty yards of the back of their campsite. They're grouped up around the fire pit, and there's open ground for about thirty yards across. We should be able to get them in a crossfire. With Lawrence and Ben coming in from the front, we'll have them surrounded; we just need to keep them from getting under cover before we get the drop on them."

"Let's get to it," Ben said, "before they start looking through the wagons."

They each took the positions Wiley had indicated and started closing in on the campsite. James moved a little closer than he'd been earlier, so he'd have clear shooting into the campsite.

Ben and Lawrence got within fifty yards of the soldiers but couldn't get any closer because it was open ground from there to the campsite, and they couldn't risk being seen. Wiley had gone back up and over the hill, gotten past the campsite and started down the hillside toward the camp. He managed to get within about thirty-five yards of it and had a clear line of sight toward the fire pit and the wagons from behind a big tree.

The soldiers had finished eating; some of them said they were going to take a nap. They heard one tell the sergeant, "I'm going to go through the wagons and see what's there." They watched him climb up in the back of one wagon, pull the tarp off and start rummaging through the stuff. Another man climbed into the other wagon and started doing the same.

Wiley knew they couldn't let them get to the crates with the blankets and strongboxes. He also knew the other McCoys had to have seen this and would be picking out the targets closest to them, getting ready to shoot.

He stood up behind a thick tree and let his rifle barrel stick out beyond it. "Hold it right there, all of you! We got you surrounded and will shoot the first man that makes a move to a gun."

The sergeant looked in the direction of the voice. As he started to pull out his pistol, Wiley shot him in the hand, and his gun went flying. The other men started scurrying for cover and pulling out pistols. The two in the wagons dropped behind the sideboards inside the wagons. Two shots came from the men who had been lying down and hit the tree Wiley was behind.

James had been ready and fired two quick shots into the shoulders of the two men who had been lying down. Two others turned toward him and raised their pistols, and Lawrence and Ben fired, hitting each one of them in the arm.

The sergeant tried to scramble underneath the wagon as more shots came from all around them. "I told you, you're surrounded," Wiley yelled, "and if the rest of you want to stay healthy, put down your guns and come out into the clear." The ones who had been shot held up their good arms and walked toward the fire pit. The two in the wagon stayed down, and the sergeant crawled the rest of the way behind the wagon wheel. The others stayed put behind trees.

Wiley yelled again, "I said, throw out your guns, and come out with your hands up!" The men behind the trees looked at the sergeant, and he motioned for them to stay put as he came out from behind the wheel.

"What do you want?" he yelled.

"We want what you stole from us," Wiley replied. "You can give up and give us our wagons back, or you can die right here."

The sergeant came out from behind the wheel and walked over to the men around the fire pit. Wiley heard him whisper, "When I say get down, everyone drop." Then with his good hand, he signaled those behind the trees to stay down and wait.

"Okay, we give up," he yelled. "You can come out."

As Wiley started to step out from behind his tree, one of the unwounded ex-soldiers took a shot at him.

James saw where it came from and shot the man in the shoulder. When two others behind trees turned and fired at James, Wiley shot one in the leg, and Lawrence shot the other one in the arm. The McCoys got back behind their cover, and Wiley yelled out, "Okay, that's enough of that. There's only two of you left in one piece, and you're in the wagons. If you think those sidewalls will stop a bullet, you had better think twice. Now throw out your weapons and climb down from there."

The men in the wagons thought about it for a minute, and seeing all the other men were wounded, they decided they would throw out their guns and climbed out.

As the guns dropped to the ground, the McCoys stood up and came out from behind the trees, keeping their rifles pointed at the men.

Wiley came in to the camp and started gathering up all the weapons he could see. He threw them in the back of one of the wagons and went over to search each of the men for other weapons. After he had taken everything the men had on them and checked all around for other weapons, he tossed the rest of them in the wagon. "Now all of you get over around the campfire," he said.

Once they were all there, he told them, "I hope that meal was worth getting shot over." He turned to the two unwounded men and said, "You two patch them up as best you can." He went to a wagon and grabbed some first aid gear that they had brought with them and tossed it to them.

He watched them bandage the wounded. When they'd finished, he told all of them to sit on the ground and put their hands behind their backs. Those who could did what he said.

Standing on one side of the group with James on the other side, Wiley told Ben and Lawrence to tie up the ex-soldiers. "Tie their hands behind them, and tie their hands to their feet," he said. They grabbed the ropes they saw on the thieves' horses and pulled a piece they had in the wagons and did just that.

Wiley looked at the thieves, then shook his head with disgust. "You men should be ashamed of yourselves. You were honorable enough to fight as soldiers and probably were decent people before the war. Now look at you. Because the war's over, you decide to steal from people who worked hard to get what little they have. I'll bet everyone you've been stealing from started out with nothing, just like you. You're just too lazy to do some honest work and get something for yourselves. I should turn you over to the law, but I want to get back home myself, and don't have time to be wasting on no-accounts like you. So, I'm going to leave you right here and let you find your own way, and I hope those bullets you collected remind you that the best way to get anything is to work for it."

The McCoys gathered up everything that had been taken from the wagons. Fortunately, their horses were still tied to the backs of the wagons. They took the soldiers' horses with them when they left, planning to let them go before they crossed the river.

The men made it back to where they'd left the women, who in their absence, had decided to get away from the wagons and watch them from a distance. "We need to get out of here quick," Wiley told them, "and get across the river." They took the hobbles off the horses and retied the animals to the back of the wagons. Wiley and Lawrence jumped in one wagon, and the women drove the other two wagons, while Ben and James held the reins of the horses they took from the soldiers. After approximately five miles, they let the ex-soldiers' horses go and continued to the river, where they hired a flatboat to take them across.

The flatboat could only handle two wagons at a time and six horses. It took about three hours for all of them to get across. Once across, they took the road that would take them northeast, so they could cross the Cumberland River up above the Twin Lakes. After crossing it, they would head south on the east side of the eastern Twin Lake. They had close to sixty miles to travel before they reached the Cumberland River.

There was a small town just across the Mississippi, close to where the flatboat left them, but they didn't stop; it was too close to where they had left those soldiers, and they wanted to put as much distance between them and those men as they could, as quickly as possible.

"We should get as many miles as we can away from those thieving soldiers," Wiley said, "in case any of them has ideas of trying to catch up with us to retake the wagons, since they know we're headed to Kentucky."

One thing those soldiers didn't know was that they had four wagons and two women traveling with them. Wiley figured that if they did try to follow, when they reached the river, the flatboat captain would tell them that no group of four men and two wagons had come across.

They continued for two days, stopping only for an evening supper and to lay out their bedrolls and added tents the second night. On the morning of the third day, it had rained hard all night the night before and was still raining steady. They tried to travel, but the roads were too muddy. They took shelter well before noon under a large cluster of trees and set up the ladies' tent and two of the two-man tents they carried. Since they kept the horses and wagons right close to camp, and there was really no place to set up a lookout, they all slept most of the day.

CHAPTER 8

SNAKES IN THE ROCKS

On the morning of the fourth day after their encounter with the so-called soldiers, they decided they would try traveling on the road again. The road was still very muddy, but they were able to travel on it. Following the track between two hills, they came to a place where the road had been washed away by flash flooding. The water had washed big rocks and pieces of fallen trees that had hung up where the road crossed the runoff path. There was lots of mud, and it was very slippery to maneuver on foot, let alone trying to get a wagon across the washed-out area.

The men pitched in and cleared enough of a path to get the wagons through, but there were still a few large and many smaller rocks scattered throughout. The first two wagons made it, but they had to help pull them through the washed-out spot by tying ropes from the wagons to the saddle horns of the horses they were riding. The third wagon was in the middle of the washed-out area, and the fourth wagon was behind it, waiting to get across, when it became apparent that the rain had also destroyed the den of some rattlesnakes.

Four of them had slithered down the wash and made it to where the road crossed it, hiding among the debris stacked up by the water. No one had noticed them when the first two wagons crossed, but apparently the passing of the wagons and horses disturbed their resting places. As the men tried to cross with the last two wagons, the snakes coiled tight and rattled their tails. This startled the horse hitched to James's wagon, and it reared up and then bolted forward.

James was knocked off-balance and lost his grip on the reins. The ropes Wiley and Lawrence were holding to wrap around their saddle horns were jerked out of their hands, as their horses spooked.

James's wagon horse took off, going as fast as it could. The wagon nearly tipped when it hit a big rock with the back wheel, but it righted itself, and the horse dragged it across the washed-out area. "Whoa!" James called, but the horse didn't listen.

At the same time, Ben's wagon-hitched horse decided the snakes were too scary to stomach and took off running after the wagon ahead of it.

As the track was so slippery, the wagon slid wildly, tossing Ben from one side of the bench seat to the other. During this sliding around, one of the wheels hit a big rock off to the side and broke the wheel. The horse was still able to keep the wagon moving forward until the wheel crumbled. Ben managed to stop the horse before the wagon tipped over and any more major damage happened to the wagon.

When James was finally able to gain control over his terrified horse, the rear axle of his wagon was busted, and the wheel was about to come off.

Wiley and Lawrence made sure the men were okay and the horses weren't hurt. After looking over the horses and the wagons, they decided the horses were fine, but the wagons were not able to travel.

They went back to the washed-out area and looked around for the snakes, dispatching them with two shots each from their pistols. Satisfied the snakes wouldn't bother them anymore, they went back to the wagons to figure out what they were going to do.

Wiley rode to the two wagons that had made it safely across, the ones driven by the ladies. He told them to just sit tight until they figured out how they were going to fix things. He looked around as he rode to the top of the hill to get a look at the other side. There he saw clumps of trees growing along the eastern bottom of the slope in large groups of five to ten acres per group.

On the southern end of the hilltop were some rock formations that would make a good lookout point. There was plenty of grass growing underneath the trees, at least those he could see under. Having seen what he went there for, he headed back to the wagons.

The men were still trying to assess the total damage, and things didn't look good. Ben turned to Wiley and said, "One wheel is shattered on one wagon, and on the other wagon, the axle is broken completely through, right in the middle of the wagon bed."

James shook his head with disgust. "These two wagons can't go any farther until we get them fixed," he said.

Wiley told them what he had seen on the other side of the hill. "I figure we can make a camp down in those trees and place a lookout up in that rock formation over there," he said.

"We'll have to go to the nearest town with our other wagons and haul back an axle and wheel. We should probably pick up an extra wheel or two, in case those on the broken axle are bent, or for if we have any future problems. The nearest town, I think, is going to be at the Cumberland River, about twelve miles, I think. Me and James will go to town with the women and put them in a hotel while we come back and get these wagons fixed. Any objections?"

Lawrence looked surprised and flustered. "It's his wagon that needs fixin,'" he said, "and since Cassie's been ridin' with me all this time, I want to be the one to ride in my wagon with Cassie."

The other men looked at him, all of them grinning. "Well, well, look who's gone sweet on that young woman," James said. "If that's the case, I wouldn't want you getting jealous of me just because Wiley said I should ride with her."

Lawrence quickly tried to defend himself. "No, it's not that," he said. "It's… it's that I was kind of hoping to get to know her a little better, an' this would be a real good chance."

James chuckled. "You sure should get to know her better, just you two in the wagon for all that time, then checking her into a hotel room. Probably will buy her some fancy perfume and take her for a walk along the riverbank around sunset too."

Wiley grinned broadly. "Okay, Lawrence," he said. "Don't get all flustered. You can drive your wagon since she's riding on it." Lawrence's face had gone burning red. He turned away to hide it. The men finding out he was kind of sweet on Cassie embarrassed him.

They unhitched the horses from the two broken wagons, and everyone went to the campsite Wiley had spotted. They found a good place to post a guard that was fairly hidden from any eyes looking from the road or from the hillsides.

There was a small creek running at the base of the next hill, where the trees were the thickest. There was a lot of grass around the trees and enough room for all of the horses. They could put up one of the two-man tents. They decided they would share watch duties over the wagons from the rock outcropping up above, until the others came back.

Lawrence and Wiley brought one extra horse each along for the trip to the next town, climbed up in the wagons beside the women, and started out down the road toward the Cumberland River.

CHAPTER 9

STOPPING CURIOSITY

At the campsite, Ben and James began to hobble all of the other horses and get the things they would need from their two wagons for their camp. They set up the camp as far back under the trees as they could get, made a fire pit, and decided to make something to eat. They also decided on making six-hour shifts for the lookout up in the rocks over the broken-down wagons. While they were eating, Ben was thinking about what people traveling down the road would do when they saw their broken-down wagons, full of supplies, with no one around them. He was sure anyone passing would get curious and want to have a look inside. He was trying to think of a way to stop that from happening without having to stay down at the wagons. He asked James, "Can you write?"

James kicked the ground with the toe of his boot. "I can a little," he said. "I did graduate the second grade. Why ya asking?"

"I was just trying to think about how to keep people from nosing in our wagons without us having to stay down there with them. I bought a small chalkboard and some chalk from the general store before we left, cuz I was hopin' to learn how to read and write, even learn to cipher, so's I didn't get tricked out of my money by some fancy no-good lawyer or somebody I try to do some business with. Can you write a sign?"

James sighed. "I think so. At least I'll give it a try," he said.

Ben went down to his wagon and dug through it until he found what he was looking for, then went back to their campsite. He handed the chalkboard and chalk to James. "Here ya are. Let's try and think of a short sign that's to the point." They each got a second portion of food and started pondering what to write while they ate.

After a while, Ben said, "How about 'Gone to town for parts. Be back soon. Stay away from the wagons.'"

"Naw," James said. "It has to be shorter. I have to make big letters, so someone can see it from a distance and still be able to read it. Besides, this chalkboard is too small to write that much in big letters. And I don't think that would make anybody think twice about taking a peek at what might be inside."

James stared at the ground for another stretch, thinking. "How about, 'Stay off wagons or get shot,'" he said.

"Yeah, that's it," Ben said. "Good 'n' short, and to the point."

James took the chalk and did his best to print the words they'd decided on large and clear.

He wrote STAY OFF WAGONS on the top half of the board and underneath that, OR GIT SHOT. The six words were so big they took up the whole sheet of chalkboard.

Ben said, "Looks good and clear to me," and they agreed folks should be able to see that from a decent distance away and get the message. Ben took the sign down to the wagons and decided to put it on the one that was still mainly upright. He set the chalkboard on the sidewall facing the road, putting a nail through the frame at the top to hold it up. Satisfied with his work, he put his hammer and chalk back in his wagon and went back to camp.

The next two days passed without incident. They did have two riders pass one time and look at the sign. When they did, they stopped and looked around until they saw the rock outcropping and someone sitting there.

It was Ben, and when he waved his rifle, they just continued down the road. The next visitor was a wagon that came by carrying a family that looked to be moving, and they slowed down to read the sign but kept on going as soon as they had.

CHAPTER 10

MASQUERADING SOLDIERS RETURN

The masquerading soldiers that the McCoys had left tied back across the river had taken only a few hours to get themselves free. The McCoys had forgotten about their fire pit in their hurry to get out of there. There was no flame or any smoke coming from it, so it never crossed their mind that there would still be hot coals.

One of the unwounded men managed to wiggle over to the pit and kick out some coals and burn the ropes around the hands of the other healthy one who still had the use of both his arms.

Once free, it took them several hours to walk out to the road and start heading toward the river, knowing the closest town would be just across. It took them the rest of the day to cover five miles on foot, helping one another to walk, and it was almost two days before they spotted a couple of their horses that had wandered not too far from the road but were a good distance from where they had been released. They went to them and grabbed their reins, then mounted up and rode around the area, looking to see if they could find any other horses. They found seven in total, and that was just as well because a couple of the men were hurt bad enough that they needed someone to help hold them in the saddle from behind.

When they finally made it to the river crossing, the flatboat captain told them he wouldn't charge them because they were soldiers and needed to get to the doctor in town.

During the crossing, the sergeant asked him if he'd seen four men and a couple of wagons, or if he had taken them across.

"I take a lot of people across almost every day," the flatboat captain told him.

The sergeant described the McCoys, and the flatboat captain said, "I can't say as I recollect any one group like that, but I have taken several wagons across. A few singles, but at most they had only two people. There were a couple of groups of eight wagons, one group of four, and whenever there was any more than one wagon, I do remember that those all had women in their groups."

His answer made the sergeant unsure if they had gone this way. The flatboat owner then said he did remember in one of the groups that had four wagons, they had four men and two women who said they needed to cross the Cumberland River above the Twin Lakes.

Once on land again, the fake soldiers thanked the captain, and he told them where the doctor was in the nearby town. The doctor cleaned their wounds and bandaged them. A couple of the men were told that they needed to stay in his office for a few days till they got their strength back.

He had a sort of infirmary set up in a couple of rooms of the building he occupied, so he gave them cots and told them he would have the hotel send over some food. The ones who were not so badly wounded told the doctor they didn't have any money or anywhere to sleep, and he offered them the use of a small hayloft in back of the building and said he would give them some blankets, so they could bed down there till their friends were able to travel. The doctor told them it shouldn't be more than three or four days at most. Right now, he was going over to the hotel to see about getting them something to eat.

When he left, the sergeant told the men he was heading out when the doctor let them leave and asked if any of them wanted to go with him.

"I'm going to try and catch up with those sons o' bitches that shot up my hand," he said. "I aim to take back them two wagons full of supplies." The men started moaning and groaning and mumbling among themselves, so he said, "Speak up! I can't understand what you're mumbling about."

"Well, Sarge," one said, "I don't hold a grudge, cuz we was wrong. We had their property, and I feel lucky that they didn't kill me, which they could have, I'm sure."

Another man said, "They shot us where they wanted us to be shot. Them boys got real good aim. So, I'm not going with ya. I don't know about the rest of these boys, but you can count me out."

The sergeant looked at him hard. "Well, you're a free man and can do as you please," he said, "but I'm going to try to find them, even if I have to go by myself."

In the end, three said no, but four of them said they'd

go along, because even if they didn't catch up with them, at least they wouldn't be traveling alone across Kentucky.

On the fourth day, the two unwounded men, the sergeant, one of the other men shot in the hand, and the one that got shot in the leg felt they were ready to ride again. They thanked the doctor, and the sergeant told him, "If we ever get back through here and have some money, we'll come pay you."

The doctor shook his head. "No need," he said. "It's the least the town can do for soldiers who helped fight to make us a country free of slavery." And they thanked him and set out on the road that would take them north of the Twin Lakes and the Cumberland River.

CHAPTER 11

GETTING TO KNOW THE LADIES

On their way to town, Lawrence and Wiley talked at great length to the women riding with them. Wiley asked Claire why they were leaving their home. Claire decided to give him her version of their situation.

Responding to his question she said, "We're from Tennessee and we had a small ranch that was burned out by the North's soldiers. We were on our way to my husband's sister's place when we got attacked by those bandits. I never really liked my sister-in-law, so I really didn't want to go there, plus we would be a burden to them on top of it. I wanted to start another ranch, our own, and do some farming too.

"With the money the sheriff gave me now I can do that; I just have to find a place I'd like to live, a pretty place that is still free from too many other settlers."

Cassie told Lawrence of the life they'd had on the ranch in Tennessee. She said, in reply to his question about what was her life like before they'd left they're home, "The closest town was about ten miles away, we didn't get there very much. I've had never had a suitor or gone to school, but I would like to learn what was offered in school. My mother taught me a little bit of how to read and write, but we didn't have very much time for it, as there were always a lot of chores to be done on the ranch to keep us alive and prepared for winter."

The town where they were headed was a lot farther than they had thought. The Cumberland River was farther still. They would need to travel a good forty miles from where they had broken down, and it took them two days to get there. But Lawrence couldn't have been any happier that it was that far away. It meant he had all those hours to talk as much as he wanted to this pretty girl sitting beside him.

He found himself being able to relax around her and speak from his heart. He told her about his life before the war, going to school and being the best pupil in the class, and that his teacher wanted him to go on to high school and college because book learning came so easy to him. He also told her his heart wasn't in going to school, but that he could teach her what he knew—or at least he thought he could.

He explained that he enjoyed himself most out in the wilderness trapping and hunting or fishing. He liked raising horses and cattle, and that's what he planned to do when he made it back home. That he knew it was going to take a lot of work, but he wasn't afraid of hard work, he'd learned that everything that someone did in life took a lot of work to be successful. What he couldn't tell her that he already had enough money to do everything and still have lots of money left over. There would be plenty of time to do that—later.

Wiley told Claire of the ranch he had started with his wife before she died, and how they had hoped, one day, to raise the finest Kentucky thoroughbreds in the state. Although the ranch was in a good location for that—there was lots of Kentucky grass for the horses to eat—of the five-hundred acres he had claimed, he had only managed to clear some of the land for farming and put fences around a hundred and fifty acres. He had gotten a few horses and some cattle, but the operation wasn't anywhere near as grand as what they had dreamed about before his wife got sick.

Wiley kept his eyes trained on the road when he talked of his wife. Claire could feel the pain in his voice when he said, "When she passed, I didn't feel like continuing with our dream. So, I just planted a few vegetables, enough to get me through the winter, and raised enough beef to have something besides what I got from hunting. I tried losing myself in fixing up the place the way she would've liked it, but when I finished, it still felt empty. Then the war came, and I just left to join the fight. I had nothing to keep me there, and I wasn't getting over losing her."

Wiley had started to notice what a fine woman Claire was, both beautiful and educated, and strong-minded as well. She wasn't one to just give up, like he had. He thought that this woman would make a fine wife for someone. She'd keep the lucky man well motivated. She seemed more encouraged about what awaited her in the future than worried about it, unlike how she'd been when he first met her. Probably, he reckoned, it was because of the money the sheriff had given her, she could make her own decisions and wouldn't have to depend on charity from other people.

They slept alongside the road that night, making a quick camp and only setting up a two-man tent for the ladies and just their bedrolls and saddles from the wagon for pillows for the men. Wiley slept fitfully, having dreams of his past wife and Claire together in the same dream. He woke several times and looked at the tent, conflicting feelings going through his head. He loved his past wife and was now pondering over another woman in that same capacity. He looked over to Lawrence and saw that he had what looked like a smug grin on his face, knowing he was sleeping near the woman that he hoped to make his. He thought, *How come I'm the one so troubled about a woman that doesn't even know if she wants another man.* Rolling onto his side and facing away from the tent, he hoped that would help him block all the thoughts passing through his mind and let him get some sleep. By morning, he felt as if he hadn't slept at all.

Chapter 12

Teaching the
Ladies to Shoot

On the afternoon of their second day of traveling, they still hadn't reached town, so they stopped to make a meal. Wiley had decided to show the women how to use a rifle.

While the women were cooking up the victuals, he and Lawrence took a couple of the carbine rifles out of the wagon along with a box of bullets. They walked out away from the road and set out some sticks and some of the thicker branches that had fallen off the trees to use as targets.

They set most of them at fifty and seventy-five yards away, and a couple at a hundred yards. Wiley also put a few around twenty and thirty yards, just in case they couldn't shoot at all. For themselves, they propped up four thick branches with rocks at about a hundred yards, and four more at about two hundred fifty yards. The last two targets they would use were trees at least four hundred yards out.

Claire had decided to make a big pot of beef stew so

that they would have some left over to eat the next day. While the stew was cooking, Wiley asked the women if they'd like to try and see if they could hit some of the closer targets that they had placed on their makeshift shooting range.

"Don't worry if you didn't know how to handle a rifle," he said. "We'll show you. I think it's about time you learned how to shoot one for your own protection."

Claire and Cassie exchanged a meaningful glance, and Claire gave Cassie a knowing wink. Claire said, "Okay, we'll try to learn how to use a rifle."

Wiley showed them the bullets and how to put them in the guns, then how to cock the rifle. Claire smiled and winked again at Cassie while he did this.

Lawrence gave Cassie his rifle and seven bullets, then helped her to put them all in the rifle. He showed her how to align the sights on the top of the rifle with her target, which he was really happy to do, because it gave him an excuse to stand behind her and put his arms around her, holding the gun in position. And he could lean his head right next to hers as he showed her how to align the sights.

Cassie giggled. She felt slightly embarrassed as he pressed up against her from behind. He told her to make sure that the butt of the rifle was placed well, and that it needed to be just inside the joint of her shoulder and pressed tightly against it, because when she pulled the trigger, it was going to kick back with some force. "I'll help you with the first shot," he said, "and after that, it will be up to you to do it by yourself."

He lined up the sights on the branch around twenty yards away and put his finger over hers on the trigger.

"Squeeze the trigger slowly," he told her. "Don't jerk it. Keep your eyes open, with the target in the sights, as you do it."

The first round went off, and pieces of bark went flying from the branch.

He let go of the rifle and backed away from her. "Now, you do it by yourself," he said.

She lifted the rifle and seemed to have some trouble keeping it up and steady, but finally was able to hold it still enough to pull the trigger.

Dirt flew up from the ground behind the target. The kick from the rifle almost knocked her off her feet. "Ow! That hurt!" she moaned as she rubbed her shoulder.

"You need to keep it tighter against your shoulder next time," Lawrence told her, "and it shouldn't be so bad."

She looked at him like he was crazy and continued rubbing her shoulder.

But soon she was ready to try it again. Cassie placed the rifle tightly against her shoulder this time and took aim at a little bigger branch at about the same distance. When she squeezed the trigger, the branch exploded into pieces, and the kick from the rifle wasn't nearly so bad.

She had the biggest smile on her face, as she yelled, "I hit it! I did it!" and jumped up and down. She tried one more target about thirty yards away and missed. When she tried again and hit it, she raised the rifle with both hands above her head as she yelled, "I did it again!" Then she got brave and tried to shoot the next two targets farther away.

First, she tried the target that was fifty yards away; twice she missed but was close. Lawrence gave her more bullets, which she loaded into the rifle herself. Then she decided to go for the farther target at seventy-five yards, which was a larger branch, and on her third try, the wood pieces went flying in the air.

She turned to Lawrence and said, "That other one was just too small, but how's that, for the first time shooting a rifle?"

He smiled. "That's a lot better than most first-timers I've seen," he said.

Now, it was Claire's turn. She let Wiley treat her the same way Lawrence had treated Cassie, standing behind and against her, leaning his head against hers to line up the sights. Even though she still felt she didn't want another man in her life, she enjoyed the feel of this big man against her, his head so close to hers.

He aimed the rifle at the first target close to them, put his finger over hers on the trigger, and squeezed. The target shattered into several pieces. When he backed away, she felt a little disappointed that he didn't stay next to her for at least one more shot.

He told her to pick her targets and fire when ready. She took aim at the next closest target and fired, hitting it. Then she skipped to the one seventy-five yards away. The first shot she missed just slightly, but the second shot made pieces of bark go flying. Then she picked out a target about one hundred fifty yards away and fired three shots quickly. Two of her shots made wood chips fly in all directions, even though all three were made in less than a minute.

She turned and gave Wiley a look a mischievous child might make. "My, what a good teacher you are," she said, handing him back the rifle. He looked at her, shocked and stunned, before realizing he'd been hoodwinked. He laughed. "There sure is a lot about you that I don't know," he said, "but I like what I'm finding out."

Her smile was ear to ear. "You best be careful around me," she said. "You never know what I might know how to do." They all laughed together for a little while.

Then Lawrence and Wiley wanted to show off their marksmanship. They made a bet on who could hit the farthest target and started with the hundred-yard targets, each firing three shots and hitting all of them. They went to the two-hundred-fifty-yard targets and fired three more shots each, hitting all again. They could tell they hit them because they were knocked out of the rocks that held them in place. They decided to try the four-hundred-yard targets. Lawrence hit all three shots, and Wiley hit two with dirt flying beyond the target on his third shot, leaving the branch still standing.

"I win," Lawrence said. "I hit all three and you missed one."

"Huh," Wiley said. "The bet was who could hit the farthest target." He went back to the wagon and took out his buffalo gun, a .50 caliber Sharps rifle and came back to the group. "You remember those trees way out there?" he said. "Well, I'm going to hit one of 'em."

He stepped out in front and took aim toward a tree that was at least six hundred yards away. He could barely see the trunk lining up the sight bar, but he could tell it was there for the wider and irregular shape it gave. He held the rifle steady, slowed his breathing, exhaled, and squeezed the trigger.

A couple of seconds later, they all heard what sounded like a cracking of wood and saw a big chunk of bark go flying in the air. Wiley turned to Lawrence and smiled. "I believe I just won the bet for hitting the farthest target," he said.

"That's not fair, I don't have a buffalo gun," Lawrence said, laughing.

"You're welcome to use mine," Wiley said.

Lawrence countered with, "That tree is just a blur to me. Your eyesight is just too good for me to compete with."

Wiley shook his head. "C'mon, give it a try!" he coaxed.

Lawrence looked at him, then at the ladies, and said, "No, that's okay. That gun kicks like a mule. You win. Besides, I'm hungry! The idea of stew sounds mighty good right about now." And they all laughed.

Cassie grabbed Lawrence's arm and started pulling him toward the fire, proud of his chivalry. "Yeah, we're hungry too. Let's go eat," she said. They went back to the wagons, and the women dished up the stew. They all ate heartily. Not a morsel was left for the next day's meal.

The women cleaned the plates with some of the water they had in the barrels carried in the wagons, since they were not near any stream. Once everything was put away, they started out again down the road.

They made it to the town a little bit before dark. While they were coming onto the main street of the town, they saw a sign saying *Tennessee River 100 yards,* and an arrow pointing to the right. Then they saw the sheriff's office, a telegraph office, a mercantile store, a saloon, and a hotel with a restaurant on the bottom floor.

They stopped in front of the hotel and Wiley went inside. He asked the desk clerk if they had any rooms, adding that he would need two rooms with two beds in each. The desk clerk told him they had a couple of rooms for them and asked if they had any baggage.

"Nothing that we can't carry ourselves," Wiley said. "Is there a livery stable somewhere close by?

"As a matter of fact, the livery is just behind the hotel," the clerk said.

"Do you also furnish hot baths?"

"Of course," replied the clerk.

"Then we'll take two rooms with two baths in each, as soon as you can have them ready," and Wiley placed a fifty-dollar gold piece on the counter.

The clerk's eyes got really big as he looked at the coin. "I'll have everything ready for you in a jiffy," he said. "If you want to take your wagons around the back, I'm sure Jesse, the stable owner, can accommodate you."

Wiley then asked the clerk if the hotel had an arrangement for laundry and was told their clothes could be washed and dried and ready by the next morning.

"Would you like your change from this gold piece?" the clerk asked as Wiley turned to go.

"No, just take out whatever it is we end up spending here," Wiley replied. "I'm sure we're going to want to eat a little later tonight, and for sure tomorrow morning. I'll get the change then."

Wiley went back to the wagons and drove around the back of the hotel to the corral. There stood was a man working a bellows and pounding on some horseshoe iron.

"Howdy, are you Jesse?" Wiley asked him.

The man turned, wiped some sweat off his forehead, and said, "Yes, sir, what can I do for you?"

"Well, I hope you can do a lot for me," answered

Wiley. "I need a place to park our wagons for the night and to rest, water an' feed our horses. I'm also in need of a couple of wagon wheels and an axle for a wagon, the same kind of wagons we have here. Do you have any for sale?"

"I sure do," Jesse replied. "Although, it'll be easier for you if I just sold you two new wagons. Them wagons are mighty heavy and tricky to hold up while you're a puttin' the wheel on, let alone trying to change an axle. Plus, you're going to need the tools to do it with."

Wiley thought about that for a minute and figured he was probably right. They did have two extra horses with them, as they had each pulled one behind their wagon, just in case something happened.

"How much you want for the wagons?" he asked.

The livery owner looked him over, sizing him up for how much he could ask him to pay. "You give me forty-five for each wagon, and I'll throw in the night's stay, feed for the horses, and the two wagons guarded overnight," he finally said. "I'll even throw in the harnesses you'll need for your horses."

Wiley was sizing him up as well. "Let me see the wagons, and I'll tell you yes or no," he said. They walked behind the blacksmith shed, and he pointed at two wagons he had there. They were pretty well-built and in good shape—not brand-new, but darn near.

"I'll give you seventy for everything," Wiley said.

Jesse shook his head. "Mister, a man's gotta make a profit," he said, "and I build them wagons myself."

Wiley smiled. "Well, then everything's profit, except the wood."

The livery owner laughed. "I guess the hard work I

put into them doesn't count for nothing? Make it seventy-five and we got a deal. Those are two real good wagons, and I'll give you new harnesses for them."

"Okay, I suppose we can do that," Wiley said. "You will make sure no one touches our wagons tonight, right?"

"No problem, mister. I sleep right over there," Jesse said, and indicated a small building to the side of the blacksmith area.

Wiley told the women to grab what they wanted out of the wagons. He turned to the livery owner and handed him a fifty-dollar gold piece. "I'll pay the rest in the morning when we're ready to leave," Wiley said.

Jesse's eyes gleamed as he took the coin. "Okay, that'll be just fine," he said.

Inside the hotel, Wiley asked the clerk, "Would you send a couple of razors and some shaving soap up to the room?"

"It's already been done as part of the bath service," the clerk said. "We give you the option of shaving yourself, if you like, by leaving a wash basin, towel, razor, and a mirror on the vanity that's in the room."

"That's some nice service there, thank you kindly," Wiley replied.

The ladies' room was straight across the hall from the men's.

"You can put the dirty clothes you want washed and ironed outside the door," he told the women, "and they will have it ready in the morning. The kitchen closes at nine-thirty tonight, if you want to have something more to eat or some dessert. Me, I'm going to have me a long soak and a shave. If the place is still open when I'm done, I smelled some apple pie baking downstairs I'd like to taste. Maybe we'll see each other later. If not, see you in the morning. Have a good night's sleep."

They went into their rooms. Claire and Cassie set out clean clothes and flopped down on the beds. The tubs were nearly full of hot water, and there were two buckets of hot water beside each one. They both undressed and put the clothes they took off outside the door, then slowly slid into that wonderful warm water, leaned back, and closed their eyes. "Ah!" said Claire. "That feels so good! I could stay in here all night, if the water would stay hot."

When Wiley and Lawrence climbed in the tubs, they both almost fell asleep. But Lawrence remembered what Wiley had said about apple pie. Pulling himself from the sleepy trance the hot bath put him in, he smiled at Wiley and said, "Apple pie. I'm going to get some."

And that inspired both to set to scrubbing the dirt off of themselves. Lawrence finished first, climbed out, and dried off, and then put on the clean clothes he had brought from the wagon and started to shave.

When he finished, Wiley was ready for his turn with the mirror. They were both ready to go downstairs by about eight o'clock.

Lawrence knocked on the ladies' door. "We're going down for some pie," he said. "Are you coming?"

They heard some movement inside, and a voice said, "We'll be down in a minute. Go on ahead. We'll meet you."

When the waitress came to their table, the men ordered four pieces of hot apple pie. She asked, "Would you like to try it with the newest craze? We've gotten the recipe for it from back east, and since the war ended, we can finally get all the ingredients. It's called ice cream."

"Really, you got some of that stuff?" Lawrence replied, excited. "I heard it was cold and creamy and sweet like candy, but I just thought the guys talkin' about it were jus' pullin' my leg!"

"Oh, it's real all right," said the waitress, "and we're the farthest town west that's got it that I know of."

Lawrence was beside himself with delight. "Can you put it on all four pieces of pie, please?" he said.

"You boys must really either miss apple pie or have a big sweet tooth," the waitress said with a smile.

Lawrence smiled back and said, "We could eat it all, but we have two women coming to share it with."

She winked, and said, "Well, lucky them," and went off to give the order to the kitchen.

The cook handed up a whole pie, cut into four pieces, to the waitress. She took it over to the counter, put each piece on a plate, and handed the pan back to the cook. Then she put two scoops of vanilla ice cream on each, and took them over to their table, and as she went back to get their forks, the women came down the staircase. They were dressed in one of their new dresses.

The men stood up, took their hats off, and held them in front of them. They'd already once witnessed the difference a bit of soap and water and pretty clothing could make on the women they were traveling with, but they just couldn't stop staring at the beautiful women coming down the stairs.

When they started walking toward them, Wiley almost tripped trying to reach the chair he was going to pull out for Claire to sit in.

Lawrence just stood there until Wiley tapped him on

the arm and said in a low voice, "Pull out her chair so she can sit down." He managed to grab the chair and pull it out just as she arrived.

"Thank you," both ladies said as they sat down. As the men scooted their chairs in, the ladies rose just a little, so they could be seated at the right distance from the table. The men hung their hats on the closest hat pole and took their seats.

Cassie looked down at the apple pie. "Oh my, we had better start eating this or we're going to have ice cream all over the table," she said.

Claire's eyes were wide as she took in the food on her plate. "I think this is too big of a piece for myself. I don't think I can eat all of it," she said.

Lawrence put her fears to rest. "Don't worry. You can pass any leftovers right over here," he said. Then it dawned on him, "You know what ice cream is?"

Cassie winked at him. "I've heard about it but never tasted it," she said. Then, smiling, she added, "But then again, I only heard about it when the waitress talked to you as we were coming down the stairs." They all laughed and started eating their pie. Everyone commented on how good the ice cream tasted. When they were finished, Lawrence asked Cassie if she'd like to take a walk around the town, maybe down by the river, which was only a hundred yards away from the end of town.

Wiley gave him a serious look. "You just be careful," he said, "because we don't know nothing about this place. Don't be gone very long."

Cassie answered, "Sure, I'd like to go for a walk around the town, and we'll see if I want to go down by the river when we get over that way. Of course, if it's all right with my mama."

Claire looked Lawrence dead in the eye. "I think you'll be all right with him. He seems like an honest boy. I think I can trust him to protect you." She smiled at him.

Wiley stood up as Cassie stood to leave and sat back down when she was gone. When his eyes met Claire's, the two seemed to melt into each other's gaze.

"Would you like to take a stroll around town with me?" he finally said.

She smiled. "There's not much of a town to see. I suppose we can take ten minutes and walk around it twice."

They went out the front door and started in the opposite direction from Lawrence and Cassie. It was a nice night: warm, but not humid, and there was a slight, gentle breeze. The sky was clear, the moon was bright, and stars were everywhere.

As they walked, Wiley tried to make conversation. "So, you're going stay on at my place? At least till you figure out what you're going to do with your life? What I mean is, if you do stay there, you won't have to worry about men bothering you, and you'll be in a safe location, and Lord knows, my homestead could sure use a woman's touch after all this time."

She stopped walking to turn and look him in the eye. "So what you're saying is, if I come with you, I have to clean your house?"

His face reddened. "No, I didn't mean it to sound like that. I mean, I would love to have your company, and I could use some help. Plus, you wouldn't have to stay in a hotel or where you didn't know anybody."

"It sounds interesting," she said coyly. "Course, I need to see your place to know what I'm getting myself into.

Besides, who knows what I may have to show you! I know how to fight too, you know, not just shoot a rifle."

His expression relaxed some. "Oh, well you don't have to worry none. I'm a gentleman, I would never force myself upon you. I was taught if a woman says no, it means no, and to leave it at that."

To Claire, he sounded like he was trying to say he felt something for her. But she wasn't ready to tell him she felt something for him too, because she just wasn't sure what it was she felt. "If you don't mind, I'll just let time take its course, and we'll see how it turns out."

He tried to look deep in her eyes but wasn't sure if he saw what he was hoping to see. "I suppose that's the best answer I could hope for," he said. "You'll see that I'm not a bad man. I'm honest and a hard worker. I don't have to tell you this, because you'll see as time passes."

• • •

When Lawrence and Cassie reached the end of town, Lawrence said, "The river is just down there," and he pointed at the sloping ground ahead of them. "It's almost a full moon, so we should be able to see pretty well. You want to go look at it in the moonlight?"

"Okay, but we can't stay very long. You know what my mama said."

Lawrence smiled. "Yeah, and Wiley said so too."

They walked down to the riverbank, where the moon was reflecting off of the water, giving it the appearance of a much larger river. The crickets were chirping, and the water was flowing, and it all gave them a nice and peaceful feeling. There was a flatboat dock close by. They sat down on some crates there and looked up at the stars.

He said, "Sure is nice and clear tonight. Means it's not going to rain tomorrow." He folded his hands in front of him.

He was trying to get up the courage to lean over and kiss her, but he just couldn't figure out how to get to that point. So, he just continued looking up and gathering his courage, until he finally said, "Would I offend you if I tried to kiss you?"

She looked down from the stars and at his face. He still hadn't the nerve to look at her, not after he'd said what he did.

She put her hand on his arm and said, "That all depends on how you try to do that."

As her words sank in, he turned to face her, scared as a schoolboy. "Then just how should I do that?" he said.

She smiled. "Maybe if I kissed you, it would be better," she said.

She leaned over and kissed him on the cheek. He turned his face while her lips were on his cheek, and their lips met. He put his hands on her shoulders, and she put her hands on his biceps, and they gave each other a long, slow, tender, loving kiss.

When she pulled away, they both blinked and kissed again with more passion. Before things started to get carried away, she stood up. "I think we should go back to the hotel now. We've been out here for a while."

"Yeah, you're right. We should be getting back," he said. They walked back to the hotel, arm in arm. When they got there, Claire and Wiley were sitting at a table having a hot apple cider, so they ordered one for themselves and sat down.

Claire asked if they had gone down to the river.

"Yes, we did," Cassie said, "and it was just beautiful, the moonlight on the water and all the stars."

"I thought that was where you went," Claire said. "We took a stroll ourselves around the town and didn't see you anywhere."

Lawrence felt he had to say something in his defense. "Well, this here town is pretty small, and we didn't want to just walk around it twice, and I knew whereabouts the river was, so we just went to take a look and had a seat on the boat dock for a few minutes."

Lawrence didn't say anything else until he finished his cider. As he stood up, he said, "I think I'm going upstairs and get some shut-eye, since we need to get started early tomorrow. We can't leave them there by themselves all that long."

Wiley nodded. "Yeah, you're right about that. You go ahead, and I'll be up in a minute."

Lawrence looked at Cassie and said, "I'll walk you to your door, if you're going upstairs now."

She gave him her gentlest smile and said, "That would be nice. I was going to go up now anyway." They headed up the stairs.

Claire turned to Wiley with a mischievous look in her eye. "I guess I'm going to have to keep my eyes on all three of you. A woman has to watch out for herself, and a mother has to keep an eye on her children."

He grinned at her. "You don't have to worry about Lawrence. He's an upright young man," he said.

When Lawrence and Cassie reached their room doors, she put her hand on the doorknob. He touched her shoulder, and she turned toward him. He had his hat in his hands in front of him, and he reached toward her and let the back of his fingers caress her cheek. "Tonight was really special," he said, "and I want to thank you for being so friendly and such a nice lady."

She looked up into his eyes, pulled his face to hers, and gave him a nice, soft goodnight kiss. "It was a nice evening for me too," she said when she pulled away. "See you tomorrow morning, bright and early." Then she turned and went into her room, leaving him standing there stunned.

He then turned and kicked his heels together and practically skipped into his room, as happy as he'd been since he could remember. He took off his clothes, put them on the chair, and climbed into the bed, pulling the blanket up to his chin. His mind was wondering what had just been started between them as he stared at the ceiling. He was feeling very good inside.

A few minutes later, Wiley and Claire were in the hallway.

"We'll see you in the morning," Claire told him. "If we're not awake when you get up, knock on our door, so we won't be holding up our return."

She leaned forward and gave him a light kiss on his lips, said goodnight, and went in to her room. Wiley smiled to himself. *This is one proper woman.* He felt a sense of excitement rise up in him. He was pretty sure she had more than just a little interest in him.

In the room, he shucked his clothes very quickly, tossing them on the chair, and climbed into bed. He didn't say a word to Lawrence, just turned on his side, smiled to himself, and was asleep in less than five minutes, feeling content and happy.

The morning came too quickly, it seemed to

everyone, and it was hard for them to get out of the comfortable beds. Finally, Wiley put his pants on and went into the hall and knocked on the ladies' door. "Rise and shine, people!" he said. "We got a long way to go and need to get a move on. We'll meet you in the restaurant for breakfast." He went back into his room to finish getting dressed.

When they all assembled in the restaurant, they each had a big breakfast of steak and eggs, fried potatoes, and flapjacks.

The men were finishing their third cup of coffee when both women gave up on their pancakes and said that they couldn't eat any more. "I've eaten so much," Claire said. "I won't need another morsel all day, and probably won't be good for anything because I can hardly move. It's a good thing all I have to do is ride in the wagon."

Wiley said he was going to take care of the bill and headed toward the front desk. The women finished the last of their cups of coffee, patted their napkins daintily on their lips, and stood up.

"Let's just waddle out of here and get to the wagons," Cassie said. The three of them laughed and walked to the door.

Wiley collected his change from the gold piece he had given the clerk the night before and came to join them. Lawrence held the door as they walked out, everyone feeling very satisfied with the restful time at the hotel.

At the livery, they found all four wagons hitched up and ready to go. Wiley paid the owner the twenty-five dollars he still owed him and said he appreciated that he had everything ready for them.

Wiley helped Claire up onto her wagon, and

Lawrence helped Cassie up on hers. Lawrence asked, "Are you sure you can handle the wagon?"

"I think so," she said. "I didn't have any trouble with the ones that we had."

The men climbed up on their wagons, said thanks again to the livery owner, and added that they should see him again in a couple of days.

They headed down the street back the way they had come, and in a couple of minutes, the town was behind them and they were on their way back to James and Ben.

The weather was nice, and they kept moving till it started getting close to sundown. Wiley's wagon was in the lead, and Lawrence's was bringing up the rear.

When they stopped, Wiley asked if anyone was hungry. There were all still full of breakfast but agreed they would like to stretch their legs a little bit. When they climbed down from the wagons, Claire and Cassie both complained about how sore their rear ends were.

"I don't know about you," Wiley said, "but I have a funny feeling. If you're up to it, I'd like to keep going for as long as we can see the road."

Claire gave him a worried look. "You think there might be trouble with Ben and James?"

"I don't know, but something's just bothering me. It's just a feeling in my gut, and I can't seem to shake it."

"Well," she said, "if your intuition is telling you we need to get there, I say let's keep going. I always trust my intuition, and it hasn't let me down yet."

Lawrence was wondering if they weren't asking too much of the ladies. "If you get too tired, we can tie the horses that are pulling your wagons to the back of our wagons, so you can lay down in the back," he said.

"We've got plenty of blankets. In fact, I think I can help out your sore bottoms." He rummaged in his wagon and grabbed a couple of blankets; he folded them lengthwise to fit the bench and put one on each of the wagons as a cushion.

The women were sharing the same thought. *Why didn't we think of that several hours ago?*

"Thank you," Claire said. "It looks nice and comfortable now." And they climbed on the wagons and started back down the road. They kept traveling all through the night because the half-moon was nice and bright, and the skies were clear.

At about midnight, the women said they were tired and wanted to lie down, so Lawrence pulled his wagon in front of the third wagon, and they tied pull ropes to the pulling horses of the women's wagons and tied them to the backs of the men's wagons. They pulled out a few more blankets to make a mattress in each wagon and gave them two each to wrap up in. The women slept until after the sun was high in the sky.

When they finally woke and were looking around, Wiley stopped his wagon. Claire asked how far away they were from where they left the wagons.

Wiley said, "I can't be sure, but I think we've only got maybe three or four hours to go. You wantin' to eat something?"

Claire shook her head. "If you think that's all the farther it is, we can wait to eat when we reach the campsite." They untied the horses from the backs of their wagons, the women got up in the driver's seats, and they kept moving.

CHAPTER 13

UNDER ATTACK

On the afternoon of the fourth day, James was on guard duty over the wagons when he saw five riders coming down the road. When they saw the wagons, they started trotting their horses at a fast pace. Three of them were bandaged on various parts of their bodies, and one of them had a military sergeant's hat on.

They stayed in their saddles and started looking around the area, one of them pointed in James's direction. He waved his rifle, expecting them to just keep on going, but they turned and went back to the top of the hill they had just come from. James could tell they were trying to get a good look around to see where the rest of the people were, but they couldn't see over the rock outcropping where James was.

Then he realized they were the same men they had left tied up on the other side of the river—at least some of them were. The men started riding along the crest of the hill, heading down below the area where James was sitting.

James hollered over to Ben. "We got company, and you better get out here."

Ben was stirring the pot of soup he had started to make, but he put down the ladle, grabbed his rifle, and ran up to the rocks to see what was going on. When he reached James, he pointed in the direction of the riders, and turned just in time to see three men on horseback dropping out of sight behind the hill.

"Them's those boys we left tied up on the other side of the river," he said. And I'm sure that must've been the same sergeant who was running that group."

"They're trying to get down below an' come up around behind us," Ben said, swiveling his head trying to follow the course they'd be taking. One of us needs to get down there by that group of trees on the edge of the hill, so we can see them coming up from below. I'll bet they're going to try and take the stuff in the wagons and kill us while they're at it." James nodded.

"I'll run over to the trees," Ben continued, "and you should stay in the rocks, in case they come back around the other way."

He made it to the trees without seeing the riders and took up a position behind the biggest tree. After a couple of minutes, he saw two men on horses headed to a place on the other side of the hill, below his line of sight. He looked back and saw three other horses and riders working their way up toward a gully that had been formed by the runoff that had washed out the road. He saw them go into a copse of bushes and trees, but they didn't come out.

The terrain ahead of them was too rough for horses, so he was sure they dismounted and were now on foot. He waved over to James and pointed at the gully.

James got into position behind the rocks. He got a

glimpse of them moving; they weren't doing well on the rough terrain. He heard rocks tumbling down into the wash and knew they were trying to make their way up. They would still have to get across about seventy yards of open ground, from the wash coming uphill, to get to him. He was sure they were going to try to get behind the closest trees to the open area.

The sergeant's men were having trouble getting through the wash because of their wounds. Most couldn't use both arms very well, and one of them had a bad leg, so it was rough going for them.

When they finally did clear the wash and got behind the trees, James hollered at them, "You boys need to get back on your horses and ride out of here. There's nothing here for you but a bullet, iffen you keep coming toward me. Stay away from them wagons."

The sergeant decided to try and give him a scare. "Now, you know we can't let you take off with that stolen stuff you have in your wagons. If you'll just let us go get it, we'll let you live."

But James was determined to show them he had the advantage. "First of all," he said, "that stuff is not stolen. It's ours, and we worked long and hard for it. I'll be damned if I'm going to let you take it from us. From where I'm sitting, I think it'll be me who lets you live, if you leave. But if you come any closer to me or the wagons, I'll put a bullet in you."

Just then, Ben heard a noise coming up the hill toward him and cocked his rifle. The men were approaching, crouching down and trying to stay low. But still, they made easy targets. He sent off a couple of shots into their path, and when the dirt went flying about ten feet ahead of them, they stopped and saw Ben aiming directly at them. They froze, and Ben said, "Put your hands up and walk toward me."

Suddenly, he heard shots on his other side; the men in the trees by the ravine had started shooting at James. When he turned to look, the men took advantage of his distraction and ran below the hill's crest. When he looked over at James, he could see he was well hidden behind the rocks and taking aim.

James was focused on the closest man to him, even though he could only see a small part of him sticking out behind the tree he was trying to hide behind. When he fired, he saw pieces of bark flying.

Two more quick shots at the others missed their mark. He heard the sergeant tell them to pull back into the ravine, and they hustled back down before he could get another shot. He heard the sergeant yelling at them to get to the horses and meet up with those other two at the bottom. He thought he was going to get another shot at them when they went back across. But apparently, they'd realized they'd been too exposed and took a longer route, one down lower on the other side of the hillcrest, where he couldn't see them.

The sergeant told his men to take the long way around, to let the shooters see them heading away. The plan was to go around below the top of the hill, and then try to get above and get a good look at the layout.

They rode down alongside the ravine to where the hill was lazily sloping to rolling prairie land. They rode over the low part of the bottom of the hill and started heading back up the hill on the far side of the crest, so they could stay out of sight until they were ready to be seen.

Then they rode a little way out in the open and let the McCoys see them, then turned back in the direction they had come from.

James saw them. "They've regrouped up on top the hill," he hollered, and Ben joined him.

James pointed out where they were, and said, "They kept going along the crest of the hill, almost to the road they had come down on, then turned and went down the far side, as if they were heading back the way they came."

Then he added, "Looks like they decided they can't do what they wanted to."

Ben said, "I don't think they're going to be leaving that easily. I think that's just what they want us to think, but they're probably going to try and do something else, probably when it gets dark.

He and James exchanged a grim look. "I sure hope Wiley and Lawrence get back here quick," James said, "otherwise this is going to be a very long night."

Ben started thinking of ways to get themselves into a good defensive position without the outlaws being able to sneak up on them. The next hill over, the one where they had made their camp at the bottom, was a little higher than the one they were on. At its crest, they would still be able to see the wagons and stay within shooting distance, although it would be some long shooting.

He saw farther up the hill was some cover; granted, not much, but enough a man could hide up there at night.

He was thinking also that it had better be him or James up there, because it would be a good spot for the ex-soldiers to pick them off in the rocks where they were now.

"Look up there on that next hill," he said. "You see those rocks an' the couple of trees? One of us needs to get up there. We should still be able to see the wagons too. We need to move there, because if *they* get there, they'll have an advantage on this spot. I'm going to go see what I can, and I'll be back in a few minutes." He reloaded his gun and stuffed his pockets full of shells. "Keep your eyes open," he told James. "I expect them to try to get above us, and then come down on us tonight." Then he went down toward their campsite and checked on his soup, gave it a few stirs, added a little water, and headed up the hill.

It took him a few minutes to hike there, as the terrain was pretty steep. It was a good spot because there was about a hundred yards of open ground around it. Although, they could still get within that distance before he knew they were there, unless he got lucky and saw them coming from a long way off. But he didn't want to count on being lucky.

He found a couple of spots that looked like they would be the easier approaches. Looking the land over, he decided that's how he would try to get here if he were them.

Maybe we can set a few traps for them, if they come this way, he thought. He decided he would tell James to come take a look, because he was good at setting traps for animals.

He stopped at the campsite on his way back and checked on his soup again, scraped some coals in a pile and set the pot on it, away from the main heat. When he reached James, he asked, "Have you seen anything?"

"I haven't seen nothing at all moving anywhere," was the reply.

"I think you should go out there and take a look. There's a couple of game trails they might try to follow to get up where I was; maybe you can think of a way to set up a couple of traps. They can get to within a hundred yards, or maybe a little less, before whoever's up there would be able to see them."

James agreed, and off he went. When he got to the top of the hill, he saw there were only a couple of access routes that would keep someone hidden. He walked a little farther out of sight from the lookout spot and found two places someone would most likely use as a path.

The game trail actually reduced the access route to only a couple of feet across in a few places, going under some low tree branches and in between some bushes. They might even have to get on all fours to get through this. Excellent spots to set a few traps.

He went back to where Ben was and told him to keep him covered while he went down to the wagons to get a couple of his beaver and wolf traps.

He had several different types for different sizes of animals. He decided on the wolf traps, as they were a little bigger than the beaver traps. He took three of them, crawled back out from under the tarp, and hustled back over to where Ben was.

"I'm going to get over there now and get these traps planted, so they won't be seen even in daylight," he told him. "That way for sure, if they came through at night, they won't have any idea there'll be any traps waitin' for them."

Ben had his stomach on his mind as well as his safety. "On your way over," he said, "stop and check the soup I was making, because that's all there's going to be to eat

143

today. Give it a stir and make sure the water hasn't evaporated."

James did as he was told, took a few mouthfuls, and even added some water to be safe before heading back up to place the traps.

He decided he was going to place two of the traps on each side of the middle of the trail, where he figured they would have to put their hands and feet when they got down to crawl.

He placed another one in an area that narrowed, forcing them either to sidestep or step over some bushes. Once he had them staked, he took some of the grass around the area and put it over top of the dirt he'd used to cover them. That way, they were completely hidden, and nothing would slow the closing of the trap on whatever triggered it.

He went back to the campsite and divided the soup into another small pot, grabbed a couple of spoons, filled a couple of canteens, and went back to the rocks to Ben. When he got there, he gave Ben a canteen and the soup. "I've set the traps in good spots," he said. "If they come from that direction, I'm sure they'll come across them."

It was getting to be about five o'clock in the afternoon, and the sun was starting to get lower over the hills. Pretty soon the sun would be down below the hills, and it wouldn't be long before it got dark.

Fortunately for them, the moon was going to be bright that night, as the orb was just passing into the three-quarter stage. They should have plenty of light to see in the open areas. As they were eating their soup, Ben couldn't stop thinking about how long Lawrence and Wiley had been gone. "I thought that the town was only about fifteen miles or so away from here," he said. "Must've been a lot farther than we thought. I wish they'd get back here. We sure could use some help."

Just as they finished their soup, James saw some movement on the crest of the hill, over by the road where it came into the washed-out area. Shortly after that, he saw what he thought was a hat coming into view and disappearing a couple of times, just on the other side of the crest.

The thieves didn't know it, but they were riding too close to the crest of the hill, and every once and a while, their hats were sticking up high enough to be seen. They seemed to be heading to a spot where they could come down the side of the hill toward them, hidden behind some of the trees.

Then he saw two men run down the hill toward them and scramble behind the trees.

"They're coming again," he told Ben. "I better get up on that other hill before they get into range. You'll have to keep a good eye out below on the wagons." Ben wiped his mouth on his sleeve and set down his soup.

"Once I get up there, I will be able to see everything on the above side and to the back of the wagons. We just have to hope that they haven't gone way down below us and come up from behind our campsite. Neither one of us can see anything from that side till they get over top the hill right behind and above this spot." He took his carbine and a box of shells and started heading fast to the other hill.

When James got to position, he had a good view of the wagons and up the wash, where he saw movement in the trees above the wagons.

When he saw a hat, he realized it was the sergeant. He was trying to make his way down through the trees to get to the wagons. The other two were not with him, and James didn't know yet where they would be coming from. Keeping his eye on the sergeant and his ears listening for someone coming up the game trail, he waited.

The sergeant made it to a cluster of trees about twenty-five yards from the wagons. In order to make a good shot, James knew he was going to have to be ready for the moment the sergeant made a break for the wagons, so he pulled his rifle to his shoulder and kept it pointed at the area the sergeant would have to cross.

Shadows were dropping as the sun disappeared behind the hills. There was still enough light to see clearly enough to shoot, but there would be a period of time between sunset and moonrise when there wouldn't be. Suddenly, the sergeant made a break for the wagons. He was zigzagging back and forth as he ran, making himself a difficult target. James fired anyway, two quick shots, but missed both. The sergeant made it to the cover of the wagons and got behind one of them, out of sight.

Ben looked toward the wagons when he heard the gunshots and saw a man sheltering behind the wagon that was tipped almost on its side.

The sergeant remembered that there were rifles in the wagons and began rooting under the tarp, trying to find them. And he did, but in order to reach them and find the bullets, he was going to have to get inside the wagon and expose himself to gunfire.

Ben saw the men moving toward him through the trees; it looked like a blur of dark shapes jumping between trees, staying low to the ground. He pulled his rifle up and trained it on the area, and the next movement he saw, he fired at the dark shapes. He couldn't tell if he had hit either one. He knew they would have to wait to get any closer, because there was still enough light to make them easy targets in the open.

Meanwhile, Wiley and Lawrence had traveled as fast as they dared with the four wagons and were coming up the road just a couple of hills away when they heard gunshots.

"We've got to hurry," Wiley shouted to the women, "try to keep up, but don't go past us."

Lawrence lashed his horse to make him run faster and brought his wagon behind Wiley's. Cresting the next hilltop, there were more gunshots. Someone on the next hill was firing, so they stopped the wagons and grabbed the rifles and bullets. Wiley grabbed his buffalo gun and a box of shells for it.

Wiley told the women to stay there, safe and out of sight. Then he and Lawrence jumped off their wagons, ran up to the edge of the hilltop, and got down on their bellies to try to see what was going on.

It was too dark to see much and would be several minutes before the moon was up high enough for them to see well enough to shoot or tell if they hit what they shot.

They saw some movement on the downside slope of the hill in front of them, above from where they heard the gunshots coming from.

Wiley gave Lawrence a determined look. "I'm going to work my way around up the hill, above and behind where we saw those shadows moving," he said.

He was going to try and surprise whoever it was by coming in from behind and above them. Lawrence nodded. "I'm going to stay here," he said. "I can shoot from here, if they get by you and come down this way."

The women got down from the wagon seats and kneeled by the back wheel of the last wagon. "I'm going to grab a couple rifles and some bullets," Claire told Cassie, "so we'll have something in our hands to protect ourselves with."

She climbed up in the wagon, grabbed two rifles and a box of bullets and went back down to Cassie. There, she took the bullets and loaded both rifles to capacity and stuffed two handfuls in her pockets. She handed one rifle and the rest of the box to Cassie and told her to stay where she was. And then she started off to see if she could help the men.

She started down the slope of the hill, well behind the men and far below the crest, heading toward the place where the hill dropped toward the prairie.

"No, Mama," Cassie yelled, "don't leave me here by myself!"

Claire turned to her daughter. "The men are up in front of you, so anyone will have to get through them to get to you. I'm going down around the side here to see if I can get an angle on what's going on. Maybe I can do some good. You just stay put, and you'll be okay." And she turned and headed downhill.

Feeling frightened and worried, Cassie sat on her heels behind the wheel on the side of the wagon away from the hill. She watched her mother go, then turned to look up toward the men, clutching the rifle.

It was dark enough now that the sergeant had

managed to crawl into the wagon under the tarp without being seen. He'd worked his way to the rifles, then felt around and found a box of bullets and crawled back out. He now had a rifle he would be able to reach their positions with.

He got back behind the tipped wagon and tried to see, but the moon hadn't yet risen enough. He would have to wait a little longer.

Ben could hear men making their way toward him through the tall grass, twigs breaking and boots grinding in the loose ground. He thought he saw a shadow run down below, but the movement vanished before he could tell if it was one of them. Then he heard more twigs breaking just below and knew at least one of them was in front of him, hiding in the tall grass.

Wiley made his way around the crest of the hill. As he poked his head up, he could barely see the wagon's dark outline in the open ground, some four hundred yards away. There was no way he could see well enough to make out a target.

The moon was very bright as it rose. Wiley heard movement on the side of the hill in front of him, so he crouched back down, peering in the direction the noise had come from.

He watched for a while, then saw a couple of dark forms trying to make their way through the brush. One was following a game trail, it seemed, and the other was just following the contours of the hill a little below the other one. They stopped as if they were waiting for something or someone. Then Wiley realized what they were doing was actually waiting for the moon to rise up over the hills to give them some light to see by.

Claire hurried along, almost at the bottom of the hill. When she a heard noise in front of her, she crouched down behind some brush and waited. There was nothing between her and the crest of the hill but the bush she was behind and the tall grass. The moonlight was starting to illuminate the hillside. She was surprised at how clear she could see now.

Then more noise came from in front of her, and she saw a dark form of a man creeping up toward the crest of the hill.

James was watching the wagons to see if the man was going to leave. All he could see was a dark form moving from one wagon to the other.

He kept his rifle trained on the wagons as he heard noises coming from below and behind him. Apparently, someone had stumbled on some loose rocks and had fallen.

Wiley heard the sound of rocks sliding under foot also; he looked down just as he heard one of the men scream in pain. A voice said, "Damn it! Someone put an animal trap on the trail!" He had put his hand right on it, and now it was clamped around his wrist, and he couldn't get it free.

The man below his trapped comrade turned and crawled toward him. The pair must have gotten his hand free, because Lawrence heard one of them ask, "How bad is it?"

"I think my wrist is broken," came the reply, "and I'm bleeding like a stuck pig."

The other man told him to get his belt and wrap it around his forearm and see if that didn't slow the bleeding any.

Lawrence could see the two forms just below him thanks to the bright moon; across on the other hill. He couldn't see any details, but their silhouettes were well-defined. They made pretty easy targets from where he was.

When Ben heard more noise from below, he rose up to take a look and saw a man in a kneeling position aiming his pistol at him. Just as the shot went off, he ducked, and it sailed over his head. He rose up again and fired at where the form had been, but the man had already dropped back down, so he missed him.

Ben started shooting into the grass where the man had been. The man appeared again, several yards in front of his last position, took quick aim, and fired again, hitting the rocks in front of Ben. He knew by the sound that he'd missed, and the bandit dropped again.

At that moment, Wiley decided the two men down the hillside would be coming within easy shooting distance of Lawrence, so he was going to get closer to the wagons. He got about a hundred yards from them, stopped, and saw a man's form stooping next to the wagons, then laying his rifle to rest on the sideboard. The moon was reflecting off of the gun barrel, and he could tell he was taking aim at someone. He grabbed his buffalo gun and tried to line up the sight on the end of the barrel. Using the moonlight-illuminated grass, which gave a light background behind his target, he followed the sight tip over to the shadow leaning against the wagon.

James was watching the hillside behind him because of all of the noise the two men were making at the trap he'd set. He started moving carefully toward the sounds. Lawrence already had eyes on them and got on one knee.

He aimed his rifle at the lower one on the downhill side, the one trying to wrap the belt around the man's arm that had been caught in the trap. He told them to stop where they were and put their hands up.

At that moment, James made it over the crest of the hill and saw the two men. When the pair heard Lawrence tell them to put their hands up, the one with his back to Lawrence turned quickly and started to raise his gun toward him. Lawrence pulled the trigger on his rifle and the man flew backward. He had been hit square in the chest.

The man almost landed on the one with the belt around his arm. That man used his good arm to raise his pistol at Lawrence. There was a shot from up on the hill. It had come from James. The man slumped over, dead before he rolled over.

• • •

At the sounds of the shots behind and above him, Ben saw a silhouette shadow emerging above the dull yellow straw grass. The contrast of dark and light was so distinct, he could clearly see a man getting on one knee and bringing a pistol up to aim at him. Quickly, Ben brought the end of his pistol's barrel to the center of the shadow and pulled the trigger. The man slumped forward, pulling the trigger on his pistol and sending out a wild shot and making dirt fly as he fell into the grass, face first.

Seeing him drop and then lay still, Ben came out of the rocks and started toward him to make sure he was not going to be trying to get off another shot. At that moment, the thief who had gone below and around the side of the hill where Ben had been positioned came up to the crest and stood at the top of it, taking aim at Ben. The sergeant, the leader of the outlaws, was at the wagons and couldn't see James anymore, who was heading toward Lawrence. Not having another target, the sergeant took aim at Ben. The two thieves had Ben in their sights, and he had no idea he was about to get drilled from two different directions.

• • •

In the next second, Ben heard two gunshots. One sounded far off, as it was from over two hundred yards away. The other came from the distant side of the hill from beyond where the man was standing aiming at Ben. Before he could pull the trigger, the sergeant's hat went flying in the air, and he dropped in a heap by the side of the wagon.

The man on the crest of the hill behind Ben heard both shots and before the man could think to do anything, he was lying face down in the dirt, dead from a bullet that exited through his chest.

Ben had turned to look at the wagons when he heard the sound of the gunshot on the hill. There, he saw a hat go flying into the air, heard a splattering sound, and the thud of a man falling against the wagon, then to the ground. No more gunshots were fired, so he went toward the man he had shot and checked him; he was dead, but he took his gun anyway.

Ben stayed low going up the hill. He wanted to get a look over the crest. He saw a dark form lying in the grass. When he reached the top a few seconds later, he saw another form walking slowly up the hill. When he saw a rifle reflecting in the moonlight he raised his gun.

Then he heard a voice come from the shadow; it sounded like a woman.

"Don't shoot! It's me, Claire," the voice was shouting. She was the one who had shot the man coming over the crest of the hill behind Ben, just before the man was going to shoot him.

They met at the fallen man. Ben took his gun, then looked at Claire and said, "I thank you kindly, ma'am. I didn't know that one was there. He would've got me for sure."

Claire was staring at the man on the ground. Starting to shake, she said, "I've never shot a man before."

He took her rifle and put his arm around her. "It couldn't be helped," he said. "He would've killed me if you hadn't shot him." He kept his arm around her shoulders to steady her, telling her it was okay and that she had done the right thing. They started walking toward the wagons.

James was the first to get to the two men down the back side of the hill. Lawrence showed up shortly afterward. They took the guns that were laying on the ground by the bodies and made sure the men were dead before they headed toward the wagons.

Wiley had started coming down the wash toward the wagons. Ben and Claire made it to the wagons first; even in the dim light, they clearly saw the bloody mass of what was left of the sergeant's head. Claire turned away. "Oh God, that's a gruesome sight," she said.

Lawrence and James arrived right after. Wiley joined them a few seconds later. Wiley looked around at everyone and said, "Is everyone okay?"

They all nodded. "I thought I told you to stay at the wagons?" he said to Claire.

Before she could answer, Ben cut in. "It's a good thing she didn't, Wiley. She shot one of them coming up behind me. He would've got me if it hadn't been for her."

Wiley turned back to Claire. "Well, in that case, I suppose it's okay that you disobeyed my orders," he said. "Just don't make it a habit. I don't know what I'd do if you got hurt."

Claire felt proud for what she had done, but also touched by what he said. "At least Cassie stayed put," she replied. "In fact, I'd better get back over there. She's probably a nervous wreck."

Lawrence agreed. "Yeah, let's go get the wagons and bring them down to the campsite, now that everything is over with and we're all safe."

Wiley and James followed Lawrence. Ben told Claire, "Let them get Cassie. You follow me, and I'll show you the easiest way to the campsite in the dark," and she followed him up over the hill and down to the campsite.

The others started walking down the road to get to the place where they had left the wagons, and Cassie was waiting, full of fear and worry.

Lawrence found her sitting on her heels and crying. When she saw him, she jumped up and hugged him tightly, crying and trying to talk at the same time. "Where's my mother?" she sobbed. "Is she okay?"

He stroked her hair away from her face and put his forehead against hers. "Everything's okay," he said. "Your mother is fine. She's back at the campsite with Ben," he said, giving her a reassuring kiss.

"I still need you to get in a wagon and drive down to the campsite. It's not very far."

"Okay, okay, let's go," she said quickly. "I want to see

my mother." And they all took a wagon and chirruped to the horses to get them moving.

Cassie jumped off the wagon as soon as it stopped and ran to her mother. She hugged her tightly. "I was so afraid for you," she said, "especially when I heard the gunshot that came from the direction you went."

"I'm sure glad your mother knows how to shoot a rifle," Ben said, "because she saved my hide tonight."

Cassie looked at her mother in disbelief. "Really? You really shot one of them?"

Claire's face showed her mixed feelings. "It couldn't be helped. It was either that, or he was going to shoot Ben. Didn't have much of a choice."

Cassie sighed and held her tighter. "I'm just so glad that everyone is okay. Who were they?"

"They were those fellows who we left tied up on the other side of the river," James said. "Apparently, not all of them could or wanted to follow the sergeant, because there were only five of them. That was one stubborn sergeant!"

Wiley wanted to change the subject. "Let's make us something to eat and get some sleep," he said. "We traveled all through the night. I just had this feeling something was wrong, and it turned out there was something wrong. I'm glad I followed my gut and that we kept pushing to get here as quick as we could."

Claire nodded, and then turned to her daughter. "I told you, always follow your instincts. Mine have never let me down yet. Like when I thought it best to stay hidden and wait to see what happened that day we went in the woods. We're still alive because of it."

Ben had climbed into the back of one of the wagons

and handed down some food and a couple of pans to Lawrence, who in turn, handed them to Cassie. "Here you go," he said. "Now it's your turn to do something for everyone." She returned his smile.

"It would be my pleasure," she said.

While the women were preparing their food, the men talked about where they were going and what the best route was. "We have to bury these men first," Wiley told them. "They may be scoundrels now, but at one time, they were probably good, honest people—good soldiers too.

They at least deserve to be buried, and since we're the ones who killed them, I think it's up to us to do it." The rest of the men nodded in agreement.

"We'll put them in the ground before we leave in the morning. For now, let's go drag them over down below that rock outcropping. Looks like the ground flattens out nicely. With all the tall grass, the dirt should be fairly soft and probably easy digging; besides, two of them are pretty close to it already."

The men moved the two closest bodies about thirty yards to the place Wiley indicated. Then they brought three of the horses to where the other men lay. They threw the sergeant on the back of one of them and tied his hands to his feet with rope secured underneath the horse's belly, so the body wouldn't fall off.

Then the other three McCoys went to the two on James's trap trail. They had to leave the horses farther up on the hill and go down on foot. James led the way.

Wiley helped Lawrence drag the man caught in the trap up the hill to the horses while James recovered his traps. They put him over the back of one horse and told

James to tie him on while they went back and brought up the other one. Once the second one was mounted and tied, they brought them to the grave site. They decided digging could wait till morning; no animals should bother them there overnight, being so close to where they would be camping.

On their way back to the campsite, Wiley talked about how hard it must have been for those men to have nowhere to go and no idea about what to do with themselves after the war. He guessed that if it hadn't been for that sergeant, those men probably would have found some kind of honest work.

"Dinner's been ready for a little while," Cassie told them when they arrived at the camp. "So, if it's burned or dried out, it's not our fault."

The men laughed at that, and James said, "We're sorry. We'll try to be more punctual the next time we have to go out to pick up bodies that need to be buried."

The women made anguished faces, thinking of that grisly job, and then turned back to the food and started putting it on the plates. After dinner, as the women washed the plates the men sat close to the fire, Wiley said, "Tomorrow, we'll find their horses and set them free. I think the best route for us to take would be to continue east to Gilbertsville where we bought the wagons. We can stay there a night, so Ben and James can enjoy a night in a bed at the hotel. Maybe they'll even take a bath and put on some clean clothes, since they're getting pretty ripe."

They all chuckled at this. "Just because you got all cleaned up, doesn't mean you weren't ripe when you got there!" James retaliated.

The conversation turned quickly back to more sober

topics. "The river we crossed to get away from those men we had to kill was actually the Mississippi River," Wiley said. "If we had crossed the Mississippi farther north, we would've had to cross the Ohio River a few miles later. Fortunately, we crossed down below where the two join together. At Gilbertsville, it's the Tennessee River that leads into the first of the Twin Lakes. Some miles farther, I think a few hours or so, we'll cross the Cumberland River, which goes into the second of the Twin Lakes, somewhere between Luka and Dycusburg. Traveling that way, we will stay above those big lakes, so we won't have to cross either one of them, and head south after that."

Lawrence nodded. "I hope that few hours or so is not as far as the twelve miles it was supposed to be from here to Gilbertsville." They all laughed.

Wiley had to defend himself. "Well, have any of you ever been up this way? I haven't. At least we're going in the right direction, and the places I talk about are there, even if they're little farther than I thought."

After checking to be sure the women were out of earshot, Wiley asked, "Have any of you spent gold pieces? I've spent three along the way and have some change left; but we need to be careful about spending those coins. We don't want any talk about all of us having fifty-dollar gold pieces. If you don't have any money other than those coins, let me be the one who spends them. At least that way, if any stories come out, one man spending gold coins might not be as suspicious as if all of us did."

He looked around for the women once more. They were still washing the dishes at the stream. "We need to be real careful," he said. "If you remember, that sergeant had been on one of the patrols trying to find clues about where the bounty from the raids had gone, and those coins will be a dead giveaway."

The men exchanged sober looks. Clearly there would be a price to pay for their bounty, and that price would be ongoing caution.

"I've been trying to figure out how to use this money without anyone knowing," Wiley continued. "If any of you come up with ideas, let's talk about them, because this will be serious business as we try and settle down using that money."

Lawrence spoke next. Being the one that had been to school the longest, he'd had the chance to study things about finance and the way banking and credit worked to promote businesses. He told them that he had read about how the banks melted down gold and poured it into forms, making gold bars to make wealth storage easier. "Do you think we could melt those coins and pour them into dirt and sand, maybe over pieces of rock, to make it look like it came from a mine?" he asked Wiley.

Wiley narrowed his eyes. This wasn't something he'd considered. "If we can do that," Lawrence said, "we may lose a little of the value, but we could file mining claims and bring the gold in to the surveyor's office to get a value put on it for the bank. I've also read a little bit about how an account with the bank works, and we could even deposit it in one for safekeeping. They transfer it east, to Boston or somewhere, where they keep the gold and the records of the money people have given them. They guarantee to honor any money drafts you write, as long as you have made the deposits in one of their banks. That way, if the bank ever got robbed where you deposited, the thieves only get what's in that bank at the moment it's robbed and not their customers' life savings. Your gold, silver, or large amounts of money left with them will have been sent to the main branch, and you'll still have the value you deposited in the form of credit with the main depository, specifically to protect their depositors from that kind of thing happening."

We need to know how they melt the stuff down. It must be something like the way we can melt lead and silver. We'll need to get some equipment and give it a try."

The more Wiley thought about this idea, the more he liked it. "We'll have to try taking a small amount to a survey office and see how they react," he continued. "If all goes well, then for sure we can all file for mining claims; it will have to be on property close to where we're going to live, and we'll have to buy the land that the mining claim is on. If it works, we'll have to let Thomas Sr. and Tommy know about it." A wide smile appeared on his face.

"That's a real good idea, Lawrence," he said. "I knew something good had to come out of people going to school, and you just proved it. Even though you really didn't like school, you might've learned something that will help us all have a better life."

The plan made them all feel very much more relaxed. But as the stress they'd been feeling left, exhaustion took its place. "I think it's time we turn in," Wiley said, "so we can get started back on the road as soon as we finish burying those men in the morning."

The night was thankfully uneventful. Before breakfast, each man grabbed a shovel from their wagon and set off to bury those five unfortunate souls. When they were finished, Wiley said, "I think we should say something over these men, so I'll do it. Then we find their horses. After that, we'll transfer all the stuff from the broken wagons to the new ones."

He set down his shovel and went to the side of the hill above the five mounds. When he took off his hat, the other men did the same. Holding their hats in front of them, they bowed their heads.

Wiley looked up in the sky. "Lord, I'm not a preacher, and don't pretend to be, but I'm sure that these men at one time had good hearts and good intentions. I'm sorry that we had to be the ones to bring them to you, and that they couldn't find themselves some other way to live. Ours is not to judge, but to survive. I'm sure you'll decide what's best for their souls; we've done what we thought was best for their earthly remains, and now it's up to you to do with them what you think is right. We hope we won't have to do this ever again. You know we were just protecting ourselves, our family, and our property. Amen."

On the way back to the campsite, the men chided Wiley, saying he missed his calling. He should've been a preacher.

He brushed them off. "I just said what I felt in my heart," he said, "and tried to do it as best and as short as I could."

Breakfast was ready for them when they came back into camp. They all had at least two helpings of everything, and James and Ben even had three. When they finished their coffee, they were ready to do the rest of the things that needed done before they could get on their way again. It took a while to load the contents of the broken wagons into the new ones. Thankfully, the dead men's horses were close by, tied to brush, so they didn't have to hunt for them for very long. They took off all the tack and set them free.

They hitched their own horses to the new wagons and got everything ready to move at the campsite. By the time they had cleared the camp and loaded the new wagons, it was almost eleven in the morning. It was already quite hot, and they were anxious to start on the road to Gilbertsville. They were not really in a hurry, but everyone wanted to put this sad place behind them. As far as they knew, all those who had given them trouble were either too hurt to travel, dead, or in jail, so they didn't worry about anyone coming after them. They only had to keep their eyes on the horizon ahead of them for any new dangers that could be heading their way.

CHAPTER 14

HALFWAY HOME

In the late afternoon of the second day of traveling, the town finally appeared in the distance. James rejoiced. "I can't wait to get in a hot bath," he said. Ben agreed, "Me too!"

"Yeah," Lawrence couldn't help but reply. "We can't wait for you to get a bath either!" They went right to the livery where they had bought the wagons on the first trip to this town.

"Jesse are you here?" Wiley shouted.

An answer came quickly. "Yes, sir, be right with you." Jesse came out from one of the stalls. Seeing who had hailed him, Jesse smiled. "Back so soon? I figgered you was going to be longer than this 'fore you got back here."

Wiley just smiled in reply. He asked the livery owner if he would keep an eye on their wagons again for them and told him they thought they would be in town for maybe two nights. The livery owner said he would charge four dollars a day, including care of all twelve of the horses and the wagons.

After checking into the hotel, everyone agreed to meet downstairs in the restaurant in a couple of hours. They were two to a room—Ben and James, Lawrence and Wiley, and the women. "If you want to buy something, let me know," Wiley told the men. "I'll buy whatever it is that you want."

He informed them he was heading to the mercantile and general store in the morning to stock up on supplies they were running short on. "If you see something you want in town or at the mercantile, let me know, and I'll give you the change I get from the gold pieces I spend," he said.

They all had hot baths drawn in their rooms and relished in the hot water for quite a while. When they met downstairs, everyone was quite cleaned up. They had given their dirty clothes to the hotel housekeeper and asked that she take care of the cleaning for them. And every one of them mentioned to Wiley that they wanted to buy a few other things to wear.

At dinner, every single one of them ordered the house special. It featured a large steak, a baked potato, green beans, freshly baked bread, and churned butter, along with a large piece of apple pie. The men all cleaned their plates to the point of nearly shining, while the women finished most of theirs, saying they wanted to save room for the pie.

It was decided to meet for breakfast the next morning, and afterward, they'd go around town and do their shopping as a group. After dessert, all of them were feeling fat and tired. As a group, they retired to their rooms to take advantage of having a nice bed to sleep in.

The next morning, everyone was feeling good and rested and just happy to be alive. After a big breakfast, they set out to stroll around the town to see what the shops had to offer. The women found a dress shop, and like many women with money to spend on such things, they had to look over everything in the store. The men grew restless as they waited while Cassie and Claire reviewed everything their eyes came across. "We'll just mosey on down the street and see if there's any stores better suited for us," Wiley eventually told the ladies.

The men found a general store where they bought a couple of pairs of pants and shirts each. "Can I order some supplies that we can pick up on our way out of town tomorrow?" Wiley asked the owner.

"Of course," the owner replied. "Just tell me what you need, and I'll make a list and have it ready for you."

"Do you have eggs and meat an' such?"

"Sir, we have everything from apples to zebras," the man said, then laughing at what he'd said. "Well, almost!"

Wiley gave him an order for twelve dozen eggs, and then stated, "But only if you have them in a container we can use to transport them in our wagons, so they won't get broken."

The owner grinned. "That depends on how careful you drive your wagons."

Wiley smiled back. "As long as it's not a basket, we should be able to keep from breaking them. I hope, anyway." Then he ordered bacon, fatback, some jerky, potatoes, onions, and even some tomatoes. He thought to ask the others what they might want, and the three began naming off things, including more flour, coffee, sugar, salt, and pepper. After adding to the group items, each man began listing things they personally wanted.

Ben hankered for some jam and honey. When James

asked if he could get some butter, the others laughed. When James looked confused, Lawrence said, "How are you going to keep it from melting? This weather's been pretty hot. It wouldn't last a day!"

James smiled. "I hadn't thought about that. I just thought some butter would taste mighty good on those biscuits we make."

"We have a couple of women with us, and they're in the dress shop down the street," Wiley told the owner. "I'll send them over to add anything they can think of to the order. Their names are Claire and Cassie, so if they come in here and tell you who they are, would you please add their goods on my order?"

With that taken care of, the McCoys started down the street toward the mercantile. As they were walking, Lawrence remembered his gold idea. "Why don't we see if we can find something that we can use to melt the gold?" he said. "I bet if we buy stuff to make musket balls or reload our bullet casings, we could use the same thing we use to melt the lead for the bullets on the gold.

This way no one will get suspicious about what we're buying, and we can try it and see what happens." The others thought that was a good idea. They could all get set up to do the reloading for their guns, and then each of them would have the equipment for themselves to melt their gold or make bullets whenever they were ready.

At the mercantile they picked up a couple of bow saws and new axes, and sharpening stones for the axes and their knives. Ben and Lawrence each bought a new skinning knife and sheath. They asked the owner if he sold ready-made bullets or if he had any kits for making their own.

"I have everything you need for doing reloading casings or making musket balls and ready-made bullets," he told them. "I bought a bunch of this stuff to have on hand during the war, and I've still got quite a bit."

They asked him to give them each a complete setup of all the equipment they needed for the job.

"It's going to take me a while to put it all together," he told them. "But if you want to wait, you can."

"Can you have it ready by tomorrow morning?" Wiley asked.

"It will be ready for you first thing in the morning," the man replied.

"Good," Wiley said. "We'll see you just after you open, and much obliged for your help. Oh, here's some money for what we've asked, and if it turns out to be more or if there's change, I'll see you then, and we'll square up."

At the door, Lawrence turned back and asked the owner, "Do you know where there is a shop in town that sells boots and belts?"

And he pointed them toward the end of the street to a saddle shop and leather works.

"I need a new belt and haven't had a new pair of boots since before the war," Lawrence said as the group walked toward the saddle shop.

Ben and James gave each other a tired look. They were dreading more shopping.

"We don't need anything from the leather shop," James said. "We're going back to the hotel to get some of that new stuff they call 'ice cream.' We saw a sign in the window of the general store saying they had some. I've only heard about it and figgered it was just some dreaming soldier's rumor. That sign said they even had different flavors."

Lawrence couldn't help but smile and say, "We had some last time we were here, and it's real good."

James frowned because he'd gotten to taste it first, then he continued talking. "If we see the women, we'll tell them they should go into the general store and the mercantile to add whatever they think might have been left out of the order."

At the leather shop Wiley and Lawrence each bought new belts with fancy buckles and a nice brand-new pair of boots. As they walked back toward the hotel with their goods, they decided they wanted to try some more of that ice cream too. When they got to the general store with the sign out front advertising different flavors, Ben and James were sitting at a table out front eating their ice cream, and the women were inside deciding what else they wanted. The women came out shortly after Lawrence and Wiley had gotten their own ice cream and were sitting with Ben and James enjoying it.

They, too, had gotten ice cream and when they saw all the men sitting there eating some, they laughed. "I guess all of us like this ice cream," Cassie said, sitting down at the table next to them.

Claire noticed the bulky packages. Their shape gave away their contents. "It looks like you bought some boots?" she said.

"Yeah," Wiley replied. "We splurged a little on ourselves today. It's been a while since either of us had a new pair."

Claire smiled. "We put a few more things on the order," she said. "Nothing much. Some carrots and fruit and some molasses. I also got a sourdough starter and some cinnamon. We haven't been to the mercantile, but I don't think there will be anything to add over there. We got our personal things from the dress shop and already put them in our room."

As Ben finished the last of his ice cream, he yawned. "After all this food and with the weather warming up like it is, I'm feeling sleepy," he said. "I think I'll take a nap. See you all later for dinner."

"That sounds like a good idea to me too," James said, and they both got up and started toward the hotel.

Lawrence asked the ladies if they would mind if he accompanied them in a stroll around the rest of the town. Cassie gave him an enthusiastic look. "That would be nice," she said.

He looked at Wiley. "Let me have those boots and the belt and I'll go put this stuff in our room, so's we don't have to carry it all around town." He then turned back to Cassie. "Just wait here for me, and I'll be right back."

"You'd better hurry up," Wiley said. "The ladies are almost finished with their ice cream."

Lawrence was back in less than five minutes, wearing his new boots and belt. He stood beside Cassie with his thumbs tucked in his belt on both sides of his new fancy buckle, rocking on his new boot heels, smiling.

Cassie noticed how he was standing there, brimming over his new boots. "They look real good on you!" she said, which made him beam even more proudly. He offered her his hand to help her out of her chair and said, "Let's get over to the mercantile. After that, we can just stroll around looking at the rest of the town."

At the mercantile the ladies didn't find anything they

thought was necessary, so they left the order as it was. They walked to the end of Main Street and turned back around toward the hotel. Once there, Claire declared she wanted some iced tea, saying the ice cream, along with the heat, had made her thirsty.

Wiley and Claire started to go inside, but Lawrence, who wanted to spend some time alone with Cassie, asked, "If you don't mind, I think me and Cassie will take a walk down to the river. We'll be back in little while."

"Just be careful," Claire said. "We still don't know anything about this town."

Cassie and Lawrence walked for a while in silence. Lawrence was brewing up the courage to talk about something that had been on his mind. "Do you know what your mother wants to do when you stop traveling?" he finally said.

She started talking without looking at him. "My mother and me would like to go through with our dreams of having a ranch and farm somewhere. With the money the sheriff gave my mother, we think it should be enough to buy a small place and start a new life."

Lawrence swallowed nervously. "We have a small place down in southern Kentucky, close to Tennessee," he said. "My family, I mean, or at least we did have before the war. I haven't been there or heard from them since being in the war, so I don't know what's happened to it or them. Me and James don't live that far from each other, and that's where we're headed.

Cassie nodded. "Once we get across the Tennessee River and the Cumberland River, it's almost straight south," he went on. "When we get over the second river, I'm not sure how long it will take to reach it, but I don't think it will be more than a couple weeks. You might like it there; it's a real pretty place."

Cassie kept her eyes on the road. "It's not just up to me," she said. "My mother and I have to decide together where we're going to live. I think she likes Wiley and made a deal to keep going with him. We'll have to see what it's like where he's from before making any permanent decision."

Lawrence wasn't looking at her either. "That's probably a good idea," he said, kicking a pebble. "Then you will have seen both areas and know which you like best. You can always come back to where my place is if you decide that's where you want to live."

They'd reached the bank of the river. She took his hand, "That's a real nice offer, and I appreciate it," she said, as she stepped up right close to his face, standing on her toes for him to kiss her, which he did. She held the kiss for a little while, then dropped back down, breaking it off.

"We'll see what Mama thinks when we get to your place," she said. "Who knows what she's got going on in her head right now!" Her voice was nervous. She turned away from the water.

"We should get back to the hotel. I know my mother doesn't want me to be out alone with a man for very long; she's still very protective over me." And they started walking back to the hotel.

Claire and Wiley were having their second glass of iced tea when the pair arrived. Claire had been working on waiting patiently to see how long Cassie would be gone. They ordered themselves some iced tea and sat down with them.

"About how long do you think it will take to get to where me and James are from?" Lawrence asked Wiley.

Wiley thought a moment and said, "It all depends on the roads, but we don't have any high mountains to go over or any high mountain passes, and as far as I know, those two rivers are our biggest obstacles. I think maybe two weeks, or a couple of weeks and a few days. I do think it'd be a good idea if we all went and took a nap and got a little extra rest. We have another couple of weeks still to travel before that stop."

They all started for the stairs to the second floor. As they were reaching their rooms, Wiley turned to Claire and said, "I'll knock on your door when we go down for dinner. You can join us if you feel like it."

Claire replied, "That will be fine. We'll see you at dinner."

Once inside, each of them fell asleep quite quickly, not realizing how much their traveling had worn them out. They slept soundly until almost five o'clock in the evening, when Ben knocked on both Wiley's and the ladies' doors, saying, "The hotel is serving dinner now, so James and me are going downstairs to get a table."

After another large and delicious meal, the group of travelers walked toward the river together to watch the sunset.

Once the sun had gone completely down, they all headed back to the hotel to turn in early, so as to be ready to leave early in the morning.

• • •

Daylight came too quickly. Before breakfast, Wiley paid their bill and went to the livery to make sure the wagons and the horses were ready, then went to the general store and the mercantile to settle up those bills as well.

When he came back to the hotel, everyone was already downstairs with all their things around them on the floor, waiting for their breakfast to be served. They had one last, large breakfast before they started again on their journey.

When they finished, Wiley told them it was time to get the wagons to the stores and load them up. The women said they would meet them at the mercantile, and the men carried the ladies' things to the wagons. After all the new purchases had been stored in the wagons, they were ready to leave. Wiley helped Claire climb on Wiley's wagon, and Lawrence helped Cassie climb up on his. "Y'all have everything you wanted to bring on the road?" Wiley asked.

"Yeah, we're ready. Let's move on," answered Claire. And they headed toward the river.

They went across it on one of the flatboats, and on the other side, Wiley told them there would be one more river crossing at the Cumberland River, which they'd encounter somewhere between Luka and Dycusburg. He said it should be a few hours away, and when they reached Dycusburg, they'd be about halfway through their journey.

"From there it's about three hundred and fifty miles, more or less, east to Pike County," he said. "We'll get to James's and Lawrence's homes in about two hundred and eighty miles." He took off his hat and wiped his brow. The sun had gotten very hot. "In other words, we still got a long ways to go," he continued. "I hope we get there by middle of September, before it starts getting cold, so we'll get to see the fall colors of back home in full swing." Then he started his wagon down the road, with the others following.

CHAPTER 15

CUMBERLAND CROSSING

They made it to the Cumberland in about three hours. It was a fairly wide river but looked like it wasn't too deep or too fast moving where the road crossed it. Wiley climbed down from his wagon and told the others to wait while he walked across to check the bottom.

When he first stepped into the water, he thought it was going to be fairly easy to take the wagons through it. At about a third of the way across, the water was about thigh deep and had a fair to strong current. Up until that point, the bottom seemed fairly hard, but there, he ran into some larger stones and small boulders and pockets of soft sand where he sank to his waist. He made it across and returned, but it was clear that at some points the water was going to come up almost to the wagon beds.

He grabbed one of the horses he had tied behind his wagon, put a saddle on it, and rode it through the river to see how the horse might react to the water. It stumbled a couple of times but never fell. It did get a little startled when it sank down to its knees in a couple of soft places, but it managed to get through the sand there without panicking. He tried moving upstream a little on the way back across and found the going a bit easier with no real sinkholes. He decided that the wagons should come to the edge of the water about twenty feet upstream of the normal crossing area, where the bottom was better.

"The wagons are pretty heavy, and it's going to be tough for just one horse to pull across," he told the men. "Let's saddle both horses that are behind the wagons and tie ropes to the saddle horns. Then tie those ropes to the front corners of the wagon and ride them across. That way, we'll have all three horses pulling the wagon through the water."

Wiley decided he would ride a horse on the upstream side of the wagon, and Ben would take the other horse on the downstream side. He grabbed one of the reins for the wagon horse and tossed the other rein to Ben, so both of them could help steer.

"Hold on tight to the bench," he told Claire. "Once we get them in the water, we need to keep them moving all the way across."

They started slowly across the river. The horses labored a little, but with all three doing the pulling, it seemed to go fairly smoothly, and they got to the other side without incident. He led the horses a little way down the road to make room for the other wagons and walked back to the river's edge and told the others to follow his path and method through the river.

One at a time, each of the wagons made it across the river safe and sound. Back on dry land, they unsaddled the horses and retied them to the backs of their wagons.

When everyone was ready, Wiley said, "I think that went pretty well for a change. We'll go as far as we can tonight, but we won't make it all the way to Hopkinsville.

We'll stop about an hour before sundown and make camp." And with that, they were back on the road.

The thoroughfare was called the Highway West, only they were actually taking it southeast. Despite its name, it was really only a dirt path barely wide enough for two wagons to pass side by side; in most places, one of the wagons would need to have two of its wheels off the track for another wagon to pass alongside.

They kept traveling at an easy pace and made another twenty miles before Wiley told them to start looking for a campsite. They found one about a half an hour later, in a spot with a small creek and some good grass nearby for the horses.

The women made their supper and cleaned the dishes afterwards. Everyone turned in early, as it had been a long day, and they knew there were several more ahead of them before they stopped at another town.

They broke camp early the next morning after a quick breakfast and started out once again on the long road home. They had gone about twenty miles when they saw a sign for Hopkinsville; it pointed down a road that joined the Highway West road. The sign said it was twenty-two miles to the city.

"Does anyone want to go into Hopkinsville?" Wiley asked. "Or shall we just keep going? We have all the supplies we'll need for a good while."

Since it had only been one night past their stop in the last town, the consensus was to keep traveling on the road heading south, at least until they needed to turn east.

"That suits me just fine," Wiley said. "We probably won't make it to the road east for a few days, but that road lets us bypass the need to cross the higher mountains taking us along the southern part of Kentucky. When we reach the Cumberland Mountains, we may have to drop down into Tennessee then come back up into Kentucky, to go around them. I'm sure it would be easier than trying to go across. That's probably somewhere around ten days from now, maybe more. We'll decide what to do when we get there, but for sure, we're going to have to take whatever way is going to be easier for our horses and the wagons."

It took them only two days of traveling south to get to the road that turned east across the bottom of Kentucky. They had passed few fellow travelers coming from the other direction. Everyone they met said that the traveling was fairly easy on the road that went east.

One group of travelers contained two families and four wagons. These people told them they had heard stories of highwaymen robbing folks along the road, but they hadn't been bothered by anyone.

One savvy pioneer who was driving a brace of mules offered some interesting information and a long stream of chatter. "The town of Franklin is about a two days' ride ahead," he said, "unless, of course, your horses decide to refuse to go onward like my mules did. In that case, you're at the mercy of your stubborn beasts, and who knows when you'll get there. Then you might need to dangle a carrot from a stick in front of them to get them move," and he laughed. "They'll keep walking toward it thinking they need to get closer to grab it." He laughed again. "My mules seem to like being in town and watching all the activity going on around them. Iffen you can keep 'em goin' another two and a half days, you'll come to Tompkinsville, which is just north of the old

Mulkey meetinghouse." And he shook his head. "Why people met there I have no idea, never changed anything goin' to those meetings. Only thing good came from that place is it's a good place to refer to when giving directions. Anyway, from Tompkinsville you'll need to head slightly north to the town of Kettle, then straight east across the north side of Dale Hollow Lake to Albany. Then you'll need to go south into Tennessee to get around them Cumberland Mountains. I done traveled all them routes in and out of those mountains, and the way I jus' told ya is by far the easiest to get to the other side of them when ya got wagons and womenfolk."

The McCoys were dumbstruck when he finally took a breath. He said he'd like to chat some more, but he had to get a move on since his mules were still of a mind to keep moving.

When the man headed down the trail, Wiley turned to the others and said, "Well that's one way of explaining things."

"I don't know about you," Lawrence said, "but when I get me a mule that won't go forward, I'm going to try that carrot on stick trick." There were chuckles all around as they headed on their way.

Another group of travelers confirmed what the old pioneer had said, telling them they had come across the northern part of Tennessee in order to stay away from the high Cumberland Mountains. It was pretty much straight roads across the northern part of Tennessee, and the going wasn't all that bad.

These travelers told them something the pioneer had left out, which was the direction to go once they got into Tennessee. They were to head east across an area called the big South Fork, and then head up through Elk Valley, and continue northeast to a place called White Oak. The next town would be Middlesboro, Kentucky, which was at the southwest tip of Virginia, just inside Kentucky territory. Once they past Middlesboro, they could follow the Pound River, and that would take them right past Wallins Creek and all the way northeast to within twenty miles of Pikeville and maybe ten miles from Fishtrap Lake.

Wiley took the time to write down these directions, which seemed better to follow since they were coming from folks that had just been through the areas. When he finished writing, he thanked the man for his helpful information. Since he had recently traveled this route, they felt assured they could make it without much trouble.

There was only one real obstacle—the Big South Fork River and then Boone's territory, still ahead.

The travelers they had met were right; it took them almost two days to get to Franklin, another three days to get to Tompkinsville, and another two more long days before they reached Albany. There, they decided to spend a day or two in town and restock their supplies and take a much-needed rest.

CHAPTER 16

A REST AND A WARNING

As they pulled into town, they saw two hotels and a livery right away. Wiley pulled up at the front of the nicer-looking hotel. "Wait here," he told the others. "I'll go inside and try to find out where the best livery is."

The man that came to the front desk looked a little unsavory and acted as if he was being put out because he had to talk to a prospective customer. "What do you want, mister?" he asked brusquely.

Wiley decided immediately that this wasn't going to be where they would stay. Instead of inquiring about rooms, he asked if the man could direct him to the sheriff's office.

"If you'd have just kept going down the middle of the main road, about half way down, you'd have seen the sheriff's office on the right," the man told him.

Wiley thanked him and left. "I think it might be better to go ask the sheriff where's the best place to put our horses and wagons," he told the others, "and for us to stay a couple of nights." He got in his wagon, and they all kept going down the main street of the town.

He pulled the wagon to a stop in front of the sheriff's

office and once again told the others to wait. Inside the office were two desks and what looked like four jail cells. A man was sitting at each of the desks, and both had stars pinned to their shirts. One bore the word "Sheriff" while the other's said "Deputy."

"Howdy, Sheriff," Wiley said, addressing the first man. "We just came into town and have never been here before. I thought maybe you could tell us which hotel an' which livery stable is best for us and our horses and wagons?"

The sheriff looked Wiley over, sizing him up from head to toe. He walked over to the window facing the street and checked over their group as well. He turned back and said, "Looks like you've been on the road quite a while."

Wiley gave him the information he was seeking. "About nine or ten days since we've had a break. We're headed to Pike County there at the eastern end of Kentucky, pretty close to the border with Virginia. We need to restock our supplies an' get us all a good bath and a couple of nights of sleep in a bed before we continue."

The sheriff smiled, and said, "The best hotel is called the Bluebonnet, farther down the street. You'll be able to tell by looking at it. It's a nice place and run by nice people. The owner runs the livery stable that's in back of it. That's probably the best hotel, restaurant, and livery in this county. You've picked a bad time to be trying to travel, though; there's a couple of highway gangs that are hanging out down by Three Points, where Kentucky, Virginia, and Tennessee all come together." The sheriff shook his head in disgust.

"They been hitting folks traveling west and east,

usually before they try going through the gap, but some are getting hit after they've come through it. You know, the Cumberland Gap, the way over the mountains?"

Wiley nodded.

"When they hit 'em, they've been stealing everything the people have and leaving them to walk. They've even killed a few people—those that tried to defend their belongings. It seems they hit a group in one area and hightail it across the state line before they hit another group. Then they move into a different state. But it's all been happening around there, sometimes on the flatland, sometimes in the mountains." He paused as if to see how the traveler was taking in the news, but Wiley's face was impassive.

"Sometimes they come into their campsite at night," he continued. "I wouldn't recommend going through the Cumberland Gap, if you can help it. There is a way around Boone's territory, too—that's a hard route for wagons. If you want to bypass Boone's territory, go down into Tennessee. You go south from here until you get to Porbus, then you go due east for about seventy miles. You'll pass thru Oneida, Elk Valley, and White Oak. About five miles past there, you'll reach the Yellow River. A little ways before the river, you'll find a road that kind of follows the river north, off to the side of it. If you take that road north, you'll go back into Kentucky. You'll come to Middlesboro. Just keep following the river north and you won't go into the gap." The sheriff folded his arms, as if trying to show the seriousness of his message.

"Be careful. Those varmints might be coming out a ways from the gap, since not many travelers are going through it anymore because of them. Keep your eyes open. Go upriver about thirty to forty miles to where the Cumberland River joins it, and then just keep going northeast following the Yellow River. It will take you across another pass in the mountains. That pass is not so high and hard to cross. It's a little out of the way, but a lot easier and safer."

Wiley nodded. The lawman certainly had a lot to say.

"The road and river eventually go back into Virginia for a little ways, and even changes names to the Pound River, but it's the same river and the same road. It will take you almost all the way to Pike County. The road along the river heads north, a few miles past Pound Lake. When you get to Elkhorn City, you'll be back in Kentucky. The next branch off of the river to the east leads to Fishtrap Lake, which is in Pike County, if you didn't already know that."

The sheriff stopped and took a breath, giving Wiley the opportunity to say, "Wow, that's a mouth full of directions. I think we're going to go check into the hotel and drop our horses and wagons off at the livery. I'll come back and write down all that you just told me. It's too much to remember. I don't want to get anything wrong or miss a part of it and get ourselves lost."

The sheriff nodded and raised a hand, as if about to add on more words of caution. But Wiley was too quick for him.

"Much obliged, Sheriff," he said. "I'll be back after I've had a bath. Maybe even tomorrow. I appreciate your warning about those highway gangs." And he went back out to the wagons.

He told the others what the sheriff had said about the Bluebonnet Hotel and the livery, climbed up on his wagon, and headed down the street. The hotel was painted blue and had the word Bluebonnet on the front, as expected. There was a restaurant, and the window advertised a livery in the back.

He went inside to make sure they had rooms for all of them. The clerk told him, "You're in luck, we still have four rooms, and you can take three of them."

"Then I guess we're going to take the wagons around to the livery and be back to check in," Wiley replied with a smile.

At the back of the hotel. They found a fairly large corral and stable area. Wiley stopped at the gate and hollered for the caretaker. He saw some movement back around the stables, and a man came out wearing leather coveralls and wiping his hands with a rag.

He seemed a much friendlier person than the man at the first hotel. "What can I do for you, mister?" he asked.

When Wiley asked what he'd charge to care for the four wagons and twelve horses for two days, he replied, "Your lot will take a heap of work and a lot of feed. I'll tell you what. You give me fifteen dollars, and I'll make sure they get all the oats they want. I'll brush them out, clean them off, and even make sure they all got good shoes, and you can be sure no one will touch anything in your wagons. You can give me ten dollars now and five dollars when you're ready to leave."

"Hmm," Wiley replied. "That sounds a little steep to me. But if you make sure they get good grain, and lots of it, and plenty of fresh water, and you really will check all of their shoes and put new ones on where needed, I guess that's a fair deal."

The man opened the gate and they drove the wagons

inside the corral. Wiley gave him the ten dollars, saying, "My names Wiley McCoy. We'll be staying in the Bluebonnet if you need me for anything." Reaching out to shake his hand, the livery owner said, "Nice doin' business with you, Mr. McCoy. My name's Rusty, and I'll do everything I said. Don't you worry." Then everyone grabbed their dirty clothes and everything else they thought they might need and covered the wagons up again. "Okay, they're all yours," Wiley told the man. "We're off to the hotel."

The man offered some directions. "You can go straight in the back door and straight down the hallway. It will lead you to the front room of the hotel."

"Okay," Wiley said. *The people in this town sure liked to give directions, he was thinking.* "Thanks. We'll do just that."

CHAPTER 17

THE BIGGEST STEAKS
IN THE COUNTY

Wiley signed for the rooms and arranged for hot baths and laundry service.

"We serve dinner from five till nine," the desk clerk told him, "and I have to brag, because we have the best cook in town."

About two and a half hours later, Lawrence was dressed in new clothes, wearing his new boots and belt, and was clean-shaven and smelling like lilac water. Wiley was just finishing putting on his new shirt and one of those Cattleman's-style string ties. He looked quite handsome—like a successful cattle rancher from the West. He looked in the mirror and, being satisfied with what he saw, grabbed his hat, smiled at Lawrence, and said, "Okay, I'm ready. Let's go check out the best cook in the county."

It wasn't but a few minutes before everyone had come downstairs for dinner. All were dressed in their newest clothes and looked clean and refreshed. The women had changed from their traveling clothes to nicer dresses, and each had done something with their hair.

As before, Cassie looked transformed. When she came up to Lawrence, he hooked his thumbs on both sides of his belt buckle and rocked back and forth on his bootheels. He couldn't help but smile at the sight of her and show how proud he was of his new clothes and leather accessories.

They went into the dining room, and the waitress told them to sit wherever they pleased. They found a table by one of the big front windows looking out over the street, where they could see both ways for a short distance.

When the waitress asked for their order, Wiley said, "I'm sure you can see we're not from around here, so we don't know what's best to eat. How about you give us an idea?"

She looked them all over. "I think y'all look like you'd enjoy a good beefsteak, and we got some of the biggest and thickest in the county. Our cook says if you can eat more than one, he'll give you the other ones free, but you have to finish everything on your plate and the trimmings that go with each one to get more steaks. The dinner's loaded with lots of trimmings too."

The men looked at each other with surprised smiles. "Now, this sounds like my kind of restaurant," Lawrence said. "Ask your cook if the third one is free too." The waitress laughed, "Nobody's ever been able to eat three steaks with all the trimmings. They cover your whole plate; the trimmings come on separate plates."

"I don't know about the rest of you, but that's what I'm having," replied Lawrence. The men all ordered the endless steak dinner. The ladies said they would have some pork chops.

"I'm sure we wouldn't be able to finish the steak, if it's as big as she said," Claire said, "let alone any of the trimmings, and neither of us like to see good food go to waste."

The waitress turned to leave, and then came back. "By the way," she said, "be sure and save some room for the best peach cobbler in the state."

When she brought out the dinners, they realized she hadn't exaggerated one bit. The steaks were at least an inch-and-a-half to two inches thick and very juicy. They completely covered the plate and stuck out past the edge.

She brought out four bowls with heaping amounts of the side dishes offered for the men to divide between themselves.

There was corn on the cob, long green beans, carrots, mashed potatoes with a bowl of gravy, and most of a whole loaf of freshly baked bread with butter.

The waitress smiled at Lawrence. "I'm going to watch you, to make sure you eat your fair share of the vegetables before you can get a second steak." When she left the table, they all stared down at this massive amount of food, and the three other men looked at Lawrence.

Ben said, "My friend, I think you literally bit off more than you'll be able to chew here." They all laughed and started dishing up the vegetables onto the second plate she had brought each of them.

When she came back with the women's dinners. Claire said, "I'm glad the cook understands that some people can't eat like a bear. This smells delicious!"

As the waitress turned to walk away, she told Lawrence, "I'll be watching you," and gave him a wink.

Ben poked Lawrence with his elbow. "I think she likes

you," he said as he poured gravy over his potatoes.

"Maybe she does," he answered, looking at Cassie, "but, I think my heart is already full up," and he took a big bite of steak.

Wiley and Lawrence both asked for a second steak. She brought them out another steak each, just as big as the first one, and they came with all the trimmings again and a few more slices of bread.

The waitress said, "I guess you really were hungry, but I doubt very much that you can eat a third steak." He grinned back at her, and said, "We'll just have to see about that, won't we!"

She asked the others if they wanted some of that peach cobbler. They all said yes, but they would wait a few minutes. They asked if she would bring them some coffee meanwhile. Wiley and Lawrence finished the bread and the corn on the cob, but it took them a while to finish the steak. Finally, though, they managed to eat the last pieces.

Wiley leaned back away from the table, looking like he had just finished some hard work. "Whew, I don't think I'll need to eat for week," he said, sitting back in his chair.

Lawrence's belly was bloated, and he looked like he had just finished a wrestling match. "I bet you can't even eat any cobbler," Wiley teased.

With a weak smile Lawrence said, "Maybe if I get up and walk around a little bit, I might just be able to squeeze in a piece."

The waitress came back with the coffee and saw Lawrence's defeated face. "I told you no one has ever eaten three. Can I get the rest of you some of that cobbler?"

"Okay, you were right," Lawrence told her, "but I still want a small piece of that cobbler. I just need to walk around little bit and make some room for it," he said as he stood up. "I'll be back in a minute. Just let me get a little air."

He headed toward the door, moving a little bit slow, as if it hurt to walk because he was so full. Cassie told the others that she would go out and make sure he was okay and got up to follow him. The waitress brought back cobbler for everyone. One plate, which had half the amount of cobbler the others, was placed where Lawrence had been sitting. Claire commented on how fresh the peaches smelled. "I do believe they do have the best cook in the county," she said.

In a couple of minutes, Cassie and Lawrence came back inside. Lawrence looked a little recovered as he sat down.

"I'm glad she only gave me this much cobbler," he said. "I don't think I made much room walking out there. Been a long time since I've even smelled, let alone eaten, cobbler like this. Though it might hurt, I'm going to have to eat it."

They all agreed it was the best they could remember eating. When all had finished, Lawrence said, "I feel so fat, I don't think I can make it up the stairs. Wonder if I can sleep down here." Unable to stop it before it came out, he let out an echoing belch. "Excuse me! Pardon my manners, but I think I'll keep my mouth shut the next time a waitress tells me the steaks are big!" There were chuckles and smiles all around.

CHAPTER 18

RESUPPLIED

The group went to bed fairly early, and the next morning, Wiley was up at the crack of dawn, still feeling full. He let Lawrence sleep and went down stairs and got some coffee.

"What time do the stores open," he asked the waitress, "and do you know when the sheriff is up and about?"

"Most of the stores are open by seven thirty," she said, "and the sheriff is usually in his office by that time too."

He asked at the front desk if he could have some paper and something to write with, telling the clerk he had to write down directions from the sheriff.

The clerk gave him a writing pad and a pencil and said, "Use what you need, but if you could bring what's left back to me, I'd appreciate it."

He knocked on the sheriff's door, and then walked inside. The sheriff was just pouring some fresh coffee and offered him a cup. Wiley said yes. Taking the coffee, he took a sip and set it down.

"Would you be kind enough to tell me again all those directions, so I can write them down?" he said.

The sheriff smiled. "I guess that's an awful lot to try

and remember first time you hear it!" he chuckled. He then repeated everything he had said the day before. When he was done, he said, "Remember what I told you about those gangs. When you get headed north toward Middlesboro, the area between there and east toward the gap is where most of these robberies have been, but so far nothing has happened past a place they call Cliff Canyon, just a little way outside Middlesboro. I don't know if it's one, two, or three gangs. It could be one that splits and joins back up together when they need more men to do a job. There's been stories of people being robbed by six men, eight men, and even fourteen, but at least you know to be wary of groups on horseback. And watch out for lone men too. They could be scouting the roads for the gang."

"Don't worry," Wiley said. "We'll be real careful by the Yellow River area. Much obliged for the warning and the directions. Now I have to get over to the general store and the mercantile to order the supplies we're going to need, because we'll be leaving tomorrow morning." And they shook hands and parted ways.

At the mercantile, Wiley looked around to see if there was anything important he hadn't already purchased earlier on their journey. In a dusty corner of the store, he came across a military telescope and asked the owner how far out he could see with it.

"I don't really know," the owner replied. "I bought it off a soldier who needed some money. I really don't have much call for this kind of thing, but the soldier said he could see over two thousand yards clearly."

"Can I step outside and look around with it?" Wiley asked.

"Sure, go right ahead. Just bring it back," he said, smiling. Wiley took the telescope outside and adjusted it. Everything a long way away appeared crystal clear, but anything less than a hundred yards seemed blurry.

But he thought it might be useful for him when he went hunting, and who knows for what else, so he went back inside and bought it.

He went down to the general store and placed his order. He doubled the amount of supplies they had picked up the last time they stopped in a town, thinking he would rather be safe than sorry. "Can you add anything to the bill that the people in my group might want to add?" he asked the owner.

"How will I know who's with you?" the man said.

"They'll tell you they are with a man named Wiley, and that's me," he replied.

When Wiley got back to the hotel, the others were in the restaurant having coffee and breakfast, except for Lawrence, who was just having coffee. "I see you're still full from last night," Wiley told him. "So am I, but I've already had enough coffee for this morning."

He explained to the group about ordering at the general store and headed to the livery to check the wagons and horses.

After breakfast came a stroll around the town. It was a larger town than the last one they had stopped in. There was actually a hardware store specially stocked with building supplies. Apparently, a building boom was in progress here.

There was even a blacksmith and wagon repair shop, although the liveries did their own horse shoeing. They also had a drugstore, which was run by the wife of the only doctor in town. Two dress shops also sold material for making clothes, as well as some of the modern foot-pedal sewing machines.

They went inside some of the stores but didn't make any purchases. They just talked of how they would like to have some of the things they saw when they got themselves a home to put them in.

In the general store they checked the list of things Wiley had purchased. Everything seemed fine to the men, but the women decided they were lacking in a few items, so they added more fruit, tomatoes, potatoes, and flour. Afterward, they went by the post office, and Lawrence wrote a quick letter to Tommy and Thomas Senior back at the ranch.

He told them where they were and that he thought he had found a way for all to be able to use their money. He would let them know if it worked, once they got to where they were going and tried it out. He couldn't be specific about what or how, for fear of someone seeing the communication. They needed to try melting the coins before he could be sure it would work.

At the livery, Wiley noticed that the wagons had all been cleaned off around the axles and wheels, and new grease had been applied to the axle joints and wheel hubs.

The livery owner had one of their horses in a stall by the kiln he used for forming horseshoes. "How's the shoes look on our animals?" he asked the man.

"Well," he replied, "I think these horses have come a long ways. A lot of them have chips and cracks in their hooves, and most have worn their shoes thin. I've done three of your horses so far, and I think they'll all need some trimming and new shoes, but like I said, I'll do them all. They're eating like pigs, as if they're storin' up to go hibernate."

Wiley nodded. "When you're all done," he said, "if you think that you shorted yourself, just let me know and I'll give you what you think is fair. It looks to me like you're doing a real good job on everything you said you would do. We're going to try and get out of here by around eight o'clock tomorrow morning. You think you'll be done by seven, so we'll have time to hitch up our animals?"

"Sure," the man replied. "I'll be done by tonight, so you can go as early as you want."

Chapter 19

Playing Poker

Wiley was sitting on a chair on the front porch of the hotel when the rest of the group made it back. He asked if they had found something interesting in the town or added anything to their order. The ladies told him what all was added.

Wiley was feeling a little tired. "We should probably take advantage of having a bed to sleep in," he said. "It'll probably be another ten days before we stop in a town again."

Claire smiled. "Cassie and I are going to take advantage of being able to take a hot bath," she said.

Ben looked wide-eyed and exclaimed, "Two baths in two days? Better be careful, you might just wash your skin right off!"

Lawrence was ready with a retort. "Just because we're lucky if you take two baths a month, doesn't mean everyone else can stand it that long," he said with a grin.

Claire had to defend herself. "It's not so much to get clean again. We did that real well yesterday, but a hot bath is good for tired, sore muscles and is really very relaxing. It also helps you sleep a lot better."

She went inside and asked the desk clerk if they would bring up hot water for two baths in her room, and if they had any of that perfumed soap, as she would like some of that too. She added there was no hurry because they wanted to take their baths after lunch.

"Yeah," Lawrence said. "Lunch sounds like a good idea."

James snorted. "That's just because you didn't eat breakfast like the rest of us. I, for one, can wait until later."

"Well, if you're not going to eat," Lawrence said, "then I'm going to get another piece of that cobbler to tide me over." He went into the restaurant.

"We might as well take advantage of someone else cooking for us and getting three good meals a day while we can," Wiley said. "What if we just meet down here around one o'clock and have lunch?"

They had beef stew and biscuits for lunch. Once lunch was over, the ladies went up to their room for their baths. Ben and James said they wanted to go over to the saloon to have a beer and maybe play some cards. But they needed money to do that, so Wiley went to the front desk and asked if he could get change for a fifty-dollar gold piece. Lawrence was just coming out of the restaurant and heard them saying they were going to play cards, and said he'd like to play too. Wiley gave each of them fifteen dollars and kept five for himself.

"I think I might just go there with you," he said. "I haven't had a beer in a long time, myself. Besides, I don't want you getting into any trouble with the local cardsharps. Why don't all four of us just go play poker between ourselves?"

"Hmm," Lawrence said. "But you can't play with just five dollars."

Wiley smiled. "I won't have just five dollars for long. I'll have your money to play with," he said as they started walking toward the saloon.

They went into the closest saloon, which looked like it was well-kept and clean compared to the others they had seen in town. Wiley went to the bartender and said, "We'll have four beers, a deck of cards, and some poker chips, if you've got 'em. We'll be at that table over by the window."

They took their seats and the bartender brought over their beers, cards, and poker chips. Seeing that they had money on the table, he told them they could pay when they were ready to leave. There was a rack with eight rows of chips, two rows each of the same color.

"Here's the rules," Wiley said. "We'll cut cards to see who deals, and the chips are worth fifty cents each; the winner of each hand deals the next hand. Is that okay with you boys?"

They all agreed it was.

By the time they were on their second beer, Wiley had ten dollars in chips, and Lawrence only had two left.

Wiley grinned at Lawrence. "You better win, or you're going to be out of the game, and there is no buying back in. Lose your fifteen and you're out. You'll just have to watch."

Then he turned to the others and said, "We'll stop the game when we've all finished our second beer, if that's okay with you guys?" They all agreed.

They played hand after hand, and Wiley kept winning. Finally, he said, "I've got about enough beer for two or three more hands, so if you guys think you're going to win some of your money back, you better bet big or stay home."

Lawrence had managed to get back up to ten dollars, and the others had shrunk down to around ten, so Wiley was winning with twenty dollars in chips. After three more hands, he said, "Okay, one last dance. Everyone puts all their chips in and winner takes all."

They slid all the chips into a pile in the middle of the table. When all the cards were dealt, each one flipped over their hand; Lawrence had a pair of jacks, James had two pairs—sixes and fives, Ben had three queens, and Wiley had a full house, two aces and three kings. Laughing, Wiley raked all the chips in front of him. "See," he said, "I told you five dollars was enough for me to play poker with you boys."

He stood up and finished the last of his beer. "Keep your money," he said. "It was fun just to watch you squirm." As he turned to the door, he said, "I think I'm going to take a nap before dinner. I'll see you all then." He took the cards and poker chips back to the bartender and paid for their beers.

"We've been here long enough; we'll come with you," James said, and they all finished the rest of their beers as well. Together, they walked back to the hotel.

They slept all afternoon and woke up around six in the evening, threw some water on their faces, and knocked on the women's door before they went down to the restaurant.

"I haven't felt so relaxed in months," Cassie declared at the table, "and I'm real glad we decided to stay an extra night." They had another excellent dinner and berry cobbler for their dessert this time. Wiley told the men, "Be up and ready by six thirty, and we'll have breakfast, then go hitch up the horses and get the wagons over to the front of the general store. Maybe we'll be able to get out of here by just after eight.

He then asked the ladies, "Can you be ready and have your breakfast by eight? We'll pick you up in front of the hotel and get started down the road again."

"I'm sure we can," replied Claire.

The next morning, Wiley settled the bill with the hotel after their breakfast, and the men all went to the livery to hitch up the horses, so they could get on the road. The livery owner told him, "You don't owe me any more money, although the horses did eat an awful lot."

Wiley gave him the five dollars he owed, but he took out another five dollars and said, "Here, take this. You've earned it."

The man hesitated. "No, a deal's a deal."

"Then consider it a bonus for doing such good work," Wiley said, sticking the money into his hand, "And thank you kindly. We're much obliged." He climbed up onto his wagon and led the way to the general store.

They divided up the supplies between the four wagons and went over to the hotel, where the women were waiting out on the porch. They put their things in and climbed onto the wagons—Claire with Wiley and Cassie with Lawrence—and started out going south down the road heading into Tennessee.

They had to cover about a hundred miles across the northern part of Tennessee heading due east. They traveled almost thirty miles, getting about ten miles inside the Tennessee border on the first day. They still had another ninety miles before they reached the Yellow River. The going was slow, but the road was good, and they made it to Oneida on the fourth day.

It was a small town, and they still had plenty of supplies, so they decided they would just pick up some more oats for the horses and some more sulfur matches, as theirs had gotten wet during a rainstorm. They kept traveling, making quick camps alongside the road at night, everyone feeling the desire to get this journey behind them and start living a more normal, settled-down life. Other travelers on the road were few and far between, with few words passed between them as they crossed paths. They passed through Elk Valley and made it to White Oak on the ninth day. It had taken longer than they had figured, as the last three days before reaching White Oak had been mountainous travel, which cut their traveling speed considerably slower. They were glad that they'd not encountered any dangerous situations or broken any wagon parts, but all that was about to change when they got to the Yellow River.

• • •

By the time they reached White Oak, they had only enough supplies for a couple of days. At the town's general store, they bought enough for five days, even though the merchant in White Oak told them Middlesboro was probably less than two days' ride in a wagon. Hearing this, all the men wanted to keep going. They wanted to get back into Kentucky, and James and Lawrence were feeling even more anxious because they knew Middlesboro would put them less than forty miles from their homes.

"We can rest and get cleaned up there," James offered, "so we can be presentable when we get to our homes."

The ladies groaned a little, but Cassie said, "C'mon, Ma, we can tough it out. It's less than two days away. We've been through worse."

Claire replied, "You're right. We need to be rested and presentable to meet your families, especially meeting them for the first time. Let's keep moving."

The merchant offered traveling advice. "You'll reach the Yellow River inside of ten miles. Start keeping your eyes peeled for any groups of riders, as there's been some recent attacks where gangs stole all the wagons and horses and sometimes killed people who tried to resist."

He then went to the door of the store and pointed down the road.

"Follow the road out the south end of town," he said. "It will take you directly to the river, but the road you want to take north is about a quarter mile before you get there. It used to have a sign with an arrow indicating toward Middlesboro, but some recent travelers told me that now the only sign there is the one indicating the way to White Oak. Not to worry, though, it's the last road before the river that heads north, so if you go too far and reach the river, just turn around and go back to the first road to the right."

They were on the road for a couple of hours when they came to the river and realized that was exactly what they had to do.

They turned around and headed back; after a short distance, they saw a rider sitting on his horse on the crest of a hill beyond the road they needed to take. The rider watched them for a while after they made the turn north.

When it seemed like he was satisfied they were taking that road, he turned his horse back in the direction of White Oak and went out of sight.

CHAPTER 20

FEAR OF ATTACK

The rider made Wiley uneasy. "He was probably one of the lookouts for the highway gang," he told the rest of the group. "I'm thinking he went back to them to let them know they had people traveling on the road north." Cassie and Claire exchanged an anxious glance.

"From now till we get to Middlesboro," he said, "we're going to need to have one of us on horseback a mile or so ahead an' one behind us, so that we can get some kind of warning of an attack. At night, we'll have two guards keeping lookout, and we'll take shifts to do it."

They had stayed on the road for about ten miles before they came across a good place to make a camp down in a little valley between two low ridges. It was still fairly early in the day, but when Wiley saw the place, he knew it was a good, defensible place to stop. He hadn't liked the way the rider who had been observing them took off once he saw their route.

Also, because he didn't know how far the man had to go to meet up with the rest of his gang, he didn't want to be caught out in the open in an area where they wouldn't have any chance to defend themselves. The others knew it was best not to question Wiley's intuition.

"We should form our wagons in the shape of a box," he told them, "with the back ends up over top the wagon tongues so we don't have any gaps." He placed his wagon about sixty yards off the road and said, "You can back up to it once I get my horses unhitched. We'll do the wagons one at a time."

They were still well out in the open, since there wasn't any real cover like groups of trees or big rocks. "Put the horses off to the side with mine," he told the men, "and hobble them in a group." When he was done with his horses, he began looking around for places to position guards—somewhere they would be able to see a good distance off in both directions.

On the top of the low ridge they had just come across, there were two trees big enough to use as cover, so he went up there to take a look at what kind of vantage point it offered.

At the trees, which were about two hundred yards from the wagons but not far from the road, he could see almost a mile back in the direction they had come from. Then he saw another group of smaller trees about two hundred and fifty yards away, off to the side of the road but still along the ridge line.

He checked them over and decided that would be a good secondary position for whoever was on guard at those two trees by the road.

Confident what he found would be good for what they needed, he headed back down and told the men to make their campfire outside the form of the wagons about twenty feet away and not to take out anything more than was necessary.

It would be a warm night; they would only need to put their bed rolls in the center of the box formed by the wagons, so they'd have some protection if anyone tried to sneak up during the night. Then he walked up to the ridgeline they hadn't crossed yet.

At the crest of the ridge right next to the road there was a formation of rocks, and the road had to turn slightly to go around it. He thought it would make an excellent lookout spot in the direction they were going to have to take when they moved on. He couldn't see the wagons from there but had a good view half a mile down the road. And he saw that farther up the ridge there was a cluster of larger trees with rocks out in front, so he went up there to see what kind of a lookout position that would make.

There he found that the trees grew on both sides of the ridge, and the rocks were spread out all around. There were just enough rocks to offer some hiding for a man if he stayed low.

The bigger rocks and trees spaced out around this position could offer a man safe cover from bullets if he had to move between both sides of the ridge. Even though it was about two hundred yards away from the wagons, it was very defensible.

He noted that the distance between the ridgetops was about four hundred yards, maybe a little more. Satisfied that the spot would make a good secondary fighting position, he went back to the wagons.

While he was gone, Ben went down the little valley a short distance to scout for positions and areas where someone could sneak toward the wagons.

There were some small trees, but nothing much else

to hide behind except tall grass and a few shrubs. There wasn't any real cover to stop bullets; someone would have to crawl a long way unprotected, so he pretty much discounted this avenue of approach.

James had gone up the valley doing the same thing, and he didn't find much cover for someone to hide behind until he was about three hundred fifty yards from the campsite; he was pretty satisfied that the only way for anyone to come at them would be over either one of the ridgelines. With the wagons in formation, a person couldn't shoot inside the square from the ridges or be able to hit someone below the wagon beds. He was feeling pretty safe about the choice they had made for their campsite.

Back at the campsite, Wiley, Ben, and James exchanged information about what they'd seen.

"I think we'll be okay for tonight," Wiley said, "as long as we keep our eyes and ears open at those lookout posts."

He was silent for a moment and then added, "Remember, whoever is up there at either one of the positions has a good view down the road. Tonight is going to be clear and bright with a near three-quarter moon, so we should be able to see and hear anyone coming from a good distance. If you end up shooting, make your shots count, because you're only going to get off a couple before you have to leave that spot and get to the secondary positions that have better cover. You should be able to fight for a while from there.

He had one more piece of advice. "When you go out on guard, take a couple of boxes of ammunition with you; you don't want to be out there and run out of bullets."

The women had busied themselves setting up a campfire and getting food ready to cook. There were two water barrels in each wagon, so Ben and James carried one over to the horses.

Lawrence said he would take the first watch on the ridge behind them, and Wiley said he'd go up on the one in front. It took two barrels of water to water all the horses, leaving six for themselves; fortunately, there was plenty of grass for them to chew on without having to move them around for forage.

The women decided to make some bread in their Dutch oven, since they had a lot of daylight left. For dinner, they made a large pot of beef stew. When it was ready, Ben and James ate their share and drank a couple of cups of coffee before going out to relieve Lawrence and Wiley of their watch.

The women waited to eat with them. "Do you think we'll be safe here?" Claire asked Wiley as he had his second bowl of stew.

"We'll be safer here than anywhere we've passed so far," he said, "and from what I could see from that other ridge, this is better than anywhere ahead."

When they finished eating, he told Claire and Cassie to make sure they each had a rifle and a box of cartridges beside their beds. "And put two pots of strong coffee on the fire," he added, "so we'll have coffee throughout the night."

When they were finished cleaning up, he asked them to help him and Lawrence pile rocks under the wagons. "I want to cover the outside edges of where we're going to sleep," he said. "If anyone tries to shoot under the wagons, they'll hit rocks and not people."

After about two hours of hauling and piling rocks, Wiley said to Lawrence, "We should go relieve Ben and James. They can finish these rock piles."

Lawrence was happy to agree. "With the moonlight," Wiley said, "we should be able to see fairly well for a good distance, but we may hear them before we see them. There shouldn't be any wagons traveling on the road at night for fear of these gangs. Anyone on horseback should be considered part of a gang until we find out otherwise."

They grabbed two boxes of shells for their rifles, and Wiley brought two boxes for his buffalo gun. They put a couple of handfuls of bullets for their pistols in their pockets and loaded up two of the extra quick-release cylinders, so they could just pop them into the pistols when they were empty.

When they got out to the lookout positions, they each showed the man they were replacing what they had brought with them and told them to bring the same thing when they came back to relieve them. Then Wiley explained what else they were going to do. "We're going to leave two boxes of rifle cartridges on the ground at the secondary position where we can get to them quickly if we need too," he said. "When we change our turns on watch, we'll bring two more boxes for ourselves in case we can't get to them. We'll have them on us when we come back out. You two do the same and bring two extras to leave on the ground here at our first position." They agreed on taking two-hour shifts, so that no one would get too sleepy. They wanted to maintain a good watch.

Just as the sun was starting to drop below the horizon, Ben saw a group of riders coming. He moved quickly below the ridgeline, so he couldn't be seen, and whistled and waved his rifle to let the others know someone was coming. Then he went back to his position, keeping hidden.

About a quarter of a mile before they reached him, the riders, which were a group with about ten horses, stopped and looked above the spot where he was hidden. He turned to see what they might be looking at, and he realized it was the smoke from the campfire. Two riders left the group.

One went up the ridgeline and the other went down it. The one that went down traveled well past the secondary position they had planned to use and came up to the crest of the ridge where he could see the wagons. Ben flattened in the tall grass, so he couldn't be seen. The other rider came up to the top of the ridgeline about five hundred yards from the road. Both men took a good look at the wagons and went back to the others on the road.

When Wiley saw Ben's warning, he turned to Lawrence and said, "Stay with the wagons. I'm going up to the secondary position by where James is. That way I can get on either side of the ridge when we've figured out which way they're coming from." Then he addressed the women. "Get your rifles ready and get into a lying down position where you can shoot from," he said. "Rest your rifle barrels on the rock piles, but don't let them stick out past the rocks. Try to keep your blankets covering you, so they won't be able to be see you easily." With that, he left them.

Lawrence told the ladies to position themselves to shoot at the ridge ahead of them, and he would get in position to cover Ben, and they all grabbed an extra box of shells. Ben decided he would move to the secondary position, because from there, he could shoot at the road if the men came down it. He grabbed extra cartridges. Staying on the wagon side of the ridge, he crouched low and hustled to his new spot.

When Wiley got to James, he told him to stay low behind the rocks till they could tell where the riders were coming from. "If they're going to come from up above the secondary position," he added, "you need to get up to the other position as quick as you can."

Once again safely hidden, Ben saw the group of outlaws dividing into two groups, one going up the ridgeline and the other coming toward him, probably thinking they were going to surprise these travelers while they ate their supper.

He quickly ran down to where he could be seen from the wagons, then whistled. When the travelers looked up, he pointed up and down the ridgeline, using his arms to motion that the gang had divided into two groups and were heading in those directions. When Lawrence nodded, showing he had seen him and understood, Ben ran back to his position.

Lawrence stood up and whistled to Wiley and James and gave the same signals Ben had given, hoping they would be understood. Finished, he quickly got back to the cover of the wagons. Wiley motioned for James to join him, so they could wait together for the coming attack. They took positions about fifty yards apart on each side of the ridge, behind the best cover they could find that offered a good view.

The McCoys waited in silence, as ready as they could be for what was about to come. It took several minutes before they started hearing the outlaw's horses laboring up the hillside. Ben heard them snorting from exertion a few seconds before he saw them. They were about fifty yards away, and while the sun had gone down below the horizon, there was still enough light to see. The men had rifles in their hands and had started to walk their horses up the ridge.

When Wiley heard the horses above him, he signaled for James to come near. James had heard them too and was already running to Wiley's position. As soon as he hid himself behind a good-sized tree, the horses went quiet. But they could hear something moving toward them through the brush, knocking away loose rocks.

From their vantage point, Wiley and James could still see the upper areas fairly well, but down lower in the little valley, the shadows were quickly deepening, making it hard to see.

But then, Wiley saw a sudden movement down below. It was men without horses. It looked like there was four of them. They were moving downhill, trying to get close to the wagons as quickly as they could. He got James's attention and motioned that the men were down below.

At the spot where the cover started thinning, they stopped and seemed to be waiting. At that point, they were actually closer to the wagons than Wiley and James, but Wiley and James had the advantage of being uphill and aware of their approach.

"You take the two on the right," Wiley whispered to James, "and I'll take the two on the left."

The men near Ben had left their horses behind and were coming over the ridge. He stayed hidden as they crested it and started coming down the wagon side. He counted four men moving downhill. They were passing at about fifty yards away from him, but no one realized he was there. When the cover ran out, they got down on their hands and knees and started crawling through the tall grass. At about two hundred yards from the wagons, they stopped.

Ben heard one of the men say, "I can't see anyone. I think they're all asleep under the wagons there. Those dark shapes look like people lying down."

This was followed by, "Okay, everyone, pick out something to shoot. On the count of three, we open up."

Ben picked out the two closest to him, so that he could hit one and then quickly hit the other before they realized where the shots were coming from. The men started their count. *One...two...*but before they made it to three, Ben fired at the closest man. When he heard a groan, he knew he had hit his target and aimed at the next one and fired again.

As soon as Wiley and James heard the first shot, they fired at their targets and watched them drop, then quickly fired at the next ones and heard more moans and yells.

Ben had hit both of his targets, but the other two started firing at him, and he had to duck back behind his cover. Lawrence had started shooting at those coming from below when he'd heard Ben's first shot. He couldn't really see his target, but saw the flash from the gun barrels, so he fired where he thought there would be a man.

The two of the four men coming from below who had not been hit realized they were being shot at from two different directions and decided to run in a direction no shots were coming from. They hightailed it, zigzagging downhill down the little valley and were able to move fast. They managed to get safely into the cover about three hundred yards away from the wagons.

Ben went down to check on the two he had shot. One man was face down in the dirt. The other was lying on his side and had a pistol in his hand; he was holding his leg around his thigh and started to point his pistol at him.

Ben dropped and rolled to the side as soon as he saw the gun swinging in his direction. "Drop it," he told the man. "You're not going anywhere with that leg, so unless you want to die, throw out the gun!"

The man thought about it for a second, and then said, "Okay, you win." Ben saw what he thought was a gun fly through the air and stood up, keeping his rifle trained at the man as he walked to him.

When Wiley and James realized they were not being shot at, they started making their way down to the men they had hit. All four of them were dead. Then they heard the sound of horses running back up the valley and figured that one man must have been left with the horses, and he had decided to get out while he still could.

Lawrence came running to Ben and saw the man lying there, bleeding heavily from his leg. Then he noticed the other man face down. He asked, "Where'd the other ones go?"

Ben pointed with his rifle, keeping both hands on it, down the valley. He went to the man lying face down and rolled him over, to see that he was definitely dead. He nodded at the injured man and told Lawrence, "Keep this one covered while I go back up the ridge to where they left their horses."

He was almost at the top of the ridge when he heard horses running, and one of the men saying, "We got to tell the boss what happened."

When Ben finally got to where he could view the road, he saw what looked like four riders and several riderless horses running as fast as they could, headed back down the hill to Lawrence.

Lawrence told the man on the ground, "You had better take off your belt and strap it around your leg above that wound, or you're probably going to bleed to death." The man did as he suggested, pulling it as tight as he could, grimacing in pain as he did so.

When Ben got back, he said, "Let's get this one over to the wagons." They each took a side of the man, grabbed an arm, and dragged him backward toward the wagons. By the time they got to the wagons, Wiley and James were there and had checked to see if either of the women had been hurt. "Those men didn't even get a shot off in our direction," they told him.

"We got a live one here," Ben yelled out as they got close to the wagons. "The other one's dead, and the other two got away with one man they'd left to hold the horses."

"Yeah," Wiley said. "The man holding the horses up by us got away too. That means there were ten of them in the bunch."

Ben nodded. "And I heard one of them saying they had to go tell the boss what happened."

"Tie the live one to one of the wagon tongues," Wiley said. "I'm going back out to get my rifle and the extra cartridges we left." After they got the man tied up, the other three McCoys stood around the campfire drinking coffee, commenting on how smart Wiley had been by making them stop there, finding their positions, and planning their defense. "That's why he was our sergeant in the war," Lawrence said, "because he was so good at that kind of thing." When Wiley made it back with his buffalo gun and all the shells they had left behind, Ben told him, "We have to hand it to you. You sure had us well-prepared for them boys."

Wiley just shrugged. "I just didn't want to take any chances and have any of us get hurt, even if nobody ever attacked us. I wanted to make sure we'd have a fighting chance if someone did."

"Well, it sure worked out well for us anyway," Lawrence told him.

"Not all that well," Wiley replied. "Four of them got away, but at least none of us got hurt. I don't think they'll come back tonight, but we need to get into Middlesboro as soon as we can tomorrow. I think there's about fifteen miles to go yet, and it's going to be mostly mountain road."

He drank the last of his coffee then refilled his cup. "Let's keep a guard posted at the lookout points for the rest of the night," he said. "We don't know how close the others are or how many are still left, so just in case, the same plan is in effect for the rest of the night."

The men nodded in agreement, pouring themselves more coffee as well. "We'll drop this one with the sheriff in Middlesboro when we get there, if he lives long enough," Wiley said, indicating the man tied to the wagon tongue. "Let's drag the ones we shot over here, so animals don't try to take advantage of a carcass tonight."

The four of them set out to do just that. When Ben and Lawrence came back with the partner of the man tied to the wagon, Ben said, "Let's just pile them up by him, so he can get a good look. Might keep him from trying anything."

When they'd finished, Ben remembered that he had left the extra shells at the secondary post.

"I'll go now," he said, "and take first watch at the lookout position since I have to go pick up the shells I left. Besides, we don't know how far away the ones who escaped had to go to get back to the others."

Lawrence started looking in his wagon for his extra tarp to put over the bodies, so they wouldn't have to look at them. When they had all five piled together, they stretched the tarp to cover them, taking some rocks from under the wagons and putting them on its edges to hold it down. Lawrence decided he would take the first watch on the other lookout post and grabbed his rifle and headed out.

"We might as well try and get some rest," Wiley told the others. "I know it probably won't be easy after all of this, but we need to try and get some. I want to be gone from here by first light. We'll have breakfast in town. We can get by on just coffee in the morning."

CHAPTER 21

OUTLAWS' RETRIBUTION

The four riders who had gotten away made it back to their hideout, which was an abandoned farm just outside of White Oak. They had come across the farm in May, just after the war ended, and since no one was there, they decided to take up residence.

After a little while there, the boss came up with an idea about making a living, and they hit their first travelers coming across the Cumberland Gap and brought everything to the farm.

They made a big fire pit where they burned all of the wagons they brought in. There was a large barn on the farm that they used to stockpile the stuff they were accumulating. They'd expected that the four loaded wagons they saw on the road would add quite a bit to their stash of loot.

When the four surviving looters rode up to the front of the house, everyone came outside to see what had happened. There was surprise all around when they saw several horses were riderless. This was the first time the full crew hadn't come back from a wagon raid. The people they tried to hit were ready and waiting for them, the men told their boss.

"They ambushed us when we got between them and the wagons," one said, "and we only got away by the skin of our teeth!" Everyone else was dead, they thought.

Since it'd taken them almost four hours to return, the boss decided there wasn't enough time to get back there before daylight by the time they gotten everything ready to go. He told his men to pack stuff for three or four days and be ready to go by sunup.

"These people are traveling through and will probably keep going after Middlesboro," the boss said, "so we'll get ahead of them and find us a good ambush spot ourselves—maybe around Bell County in Cliff Canyon. We'll make them pay for killing our boys."

At sunup, they were ready to go. When they reached the campsite four hours later, they found it empty.

"Those people are probably already in Middlesboro talking to the sheriff," the boss told the men. "When we get close to town, three of us are going in, and the rest will go on ahead to Cliff Canyon and get set up.

"When they leave town, we'll follow them and keep a mile or so back so we can close in quick when they get close to the entrance of the canyon. When we hear shootin' start, we'll block their escape route back down the road toward town, in case they manage to get turned around and try to make a run for it."

• • •

Just before sunup, Wiley made fresh coffee for everyone. While it was still on the fire, he roused the rest of the group out of their beds. They put the dead bodies in the wagons; two of them in two different wagons, and the last one by itself. They saddled one horse, which they put behind the second wagon. When they were ready to go, they put the wounded man on that horse, tied his hands around the saddle horn, and tied the reins to the wagon. The man was weak and sore, but he'd live long enough to get to Middlesboro. They started down the road as soon as they could see well enough to steer away from any potholes.

They didn't know about the trap that would be lying in wait for them just a little bit down the road from Middlesboro. Nor did they know that back in Independence, Missouri, the robbed general had hired the Pinkertons, a private detective agency out of Chicago, to try and find what his own men weren't able to—where the stolen gold had gone. And the Pinkertons had started to follow a fifty-dollar gold piece trail.

CHAPTER 22

MIDDLESBORO

It took about three hours to get to Middlesboro. As they were coming into town, people started staring at them. They were pointing at the bodies in the wagons, and women began hustling their children back inside the buildings. In the lead wagon, Wiley stopped one man and asked where the sheriff's office was.

"Right in the middle of town," the man told him, eyeing his grisly load. "You can't miss it on the right." Wiley stopped his wagon a little past the sheriff's office, so that the others would be able to stop right in front.

He climbed down and went to the front door of the sheriff's office. As he reached toward the knob, it opened, and the sheriff stepped out. The sheriff looked at the burdened wagons and at the man with his hands tied to the saddle horn.

"What in tarnation happened here?" he said to Wiley.

Wiley explained, and the sheriff told his deputies, "Get this man off the horse and put him in a cell, then go get the doc."

Then he turned back to Wiley. "You were really lucky you didn't get killed," he said. "There's been a bunch of killing and robbing going on around here since May. I haven't been able to figure out who's doing it, or where they come from, but it looks like you solved a lot of my troubles."

Wiley frowned and shook his head. "I don't think your troubles are over," he said. "The way those men lit out, they had somewhere to go and someone to report back to. I'm sure this isn't all of them."

When the deputies came back outside, the sheriff told one of them to go get the undertaker. "Where do you want the bodies?" Wiley said.

"Just unload them right here in front of my office," he replied, "and we'll take care of them from here."

Ben, James, and Lawrence began taking the bodies from the wagons, and Cassie and Claire clasped hands and stared at the road ahead, trying not to watch.

"We're just passing through," Wiley said, "but it's been a while since we slept in a bed and had a nice bath. I think we'll probably stay a couple of nights in a hotel here in town. Can you recommend a good one with a good restaurant?"

"The best one is the one with the name of the town across the front, the Middlesboro Hotel," the sheriff said. "It's down toward the end of the main street on the left. If I need to talk to you, I'll come down to the hotel."

They made their way to the hotel and Wiley went inside to see if they could accommodate them. He found out they had rooms with hot baths but didn't have a livery out back like the other places they had been. The livery was down the road next to the mercantile store.

They pulled what they needed from the wagons, and the ladies stayed at the hotel to get settled in their rooms while the men drove the wagons down to the livery. Once again, Wiley dealt with the livery owner, and they left the wagons and horses there for him to take care of.

As the men were walking back through town, they noticed several people leaning their heads close together and whispering. Some of them pointed in their direction. They were surely talking about how they were the people that brought in that gang of robbers.

When they got to the hotel, the clerk said, "I've got hot water in the women's tubs, and most of yours are already half full; it'll be a few minutes before we get the rest of the hot water to you."

"That's fine, we wanted to have breakfast anyway," Wiley replied, and they went into the restaurant.

When the waitress took their order, she asked if they were the ones who had brought in all those dead men.

Wiley didn't answer at first. He didn't want to seem as if it was something they were proud of having done. Finally, he said, "Well, we didn't have a whole lot of choice in the matter. If it wasn't them, it would've been us lying out there in the grass somewhere."

"Oh, my! Well, I'm glad you're all right and here for breakfast," she said. She took their order and headed back to the kitchen.

"Boy, word travels fast in his town," Lawrence said after she left.

"Yeah," said Ben, "And we better be careful walking around in it, because we don't know who might be in cahoots with those guys we brought in. They've probably got people in the towns around here watching for travelers, so stay on your toes."

By the time they had finished their breakfast, the clerk

came and told them that their hot water was ready in their rooms, so they all went upstairs to get a well-deserved bath and some sleep, since no one had really been able to rest after all that had happened the night before.

That evening, when they were all together in the restaurant, the sheriff came in to have his dinner. He went up to their table and leaned close to Wiley so no one else in the restaurant would hear and said, "I'll need you to come by the office tomorrow. There's some papers you need to sign. It seems some of those boys had paper on them, meaning there was a bounty for them, so you have some money coming to you."

Wiley offered him a look of surprise, then said, "I'll come by in the morning before I order the supplies we're going to need to keep traveling."

The sheriff and his deputies went to sit at a table with a sign on it that read, "Reserved for Sheriff."

After he walked away, Wiley leaned in close to the other men and said quietly, "What do you say we give Claire and Cassie the bounty money?" The mother and daughter exchanged a look of surprise, but the men grinned at each other and nodded their approval. Lawrence gave the women a mocking and serious look, then leaned toward them and whispered, "You ladies don't need to be making it a habit of collecting bounty money. It's not good for your health!"

In a low voice, Wiley added, "I'll sign for the money. That way, your names won't appear on any more bounty certificates. We don't need you to end up becoming famous women bounty hunters; it's not a very becoming reputation for ladies."

They all chuckled and agreed. They finished their dinner and went up to their rooms to get a long night's sleep in a comfortable bed.

The next morning, Wiley was up at seven and went down to the restaurant. He had his breakfast and coffee, then headed to the sheriff's office.

The sheriff was at his desk and had the bounty receipts in front of him.

"Hello, Sheriff. Nice morning," Wiley said. "Well, what were those boys worth?"

"You'll be surprised," he said. "Three of them had five hundred on their head each, and one of them had two fifty. The other two apparently aren't worth anything. I need you to sign each receipt. I have the money right here."

Wiley signed, and the sheriff gave him one thousand seven hundred fifty dollars in a big envelope, which he stuffed inside his shirt.

"That's pretty good money for saving my own skin," he quipped.

"Don't go around talking about how you picked up a bounty," the sheriff said. "It's not good for people to know that. I haven't said anything to anyone about it, so just keep it under your hat. It'll be a lot safer that way for everyone."

"Don't worry, Sheriff," Wiley replied. "I don't plan on making a living like this. I just want to keep on living. I got to go order our supplies now. Thanks for letting us know there was a bounty to collect."

He left the sheriff's office and started walking down the street toward the general store. When he went inside, the owner asked, "How'd you manage to kill all those men without any of you getting hurt?"

Wiley sighed. The small-town rumor mill was obviously working hard. "We were just lucky, I guess," he said, "and the Lord must've been watching out for us. We need to stock up on our supplies. We still got a lot of road to travel." He ordered everything he could think of, then told the owner that the rest of the group might add to it. He handed him a fifty-dollar gold piece.

When Wiley got back to the hotel, the rest were in the restaurant having breakfast. He sat with them and ordered coffee.

When they finished breakfast, he told Claire he wanted to talk to her upstairs in private, so they went up to her room. When the door was closed, he reached inside his shirt and pulled out the envelope. "This is the money the sheriff gave me," he said. "There were bounties on several of those men. Keep it safe somewhere, and don't tell anyone you have it. No one needs to know outside of us."

She took the envelope, sat on the bed, and spread the money out. Her eyes got wide as she counted. "There's almost two thousand dollars here!" she exclaimed.

"Yeah, I know," Wiley said. "That's why you need to be quiet about it."

"Are you sure you want me to have it? That's an awful lot of money to just give away."

"No, you keep it," he said. "It's yours. Me and the boys all agreed to give it to you. We'll be okay; we have some of our own."

Tears had formed in Claire's eyes. "I don't know what to say," she said, wiping at them. "With this and what I still have from before, I've never had so much money in my hands in my life. Me and Cassie are going to be able to get a nice place and make a real good start of it. You've really changed our lives for the good ever since we met you. I can't thank you enough for all you've done."

Wiley raised a hand to stop her. "We still have a long way to go to get to my place, but Lawrence and James's homes are only about forty some miles from here. You'll need to take a good look around once we get there, so you'll know if it's a place you might want to settle at."

"Oh, I don't think I'll want to settle there," she said. "I always wanted to raise horses and cattle. We'll look around, but I want to go along with you to your home and see what kind of country you have there, and Cassie does too. That is, if you haven't changed your mind and don't mind if we come along?"

"Of course, you're welcome to come with me and Ben," Wiley said. "I don't know about Lawrence, if he's going to want to leave his homestead and come with us. He'll have to see about that when the time comes."

Claire turned away from him. She pulled the money that was left from the other bounty out of her bodice and put it in the envelope, then put the envelope inside her shirt and buttoned it back up before she turned back towards him again. "I'm going to keep this money with me at all times," she said. "It's our future." They went back downstairs and joined the others. Now Claire was the one grinning from ear to ear, looking for all the world like the cat that had just swallowed the canary.

They went outside to the front of the hotel, and Wiley sat in a chair he found there. The others said they wanted to take a stroll around town, and Claire asked Lawrence if he'd ever been to the town before.

Before he could answer, Wiley said, "You must've

been here at some time. Your home is less than fifty miles."

"I think I came here once as a child," Lawrence replied.

"If we had to go into town, we usually went to Wallins Creek or to Baxter on account they're closer. We would sell things we had too much of from the farm and buy everything we needed in those towns, so we didn't really have to travel this far. We mostly fended for ourselves at home. If we couldn't make it and couldn't get it in one of those towns, we pretty much figured we didn't need it."

They went into the general store and found out that Wiley had ordered the same things they had picked up when they had stocked up in the town of Albany. Nothing they wanted had been left out.

The day was warming up quickly, as August days usually did. When the men stopped in the leather shop to look around, the women stayed outside. "What did Wiley want to talk to you about in private?" Cassie asked her mother.

Claire looked around to make sure no one was within earshot, then whispered, "You know some of those men that tried to rob us were wanted and had a bounty on their heads? Wiley went and signed for the money at the sheriff's office. He took me upstairs to tell me about it and gave it all to me, but I never would've believed it could be so much. Remember at the dinner table when he and the others agreed we should have it? Well, he didn't think there would be so much money either. That's why he took me upstairs, so no one would hear or see when he gave it to me. He told me to hide it and not to say anything to anyone about the money or the bounties on those men."

Cassie was surprised. "Really, Mama, they just gave it all to us?" she said.

"Yes, they did, and it's a lot of money."

"How much is it?"

Claire looked around again and whispered, in an even lower voice this time, "Almost two thousand."

Cassie's eyes opened wide, and she put her hands on her mouth. "Really? Really, there was that much? And you have it all? We really are going to have us a good start wherever we decide to settle down and make a go of it!"

Claire looked at her daughter with a little sadness in her eyes. "There is a little bit of a problem we need to face," she said.

"And what's that?"

"Well it seems that Lawrence's home is only about fifty miles from here, and Wiley's is another ninety to a hundred miles farther east. I told him that I wanted to go see where he was from, so that means we may have to leave Lawrence at his place."

She took a deep breath. "Wiley also told me that none of them know what they're going back to, or even if their homes are still there. So, we still don't know what's going to happen. I do know Wiley's a good man, and I really don't want to leave him. It's not that I'm in love. I just feel safe and protected around him, and I think that's a good thing to have for the two of us, since we're all alone now."

Cassie looked right in her mother's eyes. "I really like Lawrence and think he's a good man too," she said, "but I'm going wherever you go, Ma. Don't you worry about me putting up any fuss. We'll just have to wait and see what the Lord's got in store for us." Cassie hugged her.

The men came outside just as they were breaking off their hug; they saw both the women with watery eyes. "Is anything wrong?" Lawrence asked.

They both just looked at him and rubbed their eyes. "No, nothing's wrong," Cassie said. "Quite the opposite. We're just real happy how things are turning out for us."

They turned to walk back down the main street of town, and Claire turned to the men. "I want to thank all of you for protecting and taking care of us the way you have, and for your help in getting us back on our feet again with the money you gave us."

The men were feeling pleased and proud of themselves for what she'd just said to them. Ben said, "Aw shucks, ma'am, we just felt it was the right thing to do. We're right happy to be able to."

When they got back to the hotel, Wiley was sitting out front. The women went up to their room, and the men sat down next to Wiley. They had been sitting there for a few minutes when Wiley spoke. "I saw three rough-looking men ride into town when we got back to the hotel," he said. "They went in the saloon over there. They sure took a good look at me. I just tipped my hat as they went by, but I have a feeling they're from that bunch that tried to rob us."

Just then, the sheriff crossed the street and stepped up on to the boardwalk of the hotel. "I guess you saw those men who just rode into town," he said. "They've been here a few times over the last few months, and I've been wondering about them for a while. Nobody knows their names or where they're working or staying, but they always have money."

Wiley rubbed his chin.

"I just thought I would give you a heads-up to be extra careful," the sheriff said. "There is a place about fifteen miles north of here where the road goes through a place they call Cliff Canyon. It's named that way because it's about a quarter mile of sheer cliffs that go up about six hundred, maybe eight hundred feet on both sides of the road. It's a good place for an ambush, and there's been more than one wagon group robbed going through there. It might be a good idea to send someone ahead of you to check it out."

Wiley gave a slow nod.

"Once you get through Cliff Canyon, you shouldn't have any problems on the road," the sheriff continued. "Most of the other robberies happened down around the Cumberland Gap. I just thought I'd let you know, since you don't know much about the area around here."

"We appreciate your advice, Sheriff," Wiley said, "and I think we just might send someone ahead as you advise."

"Well, just be careful," the sheriff replied. "They're probably really riled up about losing those men of theirs." He opened the door of the hotel. "I'm going for some coffee. I missed my breakfast," he said.

From the porch of the hotel, the McCoys could see the entrance to the saloon the three men went into. Every once in a while, they noticed someone standing in the doorway, looking in their direction; they stayed just long enough to take a look at the hotel.

"I think we can rest assured those three are part of the gang," Wiley told the others, "Because they sure are interested in this hotel. Think I'll go over to the general store and see if I can get him to get our order ready before he closes tonight, if he can. I'll get him to bring it around to the livery. If he will, we'll load it in our wagons tonight and get out of here at first light."

He got up from the chair and started walking toward the store. The others went inside the hotel and sat in the restaurant by the window, so they could watch the saloon.

At the general store, Wiley approached the owner.

"I think some of the gang is in town and are watching us from the saloon on this end of town," he said. "I want to know if you can deliver our supplies over to the livery sometime today."

The owner nodded quickly. "I could have it there by four o'clock, since I have a couple of deliveries to make here in town before I close. I'll have my delivery boy bring it over. It won't look suspicious, and besides, the livery is down the street too far for them to see it from the saloon they're in."

"I appreciate that," Wiley said, and the man nodded.

"Just have someone there to receive the goods," he said. "And you have some money coming back too." He opened his cash register drawer and took out a wad of bills.

"I'm much obliged for this," Wiley said, "and we'll be there when your boy gets to the livery."

Back at the hotel, he found the others in the restaurant. He pulled up a chair for himself and told the men they'd need to be at the livery about a quarter of four to load the supplies from the mercantile. "We should eat a good dinner tonight," he said, "because we're going to miss breakfast, and it would be best if we turn in early. We'll leave before sunup. I'll have the hotel clerk make sure we're awake by five o'clock in the morning."

When the delivery boy arrived, Ben and James unloaded the goods he'd brought. They divided the supplies in the four wagons and got everything ready. All they had to do in the morning was tie the extra horses to the back and hitch the others to the fronts.

They gave the livery owner what they owed him and said, "Here's an extra five dollars to keep a good lookout on these wagons and horses tonight. We want to leave out of here just before sunup."

"Not to worry," the man said. "I sleep close by, and tonight, I'll sleep with one eye open."

When they got back to the hotel, the other four were in the restaurant waiting for them at a table. They told them everything was ready to go and that they could leave first thing in the morning.

While they were having their dinner, Wiley told them, "I'll ride out ahead when we leave in the morning, so if there is an ambush waiting on the road, I'll find it first and head back to warn you."

They were all up before five o'clock, dressed and ready, when the hotel clerk knocked on the door.

They walked as a group out the hotel's front door and down the street to the livery. The horses were hitched or tied to the wagons, and Wiley saddled his horse. He took along his buffalo gun and stuffed his pockets with cartridges for it.

He put one box of cartridges in his shirt and made sure he had two extra quick-release cylinders full of cartridges for each of his six-shooter Colt pistols. Deciding he was as prepared as he was going to get, he mounted up and the group proceeded down the street.

Once they were clear of the town, Wiley said, "I'll try to stay around a mile or so ahead." He nudged his horse, pulled him in front of the group, and let him go at a slow canter down the road.

• • •

What they didn't know was that the three men had got a room in a hotel where they could see the road heading out of town. They had posted a lookout in the window, taking shifts all night, watching to see when the McCoy group would leave.

When the lookout saw the wagons, he woke the other two, and they went down to their horses. They waited for about twenty minutes before heading down the road out of town.

After about two hours of travel, Wiley could see the cliffs where the road went into Cliff Canyon. But he couldn't see any signs of someone waiting in ambush, so he kept on riding.

CHAPTER 23

THE AMBUSH

There were eleven men waiting around the entrance to Cliff Canyon. Four were up on the lower ridges, two of them on each side a couple of hundred feet above the road and inside the canyon a couple hundred yards, and three were hiding down at road level just before the entrance. When the ones up high signaled to those on the ground that there was a rider coming, they all got out of sight and waited.

As Wiley got closer to the entrance to the canyon, he had a gut feeling that something wasn't right. He still hadn't seen anything, but he took his rifle out of its saddle scabbard anyway. He laid it in the crook of his left arm and on his right thigh, balancing it in front of him while he wrapped the reins loosely around the saddle horn. Then, letting his horse walk at its own pace, he was able to keep his hands free to hold the rifle in both hands, ready to swing and aim.

At about a hundred yards from the opening, he came around a slight turn in the road and saw movement in the brush. He got his rifle pointed in its direction before the first shots came out. He saw the smoke from the shots and fired back as he heard their bullets whizzing by.

His horse was startled and turned sideways in the road. He saw one man stand up to get a clear shot over the bushes he had been hiding behind. Wiley leveled his gun at his chest, fired quickly, and watched the man fall into the bush. As more shots rang out, Wiley's horse screamed and went down. He fell off to the side, then quickly crawled around the downed horse, using him as cover. He laid his rifle over the saddle as he saw a man trying to make his way through the brush toward him.

There was an opening in the brush that man was going to have to cross to get closer, so he trained his rifle on it and waited.

Wiley knew he was only going to be able to get off one shot before the man made it to the cover he was heading for. If the man made it across, he would be able to get above him and pick him off easily.

He saw him stop at the edge of the opening, getting ready to make a dash across it. But as the enthusiastic bushwhacker took one step forward, Wiley dropped him in his tracks, as a bullet from another outlaw ricocheted off his saddle horn. Another man had worked his way around and had a good line of sight on him.

Wiley grabbed his buffalo gun and made a run, carrying both rifles, zigzagging for some trees about thirty yards off the road. He heard shots and saw bullets plunging into the grass nearby. He managed to get to the trees and took a quick look behind him and saw a man running after him, dodging between any cover he could get behind.

Wiley turned and ran as quickly as he could into a ravine. He was moving so fast his steps were more like running jumps as he covered a lot of ground with speed. During a brief airborne second between steps, he saw a deadfall tree stuck at an angle between two other trees. As he got closer, he could see that the dead tree would be sturdy enough to hold his weight.

He wedged his buffalo gun between one of the live trees and the deadfall, then broke off a branch, leaving a short portion of it sticking out near his buffalo gun. He stuck his hat on the stub, and the branch held it so that just the top of it was showing above the dead tree. Trying to be quick to get out of sight before being seen, he scurried faster than a scared squirrel up the deadfall to the larger of the trees it was pinned between. He kept climbing the tree till he had gotten up about twenty feet above the deadfall, then worked his way to the far side of it and turned so he could see the area the man would be coming from.

The pursuing man realized the cover was thinning out, and since he didn't see his target or any brush moving, he slowed to a walk. Crouching low, he scanned the area for his quarry. He stopped when he saw the deadfall and Wiley's hat, deciding to get close enough to make one shot count. He crept quietly, keeping his eyes on the hat till he could clearly see its top three inches. At about forty yards away, he went down onto one knee behind a bush to take aim.

Wiley slowly raised his rifle. When the man got to one knee, Wiley took aim at his chest with his carbine.

When the bushwhacker fired, he saw Wiley's hat go flying in the air. And that was the last thing he saw on this earth. Wiley fired the instant the man's rifle went off. He hit him right between the eyes because the man ducked after he fired his gun.

Wiley climbed back down and picked up his buffalo gun and hat, which had a bullet hole right through the place where the top of his head would have been if he'd been wearing it. Then he worked his way back toward the road, keeping his eyes peeled for any movement that might reveal there were others coming his way.

When he got to where he could see the road again, he decided he would head through the trees and up the backside of the cliffs to see if he could get to a higher vantage point on the canyon and get a good look from above.

It took him quite a while—maybe fifteen minutes—to get to where he wanted to be. He started creeping toward the edge of the cliffs, staying low, being careful not to send any loose stones falling down the steep terrain. He finally got to a spot where he could see both sides of the canyon and the road for a fair distance, and he sat down to watch.

It wasn't long before the sun was up high enough that he saw reflections off of the barrels of the rifles where the men were hiding in the rocks below him. They were positioned between him and the entrance of the canyon. He counted four, then waited a little while to make sure he'd seen all of them. Then slowly and quietly, he crept through the brush until he was about two hundred yards from the men on the opposite side.

He planned who to shoot first, so he would have the advantage on those who would be left. He decided it would have to be the two on the far side because he was above and across from them, and they wouldn't be able to hide behind anything before he got off two shots. The other two were below him, and because of the angle of the cliff, no matter where they went, he would still be able to shoot down and stay behind the cover of the rocks. There was nothing to cover them from anything coming above and behind them. They had disregarded any thought of someone shooting at them from above and had positioned themselves badly.

Wiley loaded his buffalo rifle and kept three more shells in his left hand ready to load. Because he was so high up on the cliffs and could see pretty far on the road, he could see the wagons were coming. They must have fallen back farther than the mile he had suggested, but they were coming at a fast pace now. He figured someone must have come up from behind them on the road, making them start running their horses.

• • •

After about an hour on the road toward the canyon, Lawrence decided he would saddle a horse and fall back to keep an eye on the road behind them, letting Cassie drive the wagon. After another hour, he came to a rise in the road where he could see almost a mile back behind them and decided he would watch for a while from there. He took his horse back below the crest on the down side of the hill.

He left the horse there and walked back up to the top of the hill and hid. It wasn't long before he saw the three riders coming down the road, and he ran down to his horse and rode as fast as he could to catch up to the wagons.

When he caught up with them, he told them there were three riders coming up behind them, less than two miles back by now. They started moving the wagons faster, and soon the cliffs came in sight. Below those cliffs was the place the road went into the canyon, about two miles away. When they were a little over a mile away from the cliffs, they heard faint gunshots echoing off the canyon walls.

• • •

Wiley took careful aim and shot the first man on the far side of the canyon. He quickly got another shell into his buffalo rifle and killed the other one before the outlaw could figure out where the shot had come from.

When the other two realized the shots had come from above them, they looked around for a place that might offer some protection.

They had the cliff in front of them and nothing but low rocks around them for thirty yards. They had pinned themselves in without even knowing it. Wiley reloaded quickly, and all the outlaws saw before he shot the man closest to him was a rifle barrel sticking out between some rocks. The other decided he was better off moving and tried to scramble over the rocks, but he didn't get ten yards before Wiley shot him. The four who had been lying in ambush up above on the cliffs were now lying dead in the rocks.

When the wagons made it to where Wiley's horse was dead in the road, the men looked around and heard a shot come from high up on the cliff.

Wiley had fired his pistol into the air to get their attention. When they saw him waving them toward him, they continued into the canyon. When they got below him, they stopped and yelled up to him that three other men were behind them on the road.

"Lawrence," Wiley yelled, "I want you to go back out to the entrance and climb up on the opposite side of the canyon from me. Get in a position where you can shoot down on the road." To the others he said, "The rest of you, get farther into the canyon, then stop the wagons and block the road with them. Get behind the wagons in position to fight."

Wiley saw the horsemen coming down the road. *This'll serve them right*, he thought. We're going to use their own ambush place against them.

Lawrence went back to the entrance, jumped off his horse, and started climbing up the side of the cliff, where he found one of the ambushers dead, another a little farther up. He took his position at the second dead man.

The wagons drove several hundred yards farther into the canyon and then pulled across the road, completely blocking the way through.

The men on horseback coming up behind them had started riding fast when they heard Wiley's pistol shot, thinking it was their men pulling off the ambush. Coming to the entrance, they were riding so hard that all they saw was one horse standing off to the side and one dead horse in the road.

They had their guns drawn and were within fifty yards of the wagons when they realized the wagons were set up to block the road. The boss yelled, "It's a trap! Let's get out of here!" He pulled his horse to a stop and turned it around and tried to hightail it out the way they had come.

Before they could pick up any speed, Ben shot one of the riders and tried to hit another as they left, but he missed. Wiley and Lawrence were ready as the riders came back toward them.

As they got close, both took aim and fired. Their shots knocked both men out of the saddle. Each was dead by the time they bounced on the ground.

"They're down!" Wiley yelled, waving to the men to bring the wagons to the entrance of the canyon. He started down the side of the cliffs the way he had come up. When he made it back to the deadfall, he went to the man he had shot there and started dragging him to the road. Lawrence dragged out the man who was close to his position, then pulled the one out of the bush and put him beside the other one. He helped Wiley pile his man on the others. Wiley said, "There's two more on each side up higher," then both went back up the cliffs for the rest of the dead. When Wiley got to the place where the two dead men had been waiting to ambush him, he decided it was too hard and too dangerous to keep climbing back up the cliffs and dragging dead men down to the road, so he decided just to push them over the cliff and let them fall since they were dead anyway.

Seeing what Wiley had done with his two men, *Well, if he's not going to carry them down, I'm not either*, Lawrence thought, and pushed the one he was hauling down off the cliff over the side, got to the other and did the same.

Back at the wagons, Wiley said, "Give me a hand, Ben, bring a wagon. James, you help Lawrence." And James and Lawrence walked back into the canyon and dragged the three men who had pursued them on horseback over to where their three horses had stopped. They placed them over the saddles and walked the three horses to the entrance, stopping them at the wagons. When Wiley grabbed a rope and started tying the outlaw's bodies onto horses, the others followed his lead.

Once all the bodies had been collected, they looked around for the rest of the outlaws' horses. Some had scattered, but four were still attached to the brush. Wiley picked out the best horse of the bunch and tied it to his wagon. Then he went to his dead horse, told it he was sorry for what happened, and thanked it for saving his life. He patted the neck of the lifeless animal, then took his saddle and other gear off of it and threw the stuff in his wagon.

"These bushwhackers deserve to be left here for the buzzards," he said, "but they just might be worth some money, so we'll take them into the next town; it's not but about ten miles past the canyon from what the sheriff in Middlesboro said."

Once all the bodies had been either loaded into the wagons or tied onto horses, they started through the canyon.

It took them over two hours to get to the next town. They drew a crowd as they came down the main street, having three men dangling across the saddles of their horses and seven with their feet sticking out the end of the wagons. The sheriff was outside in front of his office as they pulled to a stop in front of it.

"What happened?" the sheriff asked them.

Wiley told him what had happened before they got to Middlesboro, and how three outlaws came into town and had followed them out of it, while the others were waiting at the entrance to Cliff Canyon to ambush them. He told him that he had gone ahead of the wagons and discovered the ambush. Then it just worked out that they ended up getting the best of the outlaws who were waiting to rob and kill them.

"I thought I would bring them in to you and see if maybe any of them had any paper on them, since those others did," Wiley said.

"I don't know right offhand," the sheriff said, "but I can take a look. Are you going to stay in town?"

"Yeah," Wiley replied. "I think after today, we'll stay the night here, if you'll just direct us to a good hotel."

"Go over to the Golden Bell," the sheriff told them. "It has a livery behind it. I'll check and see if there are any bounties to collect."

Wiley nodded. "Where do you want these men?" he said.

"Just leave them here. I'll see to it they get into the ground."

The men unloaded the bodies from the wagons, then tied the horses that held the bodies to the railing in front of his office. Wiley tipped his hat to the sheriff, and they drove the wagons to the Golden Bell Hotel. After dropping the wagons and horses with the livery owner, the group went inside the hotel, got rooms, and just flopped down on their beds. It had been a very stressful couple of days, and soon all were asleep.

Wiley woke around four o'clock, told the others that the kitchen started serving dinner at five, and was sitting at a table in the restaurant when they came down the stairs.

Lawrence and James were now very close to their homes and were feeling anxious. "We want to have another bath after dinner," James said. "We should reach our homes by tomorrow. We want to be nice and clean when we show up on our doorsteps."

The women also thought they could use another bath. "I think we need something to help us relax and be able to sleep tonight," Claire said. She sighed heavily. "I wonder how much more of this we're going to have to go through?" she said. "Pretty soon, we're going to have the reputation as 'the people who cleared the highways of all the outlaws.'"

Lawrence got up and approached the desk clerk. "Would you see to it that someone prepares bathtubs for us after dinner?" he said. "We'll get on it right away," replied the clerk.

While they were eating, the sheriff came in and walked over to their table. He was smiling as he grabbed a chair and sat next to Wiley. "Looks like Lady Luck has been favoring you from all directions," he said. "Seven of those men had paper on them, and two of them were really worth some money. You need to come by my office before you leave tomorrow and sign some receipts. You done some real favors to the people in these parts and the people down around Cumberland. We've been trying to find out who these men were and put a stop to their robbing and killing for months. I guess they bit off a lot more than they could chew in tangling with you fellers."

Then he added, "I sent a telegram to the sheriff in Middlesboro to tell him about this. He sent me one back, telling me what you brought him when you came into his town. In only a few days, looks like you boys took care of the whole gang."

The men exchanged glances. The news was a relief. The last thing they wanted to do was tangle with any more robbers and outlaws.

The sheriff cleared his throat. "I want to thank you on the part of this whole town and all the people that live all around these parts," he said. "Now we can feel safe about traveling on the road and might even have some more travelers come through—and maybe some might want to stay and settle here." Finished saying what he felt he needed to say, he stood up. "Enjoy your dinner, and I'll see you tomorrow," he said, leaving.

"Well," Wiley said, looking at the men. "Do we do the same with these bounties as the others?"

They all smiled. "Why not?" Ben said.

Wiley turned to Claire. "Looks like you ladies are going to have more money than you thought. I bet it's the first time you've traveled that you've actually made money instead of it costing you."

But she shook her head. "It's not right that you give us that money," she said. "We didn't do anything to earn it."

"I'd say you did your fair share," Wiley replied, "plus driving the wagons for us. And you did save one of our lives on this trip, that's for sure. I think we'd all agree that no matter how much money this is, that act alone is worth every penny."

Claire was blushing now. "Aren't you going to need some money when you get to your homes?"

Wiley smiled. "Don't worry about us," he said. "We have enough, at least to do what we need to do when we get home. Isn't that right, boys?"

They all grinned. "We have enough," Ben said, "and we're more than happy to let you keep whatever those bounties add up to be."

Where is this money they say they have? Claire wondered.

She hadn't seen anyone with money except Wiley. "Well, if that's the way you feel about it," she said, "I'm surely not going to look a gift horse in the mouth. We truly thank you for everything you've done for us."

They had their dinner, and everyone went upstairs feeling quite worn out. The bathwater arrived shortly afterward and they all soaked in the tubs, relaxing away their tension.

The next day, they all slept until eight o'clock in the morning. Naturally, Wiley was the first one up. He knocked on all the doors, told them he would see them in the restaurant for breakfast, and then set out for the sheriff's office.

He found the man sitting behind his desk, counting a big pile of money.

"Is all that for those men?" Wiley said.

The sheriff smiled. "Yeah, it sure is," he said "Looks like you struck gold here. I wired the governor; the governor has been so desperate to catch these fellers that the price just kept going up. He said to give you his thanks and happily sent the authorization to the bank to pay the bounties. I picked it up this morning."

"How much is it?" Wiley said eyeing the pile.

The sheriff took a deep breath. "Two of those fellers were worth four thousand each," he said, "another one was worth a thousand, one was worth five hundred and four of them were worth two fifty each, making a grand total of ten thousand five hundred dollars."

Wiley blinked hard.

"Two hadn't become worth any paper yet, but I'm sure they would have soon enough, if they hadn't been stopped," the sheriff continued. "You need to sign all the receipts, count your money, and keep your mouths shut about having it. I haven't told a soul."

Wiley signed eight receipts and counted the money the sheriff gave him, then put it into an envelope and put the bulging envelope inside his shirt. They shook hands, and he headed back to the hotel.

He found the men at a table in the restaurant, but the ladies were nowhere in sight, so he went upstairs to their room. He knocked on their door, and Claire called, "We'll be right down."

"I need to come inside for a minute, if it's okay," he said.

When she opened the door, his eyes were sparkling, and he was wearing the biggest smile she'd ever seen on his face. "So, what makes you so happy this morning?" she asked.

"Just this!" he said as he struggled to pull the overstuffed envelope out of his shirt. And he handed it to her.

As she looked at how thick the envelope was, her eyes nearly popped out of her head. She went to the bed as she opened the envelope and dumped the money on it.

Cassie squealed with delight. "Oh, Mama!" she said. "Look at all that money! We're rich! We're rich, Mama!"

"Oh my God," Claire gasped. "How much money is there?"

Feeling very proud of his men and happy for them, Wiley said, "There's ten thousand five hundred dollars in all."

The two women looked at each other, and in unison they said, "Oh my God!"

Claire started shaking with excitement, but Cassie was

starting to feel nervous. "What are we going to do with all this?" she said. "How are we going to hide it? Somebody's going to find out we have it and try to rob us!"

Wiley tried to stop their panicking. "Just calm down," he said. "You just hide it with the rest of your money. And don't worry. No one knows about this except us and the sheriff. Besides, we'll be here to help you guard it till you can get it to a bank or somewhere safe."

The two women started counting the money and crying at the same time, unable to believe what had just happened for them. "We won't have any more worries in the world," Cassie said to her mother. "This is incredible!"

But Wiley shook his head. "Now you have a different kind of worry," he said. "Like how to invest it so it stays with you."

"Invest it?" Claire said. "We've hardly ever had enough to buy our food, let alone have enough to think about investing. I don't even know what an investment is!"

Wiley just chuckled. "I'll see you downstairs when you've gotten yourselves together a little bit," he said. "Remember, don't talk about this to anyone, or even about it at the table. We don't want anyone to know we're holding a bunch of money, okay?"

Claire looked up from her counting. "Don't you worry, we can keep our mouths shut," she said, "but I doubt if we can keep from showing how happy we are. Whoever sees us will just have to guess why."

Back in the restaurant, Wiley ordered more coffee and then turned to James.

"We're about twenty miles from Wallins Creek, less

than twenty miles from your home. Did you know that?"

"I knew we were getting close," he said, "but we usually didn't come down this way.

We usually needed a bigger town than Wallins Creek, so we went the other direction to a town called Baxter." He picked up his napkin and nervously pleated it between his fingers. He'd been gone from home for such a long time. And he was well aware of the toll the war had taken on so many people.

Lawrence nodded. "We used to go to Baxter too. That means it's going to be only a few more miles to my homestead once we've left your place."

"Since we're going to reach my place first," James said, "if it's still there, I'd like you all to stay the night."

Lawrence smiled. "It'll be nice to see your family again," he said. "Maybe they'll have some news about mine."

Ben set down his coffee cup and turned to James. "I think since we're kin, although distant, the rest of us would be glad to stay one night and meet your family before we head out to Lawrence's," he said.

In the meantime, the women had composed themselves. "This is the first time I'll be happy to look a little fat," Claire told Cassie, and they laughed together as she stuffed the big envelope inside her bodice and laced it up. As they came down the stairs, Wiley noted Claire seemed to have put on a little weight around her middle. They sat down at the table wearing beaming smiles. "Well, you ladies sure look happy this morning," Ben told them. "I guess you're looking forward to getting back on the road and seeing where James lives."

"Oh yes," Claire said, "we're really happy our journey

is getting close to being over. We'd like to meet some of his family and get to see where he lived before the war. And it'll be nice when we can stop riding in these wagons and start to live somewhere."

They had a hearty breakfast, and Wiley settled the hotel bill. They went back behind the hotel to the wagons and headed the horses down the road toward Wallins Creek.

If they had no more problems, they would reach James's home by around one o'clock in the afternoon. As they got closer, James grew quiet. He'd started recognizing the countryside, and his stomach was tossing butterflies. He very much hoped his family was still there.

Chapter 24

James's Homestead

They were passing through a large valley between two rows of mountains. Far off to the east, they could see the Cumberland Mountains, and to the north what were called the Pine Mountains. Finally, a little after noon, they came upon a two-track road leading off of the main road.

"This is it," James said. "This is the road to my place." They went about four miles, passing thickets of trees alternating with open grassy areas before they finally came to a gate. James led the way through, and after several hundred yards, they saw the place. There were some chickens out in front of the house scratching around in the earth and a dog, who came up to greet them, barking happily. James pulled his wagon to a halt and jumped down. He got to the front door in four or maybe five steps, then leaped onto the porch. As he was reaching for the door, someone inside pushed it open, and he froze.

A woman wearing an apron came out wiping her hands on a towel.

"What can I do for you folks?" she said. "You're a long ways from the main road."

Then, as she looked at the man standing before her, she blinked and looked closer.

"James?" she gasped. "James is that really you?" She couldn't believe her eyes.

"We thought you had been killed in the war," she said, as she stepped forward and reached for him, then wrapped her arms around him and held him tight against her. Tears began rolling down her cheeks. "I can't believe it's you!" she said, sobbing. "You're really here."

Her tears were soaking his shirt. "I never gave up hope," she said against his shoulder, "even though everyone said if you were still alive, you should've been home by now. I just felt in my heart that you weren't dead."

James hugged her just as tightly. "I'm sorry, Ma, for being so late getting here. There were some things we had to do, but I'm here now, and things are going to be great. And don't you worry, I won't be leaving again." A few tears trickled down his cheek as well.

"Where's Pa and Junior?" He finally managed, as he let go of her and stepped away.

"They're out in the field cutting hay; your sister is in Baxter, getting us some supplies. Who are these people?"

He gave her a big kiss. "I've been wanting to do that for a few years now," he said.

She smiled at him happily, still full of joy. "But who are these folks?" she asked, pointing to the group at the wagons.

"Oh, I'm sorry. Where's my manners?" he said. "These here men are kinfolk: we fought side by side in the war, an' we've traveled all the way back here together. These two ladies we met on the road traveling. They had the misfortune of running into a gang of robbers who killed the men in their family and stole everything they had. They were just plain lucky, or they'd be dead too." And he beckoned to the rest of the travelers.

"Come on down here, fellas and ladies, I want to introduce you to my Ma."

They all climbed down from the wagons and walked up to the porch but didn't go up the steps. The men stood next to each other and took their hats off and held them in front of their bodies.

Both women curtsied, and Claire said, "Pleased to meet you, ma'am. You have a very fine son."

James pointed to Lawrence. "You remember this feller," he said. She put her hand to her mouth, and more tears came to her eyes as she came down the steps and gave him a big hug, telling him how glad she was he'd made it back. Lawrence noticed she didn't mention anything about his family. James then introduced the others by name. Wiley and Ben told her they were on their way to their homes.

"Ma, I asked them if they would stay one night when we got to my place, so they could meet my family and I could show them our farm."

"By all means, you're more than welcome to stay as long as you like," his mother said.

"Is there room in the barn for our horses?" he said.

She shook her head. "Heavens no. You've got a whole herd there, but there's plenty of room in the corral and plenty of fresh hay in the barn. With this many horses, you're going to have to put some more water in the trough."

She then opened the door wide and said, "You ladies come inside while the men take care of your horses and wagons."

James's mother led the way inside. "Are you thirsty?" she said. "I just made some lemonade, if you'd like some."

"That would be just fine," Claire replied. "We are a little parched."

She settled them in the sitting room then brought out a tray with glasses and a pitcher of lemonade and poured them each a drink.

"I'm so sorry for you to have lost your menfolk," she told Claire. "Was it your husband and sons?"

Claire cast down her eyes. "Husband and one son. It's been a bad last few years. I thought everything was going to be okay once the war ended, even though our farm was taken over and burned. That's why we left it."

It was then she told her about the awful events that had happened on the road, including the way the McCoy men had tried to make things right. "Your son and these men are immensely brave— heroes to us and to a lot of other people. On the way here, we ran into a few bad situations with bad men." She went on to explain what had been happening on their journey.

James's mother was shocked as Cassie spoke, but when she had finished, she beamed with pride. "I knew we had raised him right, but I didn't realize we'd raised a hero too," she said.

As the men got the horses and wagons taken care of, James said, "You want to ride out to the hayfield? I can show you some of the ranch at the same time."

"Sure, why not?" Wiley said. "There's plenty of time left before the sun goes down." So, they went to the house to tell the women what they were going to do, then rode out to find his Pa and brother. When they got to the hayfield, James spurred his horse toward the pair working there. His Pa and brother stopped what they were doing to see who the rider was.

When James got within about ten yards of them, he pulled his horse to a stop, jumped off and exclaimed, "Hey, Pa, I made it home!"

At first his father couldn't believe his eyes. When he was sure, he dropped his pitchfork and ran toward his son. They gave each other a long hug. James pulled away from him and turned to his brother. "Hi, Junior, I bet you didn't think you'd see me today," he said.

Junior dropped his pitchfork, and James released his father and embraced his brother.

"Well, I'll be danged!" his father said. His voice held a slight tremble. "We thought you'd been killed in the war and we just never got notified." He paused and blinked hard a few times. Then he hunted in his pockets for a handkerchief. "Sure is good to see you," he said, after wiping his eyes and forehead with it. "Have you seen your Ma yet? She'll be tickled pink!"

"Yeah, Pa, we stopped at the house first," James said. "I thought I'd show our kinfolk around the ranch, since I was coming out to see you."

James pointed at each man as he introduced Wiley, Lawrence, and Ben. "I worked with these fellers for a while on a ranch right after the war, till we all decided we wanted to go home," he said, adding, "Or at least see if there was a home to go to. We've been on the road more than a month, and they still have probably another ten days or more before they get to their places. They're going to stay the night here and get started again tomorrow morning."

"Sure, you're more than welcome to stay as long as you want, and thank you for bringing my boy home," his pa said.

"Aw, Pa, we brought each other all the way here," James replied. "We wouldn't have made it without them, or rather without us sticking together." His father gave him a curious look. Wiley cleared his throat to speak.

"You want us to help with that hay?" he said.

"Thank you, but we got most of it done already, and I only brought out two pitchforks anyway," James's pa replied. "Besides, I wouldn't think of having guests work my field on the first day they got here. Anyway, James here wants to show you around the ranch, so by the time he's done with that, we should be back at the house. We'll see you there later, but thanks for the offer."

James hugged his father and brother again. "I'm here to stay," he said, "and I got a surprise for all of you. We're gonna go for a ride, but we'll see you back at the house later." Then he climbed up on his horse and said, "Follow me, gents."

He started out at a trot, then let his horse move into a canter as the others came up alongside. "We'll go to the southernmost end," he told them, "then work our way back around. It's not a huge place, but it's enough for us." He was beaming with pride as they rode, so happy to finally be back home.

It took them a couple of hours to go around the whole place. James's father and brother were already at the house when they got back. Everyone was sitting on the porch waiting for them to come back.

Extra chairs had been put on the front porch to accommodate everyone. James took a seat and smiled at his father. "The place looks just like I remember it, except you're only growing something in a couple of fields. What happened to all the cattle?"

His pa's expression turned sober. "The North had a lot of soldiers to feed, and they kept coming back here until they had left us with only one plow horse and two riding horses. We're lucky they left us that. We can't do much work with just one plow horse. I suppose I'm lucky they didn't shoot me. If I didn't have this bad leg, I would have been fighting for the South, and they knew it."

He shook his head. "I don't know how long it's going to take us just to get back where we were, having a horse for everyone an' close to forty head of cattle. We only got four hogs right now because we butchered one a week or so back. We planted hay, so we could feed the animals we have left, hoping to sell any extra and buy some more animals, but a lot of other people are in the same situation as us—hardly any livestock—and they're mostly growing their own too, so the price for hay has dropped. I suppose I wasn't too smart about planting something we could sell."

James gave a quick glance at the other men. He wanted to just blurt out that he had enough money to do anything they wanted and was about to when he saw Wiley's face.

Wiley frowned and shook his head just slightly, letting him know not to say anything just yet, so with effort, he kept the news to himself.

His mother stood up. "Your pa shot a nice deer the other day, and I made a big batch of venison stew; it's ready, if any of you all are hungry," she said.

"I think we're all hungry," said James. "My belly has

been talking to me since we left Pa in the pasture."

"Well then, let's all go inside," she said, "and bring in those extra chairs so you all will have a seat; the ladies and I will get to dishing up that stew."

At dinner, they talked about how a lot of nearby ranches had been burned down and destroyed. James's father told them, "Many of our neighbors left because the soldiers were killing every male over the age of thirteen. And then they burned their farms and pillaged everything."

His mother added, "Most of our neighbors, even the ones living far away, suffered their wrath. Junior was lucky. He was only nine years old, and not a threat to pick up a gun. If his father wasn't so old and had that bum leg, they would've killed him too. We were lucky they left us with the house intact, and with anything at all."

James noticed that as she spoke, she seemed to purposefully turn her eyes from Lawrence.

After dinner, Wiley asked James to come with him to the wagons, so he could decide what of their supplies they could leave with James for his family.

As they stood near the wagons, Wiley said, "Don't say anything about the gold until we've left, and don't say that we have any gold in our wagons when you do." James nodded. "And don't go spending any gold pieces," Wiley added. "Try to melt it down and go file a mining claim on land somewhere close by that might have some gold or silver in the ground before you bring anything to the assayer's office."

James nodded. He knew how important it was to listen to Wiley's advice.

"You don't want anyone to know you filed a claim either, if it can be helped," Wiley said. "You should melt it all down and hide it somewhere around your house, and just take a little at a time to the assayer's office, so that things look normal."

"I think I know just the area that would be good to file a claim on," James told him. "I'll wait a week or so before I do anything, and when I do spend some money, I'll tell everyone that it came from the bounty we got for those outlaws we killed. I'll tell them we divided it up between us."

"That's a fine idea," Wiley said.

"I'm sure word will get around that I was part of the group that brought them in," James said. "I thought I recognized some folks in the last town that were gawking at us when we came in with all those bodies."

"Sounds like a plan," Wiley told him. "Let's get this stuff organized. You decide what you want to keep, and I'll see what else we can leave with you. We'll make do with whatever is left for us."

It didn't take long for them to get things ready to leave in the morning. When they returned to the house, the chairs were back out on the porch, and everyone was sitting there having a piece of peach pie made from the peaches grown on the farm.

"This is so good," James told his ma as he tasted his piece. "I've been thinking about your peach pie for a long time!"

His ma smiled at him, and then turned to the rest of the group. "You can put your bed rolls on the floor around the fireplace in the sitting room, so you won't have to sleep outside," she said.

When it was time for bed, Wiley, Ben, and Lawrence went out to the wagons to get bed rolls and a couple of cots for Claire and Cassie. The space was a bit crowded, but they all found room to sleep comfortably. James went upstairs to his old bedroom and had the best sleep he'd had in years.

The next morning, the men woke early and went to the barn to prepare the horses and wagons for leaving. When they got back to the house there was a big breakfast ready for them.

James's ma had cooked ham steaks, eggs, potatoes, and fresh biscuits for everyone. "You all need a good breakfast before you get back on the road again," she told them, "and thank you again for bringing my son back to me."

They said their goodbyes and headed back down the two-track road that would take them to the main road, and on to Lawrence's place.

CHAPTER 25

LAWRENCE'S HEARTBREAK

They had been traveling about four hours when Lawrence recognized a road he thought was the one that would take them to his family's farm.

It was also a two-track road, only it had been overgrown by grass. That wasn't a good sign; nonetheless, he was sure it was the right road.

They had been on it for a couple of miles when he told them his house should be just over the rise. When they got to the top, he stopped his wagon and just stared at the sight before him.

He could see a chimney, three burned up walls around it. Over to the side of it was a pile of charred wood that had been the barn. The corral and fencing had been mostly destroyed, and someone had even caved in the wall around the well.

Tears welled up in his eyes. He couldn't believe what he was seeing. Cassie reached over and put her hand on his hands. "Are you sure this is your place?" she said in a low voice.

He looked at her, and tears started running down his cheeks. "It used to be my home," he said.

The condition of the farm was devastating to the others as well. Lawrence seemed to be in shock but managed to get his horse moving again, and the group followed him toward what was left of the house.

He got down from the wagon and looked all around; on the ground were the charred remains of family possessions he remembered. He walked out behind the house but didn't find anything that hadn't been destroyed or burned. He went toward the burned barn and sat on the edge of a water trough with holes shot through it. He took off his hat and held it in his hands and just started crying. All he had been hoping to see when he got there was destroyed. Cassie sat down beside him. She put her arm around his shoulders and clasped him to her chest as he cried. She had no words that would help comfort him, so she just held him and let him get it out.

The men stayed out in front of the house with Claire. They all felt terribly bad for Lawrence and wished there was something they could do.

As they realized this devastation was something they could all be facing, the horror of Lawrence's loss struck home.

"I know what he feels like, seeing his dreams shattered," Claire said. "I lost my home first, before I lost my family." She gave a long sigh. "After traveling so long thinking the whole time about how things would be when he got back, this has to hurt something terrible."

After about half an hour, Cassie got Lawrence to stand up. She put his arm around her shoulders, and she put hers around his waist and started to walk him around the place. As he looked at the horrible sight they were taking in, his mind kept trying to refuse what his eyes were showing him.

When they had gone around the whole place, he stopped and pulled her to him, wrapping his arms around her. "It's gone. It's all gone. They're gone," he said, weeping onto her shoulder. After a few more minutes, she was able to get him to walk back to the wagons.

He couldn't look at the others because of the hurt in his heart and was embarrassed that he was crying like a baby. When they climbed up on the wagon, Cassie took the reins. She directed the horses back down the road they came in on as he leaned against her, still crying.

The others followed. Their pace was as slow as a funeral procession, and no one said anything for a long time. When they reached the main road, they turned east.

After a couple of hours, Lawrence looked at Cassie. His tears had dried streaks down his face, and his mouth was shaking as he tried to talk. "That damned war took my home and my family," he managed to say.

She looked back at him, trying desperately to think of something positive to offer him. "I know how you feel," she finally said. "I've felt the way you're feeling myself. We're in the same boat; we both lost everything we had and those we loved." She sighed heavily and took his hand in hers. "You still have all of us," she said, "and we're a family, at least I feel like we are. And we're going to make up for all the bad things that have happened to us. We'll find us a good life somewhere new, somewhere where we can make a fresh start and be happy once again. I'm here for you and plan to stay. That is, if you can see your future with me."

When she said that, he felt his heart stitching itself

back together. Still, he laid his head on her lap and cried some more. When he managed to stop, he said, "I'll thank God every day I'm with you."

Then he slept, lulled by the motion of the wagon, completely drained emotionally and physically. After a couple hours Wiley found a nice place to make a camp, so they stopped. The others got busy making the campsite, and Cassie and Lawrence went on a walk together down by the stream that bordered the site.

When they came back to the campsite, Lawrence had recovered some, but they could see the heartache on his face. "Well," he said slowly, "I've lost what I've been dreaming about coming back to, but I still have a good family in all of you. I think God brought us together because he knew we were going to need each other in a lot of ways." At those words, he turned to face Wiley.

"If you don't mind," he said, "I'd like to go with you to your place and help you out there."

As Wiley looked at him standing there, suffering but trying to be strong, he remembered the pain he'd felt when he lost his wife. "Sure thing. I can use all the help I can get," he said, "and I'll help you get yourself a place going when you're ready." He wanted to make some gesture of support and comfort, so he stepped forward and put a hand on his shoulder. "Don't worry," he said. "Family takes care of each other."

CHAPTER 26

JAMES'S MELTDOWN

After his kinfolk and traveling companions had left, James asked his brother and father to help him unload his wagon. He couldn't wait to show off what he'd brought with him. They pulled the wagon by hand over to the front porch, then took off the canvas cover and started stacking the items on the porch.

He had lots of new tools for construction, a couple of sacks of grain, and seed for planting.

He also had a couple of barrels of flour and cornmeal, along with some smoked beef and venison. He still had his two dozen eggs they had gotten from the last town, a barrel of oil, a small barrel of molasses, four good ropes, and the smelting equipment, which his pa eyed curiously.

Next, he pulled out all the new carbine rifles and six-shot Colt pistols, with several of the quick-reload cylinders. He had several hundred rounds for each type of gun.

When they got to the end of the wagon, there were three crates of blankets with his tents on top to take off before he could get to what he was really after. He knew he was supposed to wait a while to spend the gold, according to Wiley, but he had to at least show them the biggest surprise of all. As he uncovered the strongboxes, he told his pa, "I'll need your help with these. I can't lift them by myself." They dragged all three of them to the edge of the wagon and he told Junior to help hold the end of the box they slid off first, while he climbed down and grabbed the other handle.

"On the count of three," he said, "I'm going to pull this end off the wagon, so be ready because it's going to be real heavy."

At three, he slid the box and all of them groaned under its weight. They dropped it to the ground, but it didn't hit hard.

His pa and Junior were taken by surprise by its weight. "What the heck is in there that's so dang heavy?" his pa asked.

"Let's just get them up on the porch. Then I'll show you," James said.

They got all three boxes up on the porch and he called to his ma, who had started putting away some of the food, to come out so he could show her the surprise he brought home.

He still had his keys on his belt, so he took them off of it and unlocked one of the boxes, but before he opened it, he turned to his family and said, "Now don't worry. I got all of this from the Northern army, who got it from raiding the plantations, homes, and ranches of Southern families." They looked back at him, puzzled.

"You've heard of the Red Legs and the other Northern army groups that were killing and robbing all along the Missouri border?" James said. "Well, they were supposed to have given this to their commanders to finance their war. We found out, and by we, I mean there were twenty-two of us McCoys who formed a unit together after the South surrendered." He told them all about the stockpiles of goods, the letter that gave the information about them, and the raids.

When James was finished, he turned to his mother and looked her in the eye. "We even gave back more than half of everything we found to a mayor and a pastor, to distribute back to those who could show the property was theirs, and to help the families that had lost everything to get back on their feet," he said.

"We ended up with three of these boxes for each man, and we never killed anyone doing it. So, what we really did was take back what those soldiers planned to steal from their own army, which rightfully belonged to Southern people." He opened the box and revealed the bags of fifty-dollar gold pieces. The ends were tied, so he hefted one out and opened it. He dumped a few coins on the porch and left the bag sitting there, open.

His mother put her hand over her mouth. "My God, what have you got there?" she said.

"We're never going to need for anything we can buy, Ma," he said. "These here are all fifty-dollar gold pieces."

His pa put his hand in the open bag and stirred around the coins. "There's a fortune here in just this one bag," he said. He quickly pulled his hand out as the reality struck him. "If we spend these, someone will hear about it, and the government will come here and arrest us," he said.

James picked up the smelting equipment and dropped it in front of them. "We can't spend it the way it is," he said, "but we can sure file a mining claim, melt it down, and pour it over sand and rocks and pebbles, to make it look like it came from a mine. Then we can spend it, sure as fact. We'll have it assayed and put it in the bank to use however we want."

"We'll create a gold rush here in Kentucky," his pa said.

James replied, "Well, hopefully, before that happens, we'll get all of this into a bank. The bank will send it east to their main offices. They'll give us what's called a line of credit for its value, to draw on for whatever we need. We just have to try and get it all assayed before anyone knows we found gold. With the first batch we take in, we need to buy up as much land around us as we can, so we don't get overrun with prospectors when the word does get out."

His father looked thoughtful. He was pondering James's plan.

"What we need to do now is get this inside the house and go down to the stream on the backside of the property and haul back some dirt from there and make it look like we've been mining it," James said.

"We need to set up a mining camp at the stream, so if someone does want to come see where it is, someone from the state I mean, it will look like we found it all in one area, and the vein just ran out. After we've taken it all in to the bank, of course."

His pa said, "You know, it just might work. But we need to do this quickly before anyone comes out here and finds any coins. I've done a little prospecting, so I know how to set up a mining camp on a stream, but I've never made a claim because I never found enough of anything worth filing on. We better get these inside and get started right away."

Once they had everything off of the porch, they got the wood and buckets and the other items they would need to set up a camp and a sluice box. They loaded everything in the wagon and took it out to the stream.

Together, they built everything they needed. Then they started to run the sluice box, putting the dirt that was coming out of it into buckets to take back to the house. They had five buckets of dirt ready by the end of the day. The next morning, they started to melt down the coins. It was a slow process, because they needed a lot of heat in the kiln to melt the gold. Then a film of some kind rose on top of it when it melted that they had to skim off. Once skimmed, though, the liquid gold poured easily into the dirt they had brought, and as they stirred, it cooled and stuck to the pebbles and clumped up into nuggets.

It took almost three days working like this to do one box of coins. James and his father went into town to take their handiwork to the assayer's office. The first thing they did was go into the City Hall and file their mining claim, which was on their property, so they didn't have to worry about someone trying to take it away.

Then they went to the assayer's office. When they brought the gold inside, they had it packed in fifteen burlap bags. The assayer looked at them, puzzled, and James's pa told him, "You have to keep this quiet. We don't want to create any craziness with people getting gold fever. You can't tell anyone about what I'm about to show you." He stuck his hand in the bag and pulled out some nuggets and small pieces of rock with gold attached.

The man's eyes got real big. "That's gold," he said. "Where'd you find it?"

"Don't you worry about where I found it. I've already filed a claim. What I want to know is how much is it worth?"

The man looked it over and said, "Well, it seems this stuff needs to get cleaned up. The gold needs to get separated from the rocks and dirt better than what you've done here, although, there appears to be some solid nuggets as well."

James shifted from one foot to the other. He had to stifle his excitement, and it wasn't easy.

"I can only give you an estimate because I can't really judge the weight of it, with all that rock and dirt in there," the man said. "You need to smash these rocks and separate the gold for me to give you an accurate value."

"Okay," James's pa said, "so we still need to do some work on it, but how much do you think it might be worth?"

The man pulled out a tray from his back office and told him to dump one bag in it. He looked at it and moved it around, trying to get an idea of the concentration of gold. "I'd say somewhere around ten thousand dollars' worth in this tray," he said at last.

James and his pa exchanged a look. "If you'd like, I can clean this up for you, for a fee of course," the assessor said. "Then all you'll have to do is bring me what you find the way it is. If you'd wish, you can stay here while I clean up this first bag. It will show us how much each bag will be worth. That's if they're all about the same."

"Yeah, they are," James's pa said. "Okay, I'll stay here and watch what you do, and we'll see how much we have."

"It's going to take me quite a while to do this, so you

might want to go get a room in the hotel. If you want to stay until it's all done, it's probably going to take a week to get all fifteen bags cleaned and a precise amount put on it. Then you'll need to get it over to the bank."

James's pa nodded, then turned to his son. "You stay here while I go over to the hotel and get a room," he said. "Then you need to go back home and tell your ma how long I'm going to be here in town. You need to bring in whatever else you find in the next week."

They watched together as the man separated the gold from the dirt and rocks. Several hours later, the assayer finished the first bag and gave James's father his note for the value, and he took it to the bank. When he got back, he told James that he had best be headed home.

Back home, James told his ma how things had gone in town.

"I need to take another load into town at the end of the week," he said, "and that means that Pa is going to be in town for a few weeks to keep an eye on everything and deposit it all in an account with the bank in Boston."

Working day and night, James spent the next eight days getting the rest of the gold ready. When he was finished, he and his mother, brother, and sister went to town together.

They found his father at the hotel. "When the assayer finished cleaning up the first load," he said, "turns out there was about twelve thousand dollars' worth of gold in each bag, after paying his fee." And he shook his head in disbelief. He also showed them a deed to thirty thousand acres of the land that surrounded their property. He rented three rooms in the hotel, so the boys would have a separate room from their sister, and the family stayed in town till the gold had all been processed and put in the bank.

"It seems that vein of gold we found is drying up," James told the assayer, when he was finished. "I haven't found any in the last couple of days before we came to town."

By the time they were ready to return home, they had hired a large group of ranch hands, bought several wagons, and filled them with building supplies and fencing. They also bought a thousand head of cattle to be brought to the ranch by a livestock broker, who also sold them a hundred hogs and fifty horses to be delivered by springtime.

CHAPTER 27

ON TO PIKEVILLE

As James was getting his gold into the bank, the others were still traveling. Their pace had gotten a lot slower, as they had reached more mountainous country. The trip they thought was going to take eight to ten days was looking more like two to three weeks.

Lawrence was very depressed and really didn't have his heart into traveling or any enthusiasm for their destination. Cassie kept trying to cheer him up and coax him to look ahead in his life—to the life they were going to have together—but he couldn't shake his sadness.

On about the seventh day, they ran out of meat, and Wiley asked him if he wanted to go with him to see if they could find some game. Wiley was hoping it might help him get his mind off the ruins of his home. Lawrence agreed without any enthusiasm to go along and help.

Once they got out of sight of the campsite, Wiley started talking to him. "It's strange about how life does some mean things to good people who don't deserve it," he said. "I never told you this, but for a couple years, I felt the same way you do right now. I couldn't get over how the Lord could take away the only woman I ever loved, and with her, he took my dreams. I still had my family close by, but I lost my will to look to the future and any desire to do what my wife and I had planned. It wasn't only my dream, it was our dream, and since there was no longer an 'us', what was the sense in it? I just couldn't get any pleasure to continue building what we had worked for together." Lawrence just rode along mutely. Wiley couldn't tell if he was even listening, but he kept talking anyway.

"Then I lost my pa, and my ma moved into town because she couldn't take care of their place by herself. I was so depressed, I didn't even offer for my mother to come and live with me. She moved in with her sister and her husband instead." Lawrence rubbed his hand over his face, leaving a track of dirt, as he sighed.

"What I can tell you," Wiley said, "is that even though your family isn't there anymore, that's not what your future is about. Your future involves creating a life for yourself, and if you find you want a family, creating a way for them to have a better life than what you've had.

"You wouldn't have lived with Cassie in the same house with your parents, would you?" he said. "You would have got your own place and tried to fulfill the dreams the two of you have together, am I right?"

Lawrence nodded.

"I know it's hard right now," Wiley continued, "because of how you were thinking you were going to help your folks have a good life. Thing is, you also had to have thought about the life you want to have with Cassie."

Slowly, Lawrence nodded again.

"You can't do anything about what happened, but you can do something about what's going to happen with you and Cassie," Wiley said. "You need to start putting your thoughts toward making your own family with her, and the life you want to have together."

Wiley paused to let his words sink in a bit. "Cassie is a fine girl," he said after a few minutes, "and her mother raised her right. She needs to see a little sign of hope from you, that you're still thinking about the two of you. If you love her and still want to make a life with her, you need to let her know." A tear trickled through the dirt on Lawrence's cheek. Wiley ignored it.

"The best way I can tell you to help you get over your disappointment," he said, "is to let yourself dream about the life you want to have with her. The only way to put something behind you is to look to the future. Count your blessings. Don't count your losses."

Lawrence made a gulping noise and rubbed at his nose. And he nodded.

"Good," Wiley said. "Now, make yourself useful for a change and get up on that ridge over there. I'll go up on the one in front of us, and let's see if we can't find something to eat besides smoked meat and vegetables."

And he left Lawrence alone with his thoughts.

He had listened intently to Wiley's words; as he headed toward the ridgeline, he thought about them over and over.

The ridgeline was high enough that he could look out for a long distance. Standing there on his horse, he felt a shivering sensation go through him, as if God was showing him that grand view of the countryside so he would see that there still was a lot more out there, and all he had to do was put himself in it.

His grief had made him become distant in the last few days, he realized, and he didn't want Cassie to think she wasn't important to him anymore. He made up his mind to show her how much he really wanted and needed her.

He also wanted to show her that even if they had nothing, he could provide for her. He started doing what he liked to do best, looking for tracks and scanning the hillsides to find food.

They had been hunting for an hour or so when he saw some movement down the hill from him. He got off his horse and stealthily made his way toward the movement, then hid and waited. It took about ten minutes before he saw it again.

Wiley, up on the other ridge, had been keeping an eye on him. When he saw him get off his horse, he knew he had seen something, and he positioned himself directly across the little valley from him.

He started looking around to see what Lawrence had noticed and spotted two deer, directly below Lawrence, a couple hundred yards away.

Then he saw something else move, and this time below his own spot. Holding still, he saw a group of turkeys making their way down the middle of the little valley.

He looked back toward the deer and saw they were going to be coming clear of the brush blocking Lawrence's view. He knew that the shot would be an easy one for Lawrence, so he concentrated on getting a shot at the birds.

When Lawrence fired at the deer, the birds spooked and started running. Two of them headed up the hillside toward Wiley. Wiley saw that they were heading to a place where the brush thinned out and got ready for them. But the birds stopped in the thicker cover. They seemed to look around, trying to decide if it was safe for them to walk out. When they finally started moving again, they were side by side, a couple of feet apart, and directly in line for Wiley to shoot.

After they had taken a few steps, they stopped and looked around once more. Wiley knew if he shot the one closest to him in a soft spot, the bullet would go through and hit the other one.

Wouldn't that be great, to get two birds with one shot! He took careful aim at the bottom of the neck of the closest bird, which lined up with the chest on the second bird.

That's when he fired. When he saw the two birds flopping around, wings flailing, knew he had done it. He took his horse to the birds, picked them up, tied their feet together with a short piece of leather, and threw them over the back of his saddle horn. He made his way to where he thought the deer should be below him and headed down the hillside. He was about halfway down when he saw Lawrence standing over one of the deer.

He stopped his horse a few feet from Lawrence and the deer. "That's a nice neck shot you made," he told Lawrence. "Didn't ruin hardly any meat. Good work!"

Lawrence had heard one shot from the other side of the little valley and saw that Wiley had two birds hanging from his saddle horn. He couldn't help himself and cracked the first big smile his face had worn in days.

"I know I only heard one shot from the ridge. Here I thought I had made a good shot. You got both birds with one! It never fails, you always manage to shoot just a little better than I do."

Wiley laughed. "I was just lucky, that's all," he said. "They lined up together and stopped. I couldn't have asked them to give me a better chance. Now, let's get that buck dressed out and hauled back to camp."

They both took out their knives and went to work. They decided to wait till they got back to camp to do the turkeys, so they could save the liver, gizzards, and hearts, in case anyone liked those parts.

They both came back to the camp smiling. It was clear to everyone that Lawrence's spirit had lifted quite a bit. The hunters got off their horses, and Wiley handed the birds to Ben.

"If you want me to save the gizzards, hearts, and livers," Ben said to Claire, "I'm going to clean them up now. Speak now or forever hold your peace."

She gave him a teasing grin. "You're not going to marry them, are you?" she said. "Anyway, whatever you do, if you can save them I'd like them. I think they're quite tasty."

Lawrence was untying the deer he had behind his saddle, and Ben helped him pull it off the horse.

"Looks like you did Wiley one better this time," Ben said

Lawrence had to laugh. "Yeah, I thought I did, but turns out he still managed to shoot better than me. He got both those birds with one shot! At least I can say I brought back more meat this time."

They dragged the buck to a tree, where they hung it by its legs. Ben told Lawrence to tend to his horse, and he would start skinning it.

The sun was starting to go down, and they had a fire going by the time the animals were ready to be stored or cooked.

"Will you go for a walk with me?" Lawrence asked Cassie.

"Of course," she said. "It's been a while since we've had a walk together." She grabbed his arm and started walking with him.

After a few minutes Lawrence said, "I'm sorry for the way I've been acting lately." Cassie just squeezed his arm as a reply.

He stopped walking and turned to face her. "Would you really like to have a life with me, wherever we end up?" he said. Tears were beginning to squeeze from his eyes.

She took both his hands and looked into his eyes. "Why, Lawrence, is this a proposal?" she said. "Are you asking me to marry you?"

Suddenly he was embarrassed. Blushing, he said, "Well, I hadn't thought I was asking you to get married. I was just hoping you'd tell me you still wanted to see if you and I would be good together as a couple. But, now that I think about what I said, I guess it's the same thing. So yes. Would you like to be my wife? I do love you. I just don't know for sure how you feel about me."

She smiled at him and squeezed his hands. "I think I love you too, although I've never really been in love before," she said. "My heart sure did start pounding hard and fast in my chest hearing you ask me what you did. Now, I'm feeling all giddy inside and very happy."

He pulled her into his arms. After a while, she pulled away.

"There's only one problem," she said. "I know my mother will say I'm still young and don't really know you. So, let's just say for the moment that I would love to become your wife. Let's find out where we're going to live and if we enjoy living near each other, which is a lot different than just traveling together."

He felt really good inside upon hearing her words, because they meant she felt about him the same way he felt about her. She wondered the same things too, about whether they could be good together as a couple. He was sure of one thing, though. He would like to try.

They walked a little more and talked about what kind of family they would like to have and the kind of house they would turn into a home for their family.

They came back in the camp with their elbows wrapped together, and everyone could see they were both very happy and content. The sight made Claire feel good inside.

She could see the light as back in his eyes. She could also tell that Cassie had an extra sparkle in her eyes. They looked to her like two people beginning to fall in love.

The sight made her feel good, but also a little sad, because it reminded her of her husband and son. She decided she had to stop thinking about the past before she started tearing up in front of everyone, so she turned away and started making herself busy with dinner.

• • •

It took another five days before they were close to Wiley's home. As they took a turn off the main road, he told them, "From here, it should be about three miles before we get to my place. Some of my kinfolk were my closest neighbors, but they're still at least a mile down from my place and about a half a mile off this road."

They arrived at an open gate. Grass had grown up through it. "This here's the way in," Wiley said. "Let's go see what's there."

After a quarter mile, they came to an area that had been cleared of trees, with tall grass growing all around. They could see looked like a small house in the distance. As they drew closer, they saw that the house was covered in vines to the point of being almost buried. They stopped the wagons in front of it, and Wiley climbed down from his wagon. When he stepped onto the porch, his foot went through the wood almost to his knee.

He turned toward the others, grinning and a little embarrassed, but not hurt. He pulled his foot out of the wood, got to the door without falling through again, pulled the door open, and walked inside.

He looked around and saw dirt, dust, and plants that had found ways to get through the wooden walls and floor. The forest was starting to reclaim the inside of the house as well as the outside. He also saw where some small animals had left evidence of making their homes inside his.

He went back outside. "It would be safer if we camped outside," he told everyone. "It looks like the woods have reclaimed my house." They laughed, and Ben said, "That's okay. We're kinda used to sleeping outside by now."

Claire said, "I'd still like to see how you had the inside of your house. I realize it's not the way it was when you lived here, but I'd like to get an idea of what you thought was comfortable."

She got off the wagon and went to the front door, careful of the hole he had made in the porch and walked into the house. Despite the dirt and decay, she could tell it had once been a comfortable place to live for a couple just starting out.

She felt tears coming because she knew the memories that this place would bring to him. She wiped her eyes and went back outside.

She walked up to Wiley and gave him a big hug. "I was hoping we were going to build our own house anyway," she said. "I think it would almost be as much work to fix this one back up as it would be to build a new one. What do you think?"

He laughed. "I don't think we need to try to do something with this. There are too many surprises that will pop up, or maybe I should say, that we'd fall into." He pointed at the hole in the porch.

He turned to the others. "We don't have to stay here tonight. There's enough daylight left that we can make it to Beaver Bottom and sleep in a bed, if y'all want to. I know I'd like to for a change."

"I'd sure like to go see what Beaver Bottom looks like now," Ben said. "I figure the town would put us about eight miles from my house. We can go to the house tomorrow morning. I have some friends in Beaver Bottom, and so do you, Wiley, or at least we used to have, and it would be nice to see some of them, don't you think?"

Wiley nodded. "Well, what are we waiting for? We're burning daylight!" he exclaimed, helping Claire climb back up on the wagon before climbing up himself. He turned his wagon around and headed out the way they had come.

They made it to Beaver Bottom in about three hours and still had an hour or so of daylight left. Both Wiley and Ben used to know the owner of the livery, but the man they found was not the same man who had been there before.

But inside the hotel, they were glad to see Ole Walter McGee sitting at the front desk. He had been too aged to go off to fight the war. He was looking at the hotel register when they came in, and when he looked up, he saw Ben and Wiley standing there, holding their hats.

They could see by the way Ole Walter was looking at them that he'd found them familiar.

As he recognized them, they saw his eyes get wide and his face light up with a big smile. "You're the McCoys, aren't you?" he said. "We haven't heard anything for so long, so we thought you might've become some of the casualties of the war."

He walked out around the desk and shook their hands. "I'm sure glad you're still alive," he said. "Most of the men who made it back home were either wounded in a bad way or so scrawny, it's took them months to get back their former selves. But the two of you look real nice and healthy." He stepped forward and gave each one of them a hug and clapped them on the back as he did so.

"So, are you going to be staying in town?" he asked.

"For a day or so," Wiley answered. "We're going to Ben's place in the morning, but we thought we'd stay the night here, if you've got a room."

The man's expression turned to surprise. "If I was full, I'd find a way to make some rooms empty!" he said. "I'd send whoever was in them down the street to the other hotel. How many do you need?

"Three would be fine, and we'd like hot baths for all of us, if that's okay?"

Ole Walter said it wouldn't be a problem, then said, "Have you seen the Mrs. yet? She's in the kitchen getting dinner ready for our guests. Come on over and let me get her out here."

Ben and Wiley followed him to the door of the restaurant kitchen and waited for him. They could hear her complaining that she didn't have time for him to bother her as she was in the middle of cooking.

"Just come on. I have a surprise for you," he told her. He opened the door for her, and as she stepped through it, she saw Ben and Wiley. Her jaw dropped open. "Oh, my Lord, is it really you?" she said. "It's been so long, I thought we'd never see you again."

They still had their hats in their hands. "It's a pleasure to see you again, Mrs. McGee," Wiley said.

She had tears of joy in her eyes and a smile as big as her face could stretch and gave them each a hug and a kiss on the cheek. "You are going to stay with us for a little while, aren't you?" she said.

Without giving them a chance to respond, she added, "Well, of course you are. I won't take no for an answer, and don't you worry if you haven't got any money. We'll take care of you."

She then wrinkled her nose. "But I would like you to get a bath before you come down to supper. You've been traveling for quite a spell, haven't you?" She laughed.

"Speaking of supper, if I don't get in there quick, it's only going to be charcoal for dinner. I'll see you once you've freshened up." She hugged them once again and hurried back into the kitchen.

Mr. McGee called over a couple of bellboys and asked them to show everyone to their rooms.

After their baths, they all met downstairs in fresh, clean clothes, and went into the restaurant, where Mrs. McGee was seating people for dinner.

She hurried over and said, "Don't you all look nice. I didn't realize you had other people with you earlier; Walter told me about them after you'd gone to your rooms."

Ben told her not to worry and introduced the two women and Lawrence, and they all shook hands. Mrs. McGee leaned close to Ben, gave a sniff and said, "You smell good now, an' I bet you feel better too." Beckoning to the group, she said, "Follow me, I've been saving these two tables for you. Just have a seat, and I'll start bringing out your dinner."

When they all were seated, Ben leaned back in the chair and looked around the room. "Sure feels good to be back where someone knows us," he said. "I remember coming into town to this here hotel restaurant all throughout the years we lived here. And I remember everybody helping out their neighbors whenever they needed a hand with whatever they needed help with. I can remember helping build a few houses and harvesting hay, and even putting up some barns. I'm sure you remember helping out on a few of those places too, huh Wiley?"

"Yeah," Wiley said. "We'd come down and stay a week or more a few times, helping get things done. The people around here are good folks. They don't expect to be paid if they help you, and everyone pitches in to do whatever they can."

A man walked over to their table. Ben and Wiley stood as they saw him approach. "Hey there, Sheriff," Wiley said. The man smiled. "It's nice to have you back," he said. "Word gets around here quick." He winked. As they shook hands, the sheriff added, "I was over in the telegraph office the other day and a wire came in addressed to Wiley or Ben McCoy. I thought to myself, that's strange, they haven't been here in years, why would someone send them a wire?

Anyway, I brought it over to you. It seems it's from a James McCoy. Must be some kinfolk of yours." And he handed them the telegram. "Longest wire I've ever seen. Well, I'll leave you all to your dinner. I'm hungry myself. It's good to see you again."

The sheriff went over a table by the window, which was, Wiley remembered, the place he and his deputies always got their meals. It was nice to see that the war hadn't changed everything.

Mrs. McGee brought over some coffee while Wiley opened James's telegram. He read it first himself, and then out loud to the others:

I hope when you get this, everything is okay. Things couldn't be better here. Do you remember that bullet-making equipment we bought on the trail? We ran out of bullets here, and so we tried it. It works great.

A couple of days after you left, I went to the stream on our property and dug around in the silt and sand. Guess what? I found gold, and a lot of it! We made a claim and dug until we didn't find any more. We took all the gold dirt into the assayer's office in town. He cleaned it up for us and sent it to a bank in Boston, so it would be safe. They gave us a line of credit at the bank for the value of our gold.

We have just started building us new houses and have bought thirty thousand acres around the place and are going to have it filled it with livestock come springtime.

Yesterday, we were visited by some Pinkertons investigating gold stolen in Missouri. They had gotten Wiley's name from a sheriff in Missouri. They said they had been following a trail of someone spending fifty-dollar gold pieces. The trail had last been traced to Middlesboro. The hotel there told them we had spent a fifty-dollar gold piece, so he came out to see me and find out where we had gotten it from.

I told him how we worked on a ranch in Kansas for a few months after the war, and that's how we got paid. That we put together our money, so we could make the trip back home. That the money we had had come from one of our kinfolks, his girlfriend's father to be exact, from the sale of his former ranch, and that it was his place we worked on.

He wanted to know where the rest of the group I was with went to. I told him Pike County was where you were from, but I didn't exactly know where.

They were real suspicious of us, because we've gotten rich all of a sudden, but they couldn't hold anything against us because we had found our gold in the ground and had our mining claim. The assayer vouched for us, telling them that he had even cleaned the gold up for us, so that the bank in town could send it to Boston. The gold was probably already there in the bank in Boston.

The Pinkertons were headed to Pike County when they left, the same day I'm sending this telegram. If you need anything or any money, let us know. We've got plenty we can help you out with.

When Wiley finished reading, he looked up at the others and smiled. "Looks like James struck it rich. We ought to try our hand at doing some gold mining; we might get lucky too. Who knows?"

Ben said, "There's a stream that runs through my family's property, and some people that had been doing some gold panning near there had found some gold—not enough to get rich, but enough they filed a claim. We should go give it a try and see what we find. I can ask if those people with the mines are still around or if anyone knows how to set up a dredge or a sluice box to help us get started."

Wiley nodded. "I think that'd be a good idea to do right away, since our money is starting to run short."

At those words, Claire jumped in. "But we have all that money from those bounties," she said.

Wiley stopped her short. "No," he said. "That's your money. We'll be okay. You just need to have faith in us." Just then, their dinners arrived, and the conversation changed to how good the food looked and how hungry they were.

After dinner, they decided to go for a walk around the town to see if they'd meet any more people they remembered. As they walked, Claire again mentioned that if they needed any money, it was rightfully theirs and they could have it.

Wiley replied, "If we need some, I'll ask you for it, but as a loan. Until then, don't fret about it."

She dropped the subject but couldn't stop wondering why they had given her all of the bounties if they were short on money.

The town was pretty quiet after dark, as most places were closed, and not many people were about, so they went back to the hotel to get a good night's sleep.

In the morning, Ben and Wiley were up early and went to the assayer's office and asked about any information on how to set up a mine in a stream.

"We have a couple of books on how to set up equipment and file a claim that we can loan you," the assayer told them. "You can go down to the mercantile store, and you'll find all the materials you need to start mining."

The owner of the mercantile turned out to be the son of a man they knew before the war. He told them his father hadn't made it back from the war, and so he had taken over the business. They showed him the books of gold mining and the images of what they were going to try to build. He said he thought he could put together all the materials if they would leave him the books for a little while. He should have it all ready in a couple of hours.

From there, they went to the City Hall and found out how to make a mining claim, in case they found any gold. When the women were out of earshot, they talked about how they needed to do this as soon as possible. It had taken over a month for them to get there from Terry's ranch, but they had come with wagons, and the Pinkertons were riding horses and would be able to travel a lot faster.

They figured they had to get the gold shipped out before the Pinkertons arrived. Pike County was a large county, but it wouldn't take the detectives very long to find out where they were.

Back at the hotel, Wiley pulled Ben and Lawrence

aside and said, "I think we should all stay at Ben's until we're finished getting the gold to the bank. Since the Pinkertons are looking for me, they first have to find someone who knew where I lived before the war. Once they get to my place, they'll find out we aren't there and head to the nearest town. I'm hoping it takes them a while to make it here to Beaver Bottom."

Satisfied with their morning's work, they found the women in the restaurant having coffee and waiting for them. Before they could get on their way, they still needed to get enough supplies to last a few days at Ben's place and pick up their order at the mercantile.

After breakfast, they all went up to the rooms. Wiley went into Claire's room and said, "Will you loan me a hundred dollars?"

"Are you sure that's all you need?" she said.

"A hundred is plenty," he replied, and she turned around, pulled the envelope from her bodice, and gave the money to him.

The men got all their things together and went downstairs. They paid the bill, even though Mr. McGee said they didn't have to.

They went to the livery and paid the owner, taking their wagons to the mercantile and general store where they loaded up their supplies. They paid for everything with the bounty money and not the gold coins. When they took the wagons back to the hotel, they found the women in the restaurant having iced tea and wondering where the men had gone off to.

The men made no attempt to sit down and relax with the women. "We have a lot of work to do before sundown," Wiley said, "so we should get going to Ben's place."

The women finished their tea quickly, and they all climbed in the wagons and headed to Ben's family homestead.

CHAPTER 28

BEN'S PLACE

The road they took was fairly flat, except for the last couple of miles that had turned hilly and then mountainous. They were traveling along the base of those hills when they came to a little valley and a road that turned off to head down into it.

"This is the road to my place," Ben said. "Look against the far side of the valley. See where the trees seem to grow in a row following the bottom? That's where the stream is that runs through our property." It was clear he was proud of where his home was, and they could see why. It really was set in some beautiful country.

They followed the road for about a mile and a half and came to an opening in a fence that a side road continued through. Another half a mile on, they could see a farmhouse and a barn with a corral.

They pulled up to the front of the house and a woman came out. She was dressed in a country dress with an apron around her waist. She shielded her eyes from the sun with one hand and said, "Hello there, what can I do for you folks?"

Ben stepped down from his wagon and walked toward

her. When he got close enough for her to get a good look at him, she put her hand to her heart and sat down heavily on the steps of the porch.

They were afraid she was having a heart attack.

"Am I to believe my eyes?" she moaned. "Is that you Ben? We haven't had a word from you in so long. We thought you had been killed in the war!"

Ben sat beside her on the step. "Yeah, Ma, it's me. I've finally been able to come home," he said, hugging her. As she hugged him back, both of them started crying.

The mother-son reunion was a touching sight for everyone in the wagons. Not one of them was able to keep their eyes from tearing up.

Ben's mother told him how the place had seemed so empty without him. "Your father and I have just been going through the motions of living, thinking we had lost our only son," she said. She pointed to the fields beyond the house. "Go to him, Ben. Your father is out in the pasture cutting the last of the hay, trying to get us ready for the winter."

She turned to the others and said, "Excuse me, pardon my manners. Please do come inside."

Ben said, "Let us get our horses and wagons to the barn while you ladies go inside and keep my mother company." He introduced Claire and Cassie and said, "We'll be in as soon as we put away the horses."

They got the horses unhitched and untied and put them in the corral. Three that had been tied to the wagons were going to be their mounts. They saddled those three and walked them over to the porch, tying them to the hitching rail in front of it before going inside.

Ben's mother had made lemonade. She gave everyone

a canning jar full, saying, "I don't have any real glasses; we just drink from the jars I use for putting things by."

"Not a problem," Wiley said. "Just makes us feel more at home."

"You remember Wiley, don't you?" he said to his mother.

"Of course," she said. "You came down a few times to help build our barn and help some of our neighbors, right? Course you were a might younger then."

"Yep, that's right," replied Wiley.

Ben introduced Lawrence and then finished his lemonade in three gulps. "I'm going to see Pa," he said, setting down his jar, "and I want to take my friends out to meet him, then show them around the place before dinner."

Claire and Cassie quickly said, "We would love to help with dinner, if you don't mind." The women started talking about what food to make.

The ranch was a large place, especially for just one man and his wife. They rode for a half hour over rolling hills to a place they could see where a crop of hay had been cut. At the far end of it, they could see a horse, way off in the distance. "There's my pa," Ben said.

His father had been busy cutting the hay with a sickle and stacking it. He was stopping to get a drink from his canteen when he looked up to see three riders coming in his direction.

When they came to a halt a few yards away, Ben climbed down from his horse and said, "Howdy, Pa. How've you been?"

The man squinted his eyes a little, blinked a couple of times, and said, "I'll be damned! Hello, Son. Glad to see you made it home." He stretched his arms out as Ben moved into them. They hugged each other, swinging together from side to side for a while.

Ben let go of his father and told him, "I want to introduce some kinfolk, Pa. This here's Wiley and Lawrence; you remember Wiley from up north of Beaver Bottom? And Lawrence here is a McCoy from way over by Wallins Creek."

His father smiled. "I remember a Wiley—a young man that came and helped us put up the barn a long time ago. Was that you?"

"One and the same," Wiley responded as he got off his horse and held out his hand to shake.

Lawrence climbed down from his horse and held out his hand as well. "Pleased to meet you, sir," he said.

"Names Thaddeus," Ben's father said, "but just call me Thad."

He turned to his son. "How come it took you so long to get home?" he said.

"Well, I didn't want to come home empty-handed," Ben replied, "and I had a chance to work on a ranch for a little while and do some other things to get some money, so I could make the trip. We all worked together at the same ranch and put together our money, so we could come home."

"Lawrence is here because when we got to his place, it was only a charred ruin, and he thought he might as well just tag along since there was nothing left there."

"Well, I'm sure glad you all made it here safe and sound. I was just about finished out here. I'm getting old and can't work as long as I used to. You did stop at the house and see your mother, didn't you?"

"Of course, I did, but right now I want to show these boys around the property. We'll be back at the house before sundown."

"Suits me fine," his father said. "I'm going to stack up the last of this hay and head back to the house. I'll see you there."

CHAPTER 29

FINDING A REAL GOLD MINE

They mounted up and rode out to where the stream flowed through the property. Ben showed them a nice spot where the water dropped over large boulders and made a pond with a lot of sand and gravel around the edges. There was open ground around the sides, and it looked like the spring runoff had washed away much of the vegetation and left a beach along one bank, large enough to set up a sluice box and do some mining. They decided this was where they would make their claim; in the morning, they would bring out the tools and materials to get the mine started.

They had a fine homecoming dinner with Ben and his parents. When it was time for bed, they moved some of the furniture to make room for their bedrolls and the ladies' sleeping cots and had a good night's sleep.

After breakfast, Ben said to his parents, "I remember about people finding gold before the war in the stream that runs through our property. If I remember right, the gold was found on both sides of our property in the dirt of the streambed that had been washed down from the mountains. We have the materials to set up for mining a stream and want to give it a try around the big pond with that big drop-off. We'd like to see if maybe there isn't some gold on our property too."

His ma smiled at him with her heart in her eyes. "Always the dreamer. But don't you think I'm gonna let you take off and go prospecting all over the country. I just got you home. You're not going anywhere farther than that stream for a while!"

"Okay, Ma," Ben said. "I promise I won't go prospecting anywhere off the property." And they took the books and materials in a wagon out to the big pond.

While Ben and Wiley went over the books and the drawings for making a sluice box, Lawrence unloaded the materials and set them near where they were going to build it. It took several tries to make a successful sluice box, but they finally figured out how to get it to work.

The first few buckets of dirt went in the box; over it they poured several buckets of water. It was quickly clear to all that this was going to take a long time and a lot of hard work.

Lawrence came up with an idea. "We can make a trough to channel the water to flow into the box," he said. "We can put it in the stream up above the drop-off, so the water will run down to the box. We can even put a block at the opening up above to stop the flow of the water when we don't want it." Everyone agreed it was a real good idea and would make things a lot easier and faster.

And it did. When they got the long trough working, the dirt washed out quickly. They started making piles of the washed dirt so they could use it to pour the melted gold onto. They decided to put a wood frame around this dirt and make a hole in the center of the pile, where they would pour the melted gold, then scrape the dirt onto it and stir it all together.

At the end of the day, when they were ready to start melting the coins, they had a surprise. They had let the water run through the chute while they were building the wood frame around the dirt pile, and when they went back to the sluice box, they found a lot of shiny particles on its bottom.

"Guess what, boys?" Ben said. "We really have got us a gold mine! Look at this stuff here!"

Wiley and Lawrence inspected the shiny flakes closely, and Wiley said, "I'll be danged. Whatta you know about that!" They separated as much of the gold flakes as they could, as it was getting dark, and Ben swept them into a bandanna. Then he tied it in a knot and put it in his shirt pocket.

"This is a lot better. Now, I don't have to worry my parents about how we got this gold. Let's just keep it to ourselves and let them think we found it all right here. I'll tell them once it's safe and we're sure everything's okay."

Wiley and Lawrence said that was fine with them, and they headed back to his house.

After they'd settled the horses and were walking back from the corral, the women came outside on the porch. "Well, how did our prospectors do today?" Cassie said.

Ben looked at her with a big grin. "Make fun of us all you want but look what we got." He took the bandanna out of his shirt pocket, carefully untied the knot, and brought it over for them to see.

The ladies' eyes widened at the sight of the shining

flakes, and Cassie exclaimed, "Wow! You really found some gold. How much do you think it's worth?"

"That, I don't know," Ben said, "but I know one thing. We're going into town tomorrow to file us a mining claim."

Ben's father came out the front door in time to hear him say they were going to file a claim.

"Let me see what you found there," he said. When Ben showed him the bandanna he looked impressed. "Did you get all that today?" he asked.

"Well, actually," Ben said, "it took quite a while to get the sluice box set up, and we really only started running soil through it for about an hour. We set up our box down below the big drop-off on the edge of the big pond, and it looks like there's been a lot of gold washed over it."

His pa shook his head in disbelief. "I tried panning for gold back when people first started saying they found gold above and below our property along that stream. I worked at it for a couple of weeks, and I didn't even get half that much, so I gave it up."

"The way to do mining has improved a lot since when you tried," Ben said. "And there are now ways to work a lot more dirt a lot faster. With what we built, we can clean five or six buckets of dirt in an hour or less. The more dirt we can sift, the more gold we can find." Then he turned to Lawrence and Wiley.

"We all need to go into town tomorrow," he said, "with you too, Pa. We'll have to put our mark on the mining claim. Can you take the day tomorrow and come with us?"

But his father shook his head. "I can't go," he said. "I

have to finish cutting the hay. It doesn't matter to me if my name is on it as long as Ben has his. Besides, the three of you are doing all of the work."

Early the next morning, the three went straight to the assayer's office and had him check the gold. He told them there was around a hundred and eighty dollars' worth in the bandanna. They went over to the City Hall and filed their mining claim, went to the bank with the assayer's note of value, and deposited the gold, dividing it three ways and opening three separate bank accounts.

Back at Ben's ranch, they started unloading one of the wagons. Once that was done, they took all of their bullet-making equipment and put it in the empty wagon along with the nine strongboxes, which they covered with a tarp. When they got to the mine after lunch, they stacked the strongboxes by the box of dirt they were going to use to mix the melted gold with, then covered them with the tarp. Then they started setting up the kilns, and once they thought they had enough heat in them, they opened one of the strong boxes and began putting the coins in the ladles and waiting for them to melt.

By the time the sun was going down, they had melted almost three bags of coins.

They, too, noticed there was some kind of a film on top of the gold when the coins melted, so they skimmed it off before pouring the melted gold into the pile of dirt, fine rocks, and pebbles in their dirt box. At dinner time, they left everything there and went back to the house.

At dinner, the men declared they were going to start staying down at the mine to keep an eye on things since they were finding more gold. They didn't want anyone sneaking around, since word would probably get around pretty fast that they had filed a mining claim.

The next day, they brought a tent, their cots, and bedrolls when they went to the mine in the morning. By two o'clock, they had finished almost two boxes and made twenty-four bags to take into the assayer's office.

"I'll take it in," Wiley said, "and you two can stay here and keep working. I'll get a receipt from the assayer and tell him to keep his mouth shut about how much we're finding."

He made it to the assayer's office about three-thirty in the afternoon. "Can you put a value on this bag I have here?" he asked the man.

The assayer pulled out a tray and told him to dump it out and he would take a look at it. The assayer told him it was too full of dirt and pebbles to get a clear sense of the value. Wiley asked if he could just give him an estimate. The assayer thought a while, then said, "I really can't tell for sure, but I think somewhere around ten and fifteen thousand." Quick to follow that statement, as James's assayer had done, he offered to clean the gold for a fee.

"Go ahead and clean it," Wiley told him. "I'm going to the telegraph office and then to have a beer. After that, I'll come back and see what you've managed to do."

The man gave his head an exasperated shake. "I don't know how much I can get done in that amount of time," he said, "but I'll call in some help from my son and daughter. Don't worry, they know enough to keep their mouths shut." And Wiley nodded and left.

The telegram he sent Tommy was as long as James's note had been:

We've made it home, and it was a good thing we had

our bullet-making equipment. We ran out of money and needed some bullets. We tried the equipment, melting down some of the lead to make our own, and although we spilled a lot in the dirt and lost some of the lead, we still came away with plenty of bullets. The Pinkertons have been to James's place and are headed to Pike County.

They were following the trail of fifty-dollar gold pieces that had been spent. They have probably already been to your place because of the gold pieces that you spent to build up your ranch.

James said he told the Pinkertons we were paid those gold coins out of money that came from the sale of the place Terry's father had before they moved to Kansas. That we had to put together all our money to make the trip home and didn't have any left from the pay we got from the ranch. The only money we had was what we'd gotten from some bounties we collected along the way.

After we left, James found some gold on their property and made a mining claim. Apparently, he found a whole lot, at least that's what he said in his telegram to us. He is now busy building up their ranch and surrounding property.

He said the Pinkertons were mighty suspicious because of all the gold he'd found, but they couldn't prove anything because it had all been taken to an assay office and then put in a bank. The bank gave them a note of credit for the whole amount and then shipped the gold to a main branch bank in Boston for safety. James offered to give us some money if we needed it, to get us on our feet. END OF MESSAGE.

Wiley knew they only had a short time to get the rest

of their gold into the assayer's office and into a bank before the Pinkertons showed up, and he hoped that Tommy would understand his message. At the saloon, he got himself a beer and waited for the assayer to put a value on the bag he'd left him. After an hour he couldn't wait any longer. But when he went back to the assayer's office, he found him still trying to clean up the gold.

"This is no easy job," the assayer said, "and it's going to take quite a while. But from what I can tell, I was pretty right on my estimate of value."

"I appreciate your work," Wiley said, "and I need to tell you there's a lot more where that came from. In fact, I have another twenty-three bags in my wagon."

The assayer stared at Wiley in disbelief. "Well then," he finally said, "bring it on in. You don't want to leave that in your wagon."

"Are you sure it's going to be safe here?" Wiley said.

The assayer nodded. "I can give you my word and that of my family that we won't tell a soul. If we did, someone would quite likely kill us to take it. I can give you a receipt and put an estimated value of at least ten thousand per bag, if they're all about the same. Once it's cleaned, I will give you my assayer's note about a precise value for you to take with you to the bank."

"Sounds fair," Wiley said. "I don't know how much more there is going to be, but it looks like a lot more will be coming, so you have to keep this secret as long as you can."

The assayer gave a quick nervous nod. "I'm going to get my wife to help, so then I'll have four people cleaning it." He folded his arms to appear strong willed. "My price is twenty percent for each bag, and if you don't like it, you'll have to clean it up yourself. It takes too much work to get it in a condition the bank will take it."

Wiley thought that fee was a little high for just cleaning gold. "Let's see how much we end up with from this bag, and we'll see," he finally said.

The assayer told him he would estimate the value of each bag at twelve thousand, if they were all about the same in gold content, and then added, "This is just my estimate for my note of intake of property to you, but after my fee for cleaning, whatever the weight is, that's what I'll put as a value on my assayer's note for the bank."

Because the Pinkertons were on their way and he had no time to dicker, Wiley nodded. "That sounds fair enough to me, as long as you get it done quickly," he said. "Will you help me get the rest of it in here?"

All four cleaners headed outside to unload the wagon. Wiley left the office with a note declaring he had deposited in the assayer's office an estimated two hundred eighty-eight thousand dollars' worth of gold to be cleaned.

When he got back to the mine, it was after dark, and Ben and Lawrence had another eight bags ready. He showed them the assayer's note and assured them the man was going to keep quiet.

"I'll go back to the house and bring us some dinner," Ben said. After eating, they worked until they couldn't see well enough to mix the gold with the dirt and decided to get up at sunup and get started on it again.

It took them three more days to finish mixing all the gold. Then they burned the strongboxes and took the metal from the ashes and threw it in the pond. They had to hitch a second horse to the wagon in order to pull it to the house because of the gold's weight. After breakfast, all three went into town to the assayer's office.

"I'm sure glad you showed up," he told them. "I finished yesterday afternoon and have been sitting here worrying, sweating, and waiting. I don't like having all this gold here."

"Well," Wiley said, "you're about to have a lot more. This time we brought in a big load."

The assayer was flabbergasted. "You mean what you brought before wasn't a big load?"

Wiley grinned. "So, what did you end up with for the value?"

"Exactly what I told you. Twelve thousand a bag," the man said.

All four of them unloaded the sacks of dirtied gold from the wagon and piled them in the back room. And then they reloaded up the wagon with the twenty-four bags of cleaned gold. The assayer gave them a receipt for one hundred eleven bags and told them that, once again, he'd get all hands to get it cleaned as fast as possible.

At the bank, Wiley went inside alone and asked for the bank manager. "I'm about to bring in twenty-four bags of gold, he told the man in a quiet voice after he was shown to his desk, "and I don't want anyone to know about it. So, we're going to wait until the bank is empty, and I would like it if you sent all the tellers to lunch. We don't want this town turning into a gold rush madhouse. News is going to get out sooner or later, but the later the better."

"I understand completely," replied the manager, almost drooling at the thought of his commission from the main branch for a sum so large.

The tellers thought it was strange that they were going to close for lunch, but they obliged without much fuss. When the tellers had gone, they unloaded the wagon. The manager opened each bag and sifted through it a little; then, satisfied that it was all gold, he weighed them and asked the McCoys to stack it in the safe.

The safe was large, but the bags almost completely filled its bottom. Wiley produced the assayer's note, which verified the weight and value, and the manager deposited eight bags into each of their accounts and gave them each a receipt of deposit. "We'll be back in a few days with more," Wiley told the manager, "as long as you haven't let word slip out." Wiley knew that dangling the prospect of more gold would give the manager a good reason to keep his mouth shut.

"I won't say a word," the manager assured them, "and I'll get this gold to the main branch in Boston as fast as I can." Then he added, "Don't worry. I always have to keep quiet about gold deposits for fear of someone robbing the stage or my bank. If I don't get it to the main branch, I don't get my commission. Your deposit is protected by the bank's guarantee once it's in my safe."

CHAPTER 30

THE PINKERTONS CATCH UP

It took the Pinkertons eight days to travel from Wallins Creek to Pike County. Once there, they started stopping at every house they passed, asking if anyone knew where any McCoys lived.

But the McCoys were a clan who looked after their own.

After two days, they found a McCoy. He told them he didn't know Wiley, but there were more McCoys up north thirty or forty miles.

When they did as he'd advised, they found another McCoy. He didn't know Wiley either, he said, but he knew there were more McCoys on the south end of Pike County than there were on the north end.

They continued north, found another McCoy, and were told to go east. It was just the code of the hills. You didn't help trouble find any of your kinfolk, even if they were guilty of something.

The Pinkertons went so far east they crossed into Virginia. When they realized this, they headed back west into Kentucky. Finally, they decided that since they had come in from the west and had already been north and east, they would go south this time. After being in Pike County over two weeks, they were finally headed in the right direction, or so they hoped.

They had been searching south Pike County for eight days before they found someone who wasn't a McCoy, who said they knew of a Wiley McCoy and could tell them where he'd lived before the war. It took them two more days to find his place. They looked over the farm, decided that someone had been there, and headed south when they left, probably to Belcher, the nearest town. They arrived late, so they stayed the night. The next day, they asked around town and they found out that a group matching their description had left town heading south, but no one knew who they were. So, they mounted up and headed to Beaver Bottom.

Chapter 31

Getting the Gold to the Bank

The three McCoys each carried a note of credit of ninety-six thousand from the bank when they left town. They went right back to the mine and cleaned up everything they'd used for melting down the gold.

Then they set about doing some real mining, the way they'd found the gold flakes with the sluice box. By the time the sun went down, they had managed to separate enough gold that they each had about the same amount they'd found the first time.

When the boys got back from the mine, they didn't say anything to anyone about the large deposit they had made at the bank but showed off the flakes they'd collected. During the next week, they found three bags' worth of gold flakes, weighing a few pounds each. They told everyone they were going into town to deposit it in the bank.

When they walked through the door of the assayer's office, the man looked like he was about to have a nervous breakdown. "Don't tell me you brought another load like that last one!" he said. "We've been working night and day to get it cleaned. I don't think my nerves can take any more."

Wiley smiled. "No, not this time," he said. "It seems like the vein has kind of dried up, although we do have some we cleaned ourselves."

The man looked very relieved. "Good," he said, "because we've been working our fingers to the bone. We finished it all last night, finally. Let me see what you brought this time."

They handed over their bags of gold and he dumped it all onto the tray. The total weight was a little over twelve pounds. "Now, that's how I like to see gold come in," the assayer said. "All I have to do is put it on the scales. I get three percent for doing the assayer's note for the value. This gold is worth a hundred dollars an ounce, so minus my fee, there is nineteen thousand here.

The assayer shook his head in wonder. "You boys sure have found yourself a bonanza!" he said. "I've never seen so much gold come from one mine in my life."

They loaded the assayed gold in the wagon, covered it, and went straight to the bank.

"I have another load for you," Wiley told the manager, "and it's more than three times the size of the last load."

The manager actually started shaking. "Wha, wha— what am I supposed to do?" he said, stuttering nervously. "It won't fit in the vault. How am I going to make sure it stays safe till I get it sent to Boston?" He turned in a circle. "It can't all go on one stage. It's going to take at least four, maybe six, stagecoaches." He put his hands in his hair and clutched at the strands. "I'll have to tell the sheriff to put a couple of guards here at the bank till I can get it sent off."

All of which could attract attention. "Just make sure you tell the sheriff you had a shipment come in," Wiley said, "and that you're supposed to transfer it to Boston, and you need to have extra guards round the clock at the bank till you can get it all sent off. Don't tell him where it came from or what it is."

The manager nodded rapidly, then turned in another circle. "That's a good idea. I'll do just that," he said. "After I've checked the sacks, put as many in the vault as you can, then just pile the rest on the side of the vault, and I'll cover it with something."

Since it was almost closing time, they waited till all the employees had gone home to unload the wagon. The manager checked the bags as they filled the vault, then covered the ones that wouldn't fit. He gave them each a note of credit for four hundred fifty-three thousand dollars that was applied to each of their accounts.

Afterward, they went to the saloon across from the sheriff's office and each had a beer. From there, they saw the bank manager go inside the sheriff's office and emerge with two deputies, who positioned themselves on the benches on either side of the bank entrance. Satisfied that their gold was safe, they finished their beers and headed back to the ranch. On the ride home, they all agreed they'd best continue mining for a while for appearances sake.

CHAPTER 32

FACE TO FACE WITH THE PINKERTONS

It only took the Pinkertons a few hours to get to Beaver Bottom from Belcher. They went straight to the sheriff's office. When they asked him if he knew of a Wiley McCoy, he told them he did. He also told them that Wiley was at Ben's place and where Ben's place was. The Pinkerton's horses left the town at a run.

Within an hour, they were coming through the gate at Ben's place. The man in charge was heading up the porch steps as the front door opened and Ben's mother came out. When he told her that they were looking for Ben and Wiley, she asked why. "It's personal business, between us and them," he told her.

"Well," she said, "they left early this morning to go prospecting, and I don't know when they'll be back. Although, I figure they'll be here for dinner."

"I have a warrant to search any premises suspected of hiding what we're looking for," he said. "We're going to have to search the ranch, the house, all the buildings here, and all the surrounding area." As she took this in, he added, "Can you have anyone inside come out while we search the house?"

Ben's mother and Cassie and Claire sat on porch chairs while several of the Pinkertons searched the house.

They looked in all the cupboards and closets, rummaged the drawers and dressers, and checked the floors and walls for hidden compartments. It took a couple of hours for them to decide there was nothing there. Their leader told them to spread out and check the premises, including the barn and corral. "You can go back inside if you like," he finally told the women.

"I think I'd like to walk around with you while you search my property," Ben's mother said. "I don't want anything torn up, just so you can look for whatever it is you're looking for."

She walked with them to the barn and watched as they searched everything, even the piles of hay in the loft. It took another couple of hours before they gave up.

But the man in charge wasn't ready to give up. "We'll be staying on the property until Ben and Wiley come back," he told Ben's mother.

"That's fine," she replied, "but I don't want you in my house, and we don't have much food ourselves, so if you plan on eating, I hope you have brought your own food. You can wait up here on the porch, but when night comes, you'll have to sleep there too."

"We thank you for your cooperation," he said.

At around four o'clock, one of the lookouts signaled someone was approaching. It was Ben's father coming in from the field. When he saw all those men standing in front of his house, he started to worry that they were a gang who had heard about them finding gold and had come to rob them.

When he came to the porch, the leader of the group stepped forward, and Ben's father saw the badge on the lapel of his jacket.

He said, "Good day, mister. What can I do for you?"

The leader pulled off his hat. "We're here looking for Ben and Wiley McCoy," he said. "Do you know where they are?"

"What's this about? Are they in trouble?" Ben's father said.

"We've come from Missouri," the man replied, "sent out by Brigadier General Thomas Ewing Jr., the commander of the district of the border between Kansas and Missouri, to see if we can find information on the whereabouts of some gold that was taken from the Northern army. We've been following the trail of fifty-dollar gold pieces spent around Lawrence, Kansas."

Ben's mother and father exchanged a quick glance.

"Also," the man continued, "there was some spent over in Harrisonville and Independence, Missouri. The trail led us to Wiley and Ben. We figured, if they didn't take the gold, they could at least tell us where they got the coins they've been spending, and we can follow the trail from there."

"Well," Ben's father said, "I can assure you that Ben and Wiley are no thieves, and I haven't seen any fifty-dollar gold pieces. Now they did find some gold, but they found it on my property, down by the stream that runs through my land. As far as I know, they're down there right now, doing some mining."

The man put his hat back on his head. "Would you mind showing us where that is?" he said.

"Let me put my hay wagon in the barn and saddle my

horse. I'll be happy too," Thad replied. When he was ready, the men mounted up and followed him down toward the big pond.

When they arrived, the boys were just finishing cleaning the last buckets they had put in the sluice box.

To anyone looking at them, they were just doing what miners do, pouring dirt in the sluice box and having the water push the dirt out, leaving the gold behind. The McCoys had been working there since their last trip to town three days before. They each had a bag of gold particles about the same size as the ones they'd taken on their last trip to the assayer's office.

The leader of the Pinkertons stepped off his horse and asked, "Which one of you is Wiley?"

"That would be me," Wiley said calmly. "What can I do ya fer?"

"Well," the leader replied, "seems you and your group left Missouri a couple months after some gold had been stolen from the Northern army and you have been spending some fifty-dollar gold pieces. I want to know where you got them."

"Well sir," Wiley said, "me and my kinfolk here worked on a ranch up near Lawrence, Kansas. When we had enough money between us to travel, we decided we would make our trip home. We got paid for the work we did by the lady who was running her father's ranch." Wiley proceeded to tell the men the story of how the woman had to pay them with the fifty-dollar gold pieces her father had gotten from the sale of the place they'd had in the south before the war started.

"The money we had ran out around Middlesboro," Wiley said. "We ran into some trouble with a gang of highway robbers on the way, but it turned out we got lucky and survived. Some of them had bounties on their heads, so we had enough money to get us the rest of the way home. As far as any gold we have, everything we put in the bank came from this place right here after we arrived."

"So, you deposited gold in the bank, did you?" the man said.

"Yeah, we did, after we had it assayed by the assayer's office," Wiley replied. "We also made us a mining claim, as soon as we started finding some gold, so it's all legal. You can check with the assayer and City Hall."

"Well, if you're mining gold, you should have some here, shouldn't you?" the man said.

"Yeah, we have some," Wiley said. "Take a look. I'll show you how we been doing it."

The Pinkertons went to the sluice box and watched the water flowing through it. Wiley pointed at the bottom of the box, and said, "You see those shiny particles in there? They're gold flakes that have been washed down over this drop-off. We're pulling it out of the dirt. When we first started, we got just a little, but after a couple days, we found a whole bunch." He started sifting through the bottom of the box, and as luck would have it, there was some of the gold there left over from the last lot they'd melted, dirtied, and cleaned. He pulled out a couple of large nuggets and said, "See here, this is what we've been finding."

He handed them to the man.

The man bounced them around in his hand. "Those are pretty hefty nuggets," he said.

Ben and James brought over their bags, opened them,

and showed him what they had. He looked inside and said, "Well, I guess we've come a long way for nothing. We're going to have to go back to Lawrence and see if we can pick up a new trail. I'll stop by that assayer's office in town just to make sure what you say is true. If it checks out, you won't see us again, and we're sorry to have bothered you." He handed the men back the nuggets. He then got on his horse and told his men, "Let's see if we can get back into town before the assayer's office closes," and they took off at a run.

As he left, Ben, Lawrence, and Wiley exchanged a worried look. What would the assayer tell them? And had the bank been able to get all the gold sent off to Boston? But they didn't let on to Ben's father that they were concerned.

They packed up their three bags and stopped the water from flowing through the box. "It's time to go home for some dinner," Ben said, and they mounted up and rode back to the ranch house.

• • •

The Pinkertons didn't make it in time to the assayer's office, so they went to the sheriff and asked if he would direct them to where the assayer lived. "He lives behind the office," he said, "and has an entrance to his house in the back of his office."

Upon seeing the badge on the man standing in front of his door, the assayer said, "Hello, sir. What can I do for you?"

"We've been trying to follow the trail of some gold coins that have been taken from the Northern Army in Missouri," the leader said, "and I want to know if the

McCoys have brought you gold they claim they found in their mine."

"Yes, sir, they did," the assayer said. "I helped them clean it up, so it could be put in the bank, and it sure took work to do it. There was a lot at first, but the mine seems to be slowing down, and I haven't seen them for a few days. I can tell you this though, they didn't have any gold coins. Every bit of gold they brought me had to be separated from a mess of dirt and pebbles. You can rest assured all of the gold they brought me came from the earth."

Since the Pinkerton man didn't ask, he didn't tell him exactly how much they had brought him, and he didn't figure it was any of their business.

The leader sighed. "Well, sir, that's what I came to find out," he said. "If you can attest that it came from the earth, I guess we'll be on our way back to Kansas. Thank you, and sorry to have bothered you."

And with that, the assayer went back in his house, and the Pinkertons started back to Kansas.

CHAPTER 33

THE BIG REVEAL

When Ben, Lawrence and Wiley got back to the ranch house, they put away the horses and wagons, and Ben's father went into the hay barn to finish what he'd been doing before the Pinkertons showed up. The McCoys settled onto chairs on the porch, and when the women saw them there, they came outside.

"Well now, don't you all look like a bunch of Cheshire cats!" Claire said. "What have you men been up to?"

The men couldn't help but start laughing. "There is no way we could ever hide anything from any of you," Wiley said, "and this is just too big for us to hold in."

He reached in his pocket and pulled out his note of credit from the bank. When he did that, Ben and Lawrence did the same, then handed them to the women most important to them.

Ben's mother put her hand to her mouth and started crying, dropping into a chair. The other two had to read the paper a couple of times, then looked at each other in speechless disbelief. Finally, Claire was able to talk. "Does this paper say that you deposited over four and

323

half thousand dollars' worth of gold in the bank today?"

"No, that's not what it says," said Wiley. "It says that we deposited over four hundred and *fifty thousand* dollars, but not today." As he handed her another note for what they had deposited the week before. Ben and Lawrence each did the same.

Each of those notes said ninety-six thousand dollars had been deposited. This information rendered them once again, speechless.

When Claire finally was able to ask, she said, "So how much did you put in the bank over the last two weeks?"

"Five hundred and forty-nine thousand dollars," Ben said. "Each of us put that same amount in the bank over the last two weeks."

Ben's mother started shaking and then fainted in her chair.

Ben jumped to her side to keep her from hitting the floor. He shook her gently, and when she came back to her senses, she still was having trouble breathing. "Just relax, Ma, and take a couple of deep breaths," he said. "We're never going to have to worry about anything ever again. We can buy anything we want that can be bought."

Cassie and Claire went to their men and sat on their laps and put their arms around their necks. Tears started to flow.

"You're rich. Rich beyond anyone's wildest dreams!" Claire said.

Wiley looked into Claire's eyes, trying to show how much love he had in his heart for her. He felt more alive inside than he had in years. "No," he said, "*we're* rich. All of us are rich."

Ben's father came in from the hay barn, looking dead-tired and dirty. When he stepped onto the porch, Ben said, "Pa, I don't think you should work anymore. You're getting too old to be doing this."

His Pa smiled at him and said, "That would be nice, son, but if I don't, how are we going to eat? Someone's got to do something besides go out prospecting."

Ben smiled back at him. "My prospecting days are over, Pa," he said. "I think I'm going to retire." He laughed. When they all started laughing, his father looked around, puzzled. Ben's mother went to him. She held up the two banknotes and said, "You won't believe this. I can hardly believe it myself, but here's the proof right in your hand. You really can stop working."

He had to look at the papers several times, holding one up first, then the other. Finally, he sat down on the step without saying another word.

His wife sat beside him and put her arm around his shoulders. "Do you know how much those numbers mean?" she said.

"No," he said. "There's more numbers here than I can cipher."

"Me too," she said. "But they amount to more than half a million dollars."

He turned to her, suddenly rigid. "What's that you say? Are you telling me they found more than a half million dollars' worth of gold in that stream?"

"No, dear. That's just Ben's share," she said. "They found three times that amount."

He looked into her eyes, but he just couldn't believe it. He turned around and saw the others were all smiling and nodding. "Yes, it's true. You're a rich man," Ben said.

He couldn't believe what he was being told. He stood up, went into the kitchen, and splashed water on his face several times, and then came back outside and looked at the notes again. He sat down in one of the chairs, eyes growing misty.

Ben came to him and put his arm around his shoulders and said, "Pa, I know it's a shock and almost impossible to believe, but it's really true. We're rich beyond our imagination, and the money is already in the bank."

EPILOGUE

The McCoys went into town the next morning and brought their gold to the assayer's office, where they found out what the assayer had told the Pinkertons. He gave them a note that attested to the value of this load, and they took it to the bank, adding still more to their accounts.

Wiley stopped at the telegraph office and sent a telegram to Tommy, telling him that the Pinkertons had been there and were suspicious of them and the gold mine, but since there were no coins, and the assayer attested he had cleaned up the gold himself, they couldn't do anything. He added that if they needed any money for anything, he'd see to it they got it.

He also told Tommy the Pinkertons were headed back to Lawrence. He advised him to use his bullet maker as soon as he could. He wouldn't need money to buy bullets by making his own. He hoped that Tommy would take his warning and do something with the gold they still had back at the ranch, as quickly as possible.

The Pinkertons had arrived at Ben's place two days after the bank had sent the last gold to Boston. The leader still felt there was something fishy about the McCoys' stories. It was just too much of a coincidence to have two gold mines found by one group of men who had come together from Lawrence, Kansas. Unfortunately for him, he had no proof. No coins had been spent in any quantity, and the men had legal mining claims. He was just going to have to take his men back to where they'd started from and see if they could find another trail.

Back at James's ranch, once they had all of the gold in the bank and had made most of their larger purchases, the real work of building their ranch began. They started making trips back and forth to town, hauling building supplies for the new houses under construction—one for James's parents and one for James.

They hired men to clear the land and put up bunkhouses for the ranch hands. Once they saw how much work needed to be done on a weekly basis, they would be able to figure out how many men they would need to run the ranch.

It seemed everything was falling into place for James and his family, and their future was assured by the credit at the bank of more than four hundred fifty thousand dollars. When the word got out that they had struck gold, his family had already started to mark their property boundaries and put up fences. People began hunting all over for the shiny yellow stuff. Gold hunters went to every stream in the county and right up to the edge of the new property James's pa had acquired, but no one else found anything close to what James's family had said they found.

After a few months, things settled down. The ranch was ready for the animals that were coming, and when springtime came, the whole family came out to watch the herds arriving and beamed with pride.

A telegram from Wiley told James that his cousins were fine, and everything had gone well for them too.

They were also starting to build their ranches and creating what looked like a good life. James couldn't help but wonder, however, what was going to happen at Tommy's ranch when the Pinkertons got back there. Would they find the gold the others had? Would there be enough evidence to bring a case against those at the ranch, or maybe even to link all of them?

A couple of months went by, and Wiley sent a letter to Tommy, telling him that they were still working their mine. He also told them how they had met Claire and Cassie on the road home, what had happened to them, and that they were still with him and Lawrence. He wrote that they were starting to build new homes for Lawrence and himself, up at his old place, and had bought up all the land within ten miles around it. They'd placed orders for all of their materials and hired crews to start building and setting up fencing around the property. And they were looking to start raising a new breed of horses called "thoroughbreds." Ben also had bought as much land as he could around their place and wanted to build a new house.

Wiley told him that he had married Claire and Lawrence had married Cassie, and about how the women had become very efficient at directing people to do the work they wanted done, even though they were both pregnant. He also talked about how Lawrence and Cassie had planned to have a whole passel of children, but Claire's doctor had put a limit of two children for their family, as she was getting up in years to be having lots of babies.

Wiley also spoke of how he was handling the way his life had changed so dramatically saying, "Although, there's a lot more work than he thought to organizing and overseeing the things to be done, I still make time to go out hunting and fishing, which me and Lawrence do about every couple of weeks for a few days, just to relax and feel normal again." He told him to let him know if there was anything he might be able to do for him.

Life was good, and Lawrence realized that it didn't matter what a man had gone through in his life, as long as his priorities were to be a good person to himself and those around him, to be honest with himself for his actions and his sufferings and to ask for forgiveness where needed, to love and enjoy his family, and to take the time to do the things he likes to do. Then a man can live very happily and be content with whatever he has, rich or not.

If you're wondering what's going on with the Pinkertons and the McCoys back in Kansas…

Well, you can find out in the next saga of:
The McCoys: Before the Feud.

BACK AT THE RANCH
PROLOGUE

As soon as the last light went out in the farmhouse, Tommy saddled his horse and walked him quietly out of the barn. He didn't mount up until he was sure they were far enough away that they wouldn't be heard. He took up a fast pace, but not so fast as to burn up his horse. He figured he had twenty miles to cover to get to their camp and had to use the same horse for the ride back.

Jeb was on watch. As he saw Tommy approaching, he hollered to the others and they all got out of their bedrolls to find out what had happened.

Tommy filled them in on the situation. Then looking directly at his pa, he said, "You need to be on that side road that's about ten miles downriver, the one that comes over the hill to meet the river road, by around two o'clock. You'll need a horse saddled and ready, trailing the wagon."

He turned to A.C. and Oliver and said, "You need to get there early, set up in the trees, and to be ready to start shooting as soon as they approach Pa's wagon." A.C. and Oliver exchanged a glance. Tommy's tone made it clear that their role would be crucial.

Get the next book in the series:

Back At The Ranch
www.TheMcCoysBeforeTheFeud.com/back-at-the-ranch

You're Invited To...

As you sit here reading this you might have thought about how much others would enjoy this book as much as you have. If you'd love to share that enjoyment with others then would you leave a review?

www.TheMcCoysBeforeTheFeud.com/review

ALSO BY THOMAS MCCOY

In the *McCoys Before The Feud* Series

Before The Feud (Book 1)

A corrupt general. A stockpile of plundered Southern riches. Can a proud family reclaim the gold for its rightful owners?

Kansas-Missouri border, 1865. Tommy McCoy burns for justice. Reeling from the end of the bloody Civil War, he learns that a corrupt Northern general has raided the bounty of the Confederacy and plans to keep it. Tommy and his shrewd father vow to get back the valuables for innocent Southern families or die trying.

With time running out before the general's reinforcements arrive, Tommy risks a deadly confrontation in a series of secret raids. Can he secure the rightful Confederate property before the North deals the McCoys a final crushing blow?

The McCoys: Before the Feud is the first book in a deeply-researched historical Western saga. If you like dusty battles, a different point of view on yesteryear, and twists you won't see coming, then you'll love Thomas A. McCoy's gripping tale of justice for the people.

Buy *The McCoys: Before the Feud* to join a family's quest for justice today!

Back At The Ranch (Book 3)

Southern honor. Northern greed. The cost of failure could be their lives...

Kansas, 1865. Tommy McCoy sees a bright future ahead. After succeeding in several risky raids to reclaim the South's gold from a thieving Union general, he's finally back home with the woman he loves. But when Pinkerton detectives start snooping around, he's worried his temporary comfort will end with an execution.

To keep his family safe, Tommy devises an ingenious but dicey plan to protect his family from suspicion. After some of the McCoys refuse to take part in the high-stakes scheme, Tommy may lack the men he needs to outmaneuver the law one final time...

Will Tommy evade the Pinkertons or will his family's rightful property fill a corrupt general's pockets?

Back at the Ranch is the third book in the McCoys: Before the Feud historical Western saga. If you like go-for-broke action, clever twists and turns, and good people fighting for what's right, then you'll love Thomas A. McCoy's riveting adventure.

Buy *Back at the Ranch* to witness real McCoy ingenuity today!

ABOUT THE AUTHOR

Thomas Allan McCoy is the author of the Western Historical Fiction series The McCoy's: Before the Feud. As a direct descendant of the original McCoy family that was involved in the legendary feud between the Hatfields and McCoys, he provides a unique perspective and valuable insights regarding their traits, morals, and how family honor affected the way they carried out their lives after the Civil War. Inspired by the dramatic events that occurred within his own family history, McCoy weaves together facts and fiction to bring to life events that were happening in our country before this timeless feud from the 1860s took place.

McCoy's father, grandfather, great, and great, great grandfather were all born in Pikeville, Kentucky. However, he grew up in Southern California. In addition to writing, McCoy loves fishing, traveling, and baseball. He now lives in Arizona with his wife.

Made in the USA
Monee, IL
14 December 2021

85493110R00199